Who Comes to King's Mountain?

John and Patricia Beatty

Who Comes to King's Mountain?

William Morrow and Company
New York 1975

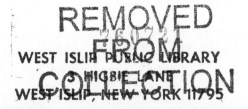

Library of Congress Cataloguing in Publication Data

Beatty, John Louis (date)
    Who comes to King's Mountain?

    Bibliography: p.
    SUMMARY: Living in the South Carolina hills in 1780, a young Scottish boy, whose own family is divided between Loyalist and rebel, must decide for himself which side he will follow.
    1. United   States—History—Revolution,   1775-1783—Juvenile fiction.   [1. United   States—History—Revolution,   1775-1783—Fiction.]   I. Beatty, Patricia, joint author.   II. Title.
PZ7.B380543Wh   [Fic]   75-11997
ISBN 0-688-22041-X
ISBN 0-688-32041-4 lib. bdg.

Contents

Who Comes to King's Mountain?

I

The Faraway Thunder

Lying on his stomach while he scooped up water with both hands, Alec MacLeod heard the baying. He let the creek water, ice-cold and swift running from the distant South Carolina mountains, run through his fingers and rolled over, reaching for his weapon set against a tree trunk. An instant later he was on his feet, his long rifle in his hands.

The dogs were closer now and coming toward him. If it was a deer fleeing ahead of hounds running masterless, the deer might be his. Venison was always a welcome change from winter's everlasting salt pork.

Alec pushed his way into a thicket beside the stream and crouched down, his rifle ready to be set into his shoulder to fire. The thicket, for all that it was winter blasted and mostly twigs, concealed him in his grease-stained buckskin coat. No deer pursued by dogs would spy him. He waited crouched on the frozen ground, and while he waited he frowned with tension.

A frown suited Alec's thin, sharp-jawed, dark face. A true black Scot, his mother called him, with his light blue eyes under heavy black brows. Already at fourteen he had the start of a black beard above his lip and along his chin. By the time he was twenty he would very likely find white hairs intermixed with his long, black Indian-straight hair, tied back today under his hat with a leather thong. Some of the MacLeods went "winter gray" at an early age.

A brown-and-white liver-spotted hound came running first to the creek bank, her mouth open in a long wild baying, her ears flapping. Alec knew her. She was Jamie Gilchrist's best hound. As she scrambled through the shallow water, followed by four other dogs, Alec got up from his crouch. There was no deer. He recognized not only the brown-and-white dog but the others behind her, all sleek and strong—all from Jamie's pack. When they were out running together, their master would not be far behind.

Alec waited for Jamie to come. Over the yelpings of the dogs running about, nose to the ground, casting for a scent over the creek, Alec heard the thudding of horses' hooves. He came out of the thicket to stand with his rifle cradled in his arms at the stream's brink. He called as loudly as he could over the sounds of the dogs, "I be here, too, Jamie. Alexander MacLeod."

A moment later a sorrel horse came bursting like thunder out from the undergrowth with a young man clinging to her back. The dogs had outdistanced the horse—which was a wonder because to Alec's eyes this was a racehorse if he had ever seen one. The rider straightened in the saddle, fighting the sweating mare. She danced in a circle while he cursed her in a torrent of furious Gaelic that made Alec grin to hear him. Plainly Jamie had got himself a new horse, one with much spirit. Though in time, Jamie would subdue her and win her, as he won all things.

While Gilchrist battled the mare, Alec stood his rifle against a stump and sat down beside the creek to play with the dogs, which flung themselves on him to be called each by name and fondled. Jamie's best dog was licking at Alec's ears when the man finally brought the sorrel at a snorting, resentful trot to loom over the boy and the frisking dogs. Alec looked up at the rider and grinned. There was no person more admired by the Scots living in the Ninety-Six Section, or at least by lads Alec's age, than braw Jamie Gilchrist. The only son of a prosperous farmer with a large grant of land from the English king, Jamie bought only the finest horseflesh to be had in South Carolina. His game-cocks were blue ones, the fiercest to be had, and his dogs the best hunters for miles in any direction. The Gilchrists lived like squires! Or lairds in Scotland.

Lanky Jamie, only eight years older than Alec, had a long, ugly, freckled face, a merry, wide mouth, and straw-yellow hair. He was not a bonny lad, but his garments more than made up for that. He rarely wore buckskin or home-spun like nearly everyone else—not he. Today his red-topped boots gleamed with wax and his coat was a lustrous bottle-green wool. Alec suspected that the cloth had come all the way from England and been tailored in a Charles Towne shop, not made by his mother, as Alec's clothing was.

"Ye have another horse, Jamie?" Alec asked in Gaelic,

though he knew that Jamie could speak English—and speak it with more ease than he could.

Gilchrist replied in Gaelic, "Aye, lad. Sweet Lass I call her, though she's got a devil of a temper right now. I bought her a week past in Charles Towne." He laughed. "I think I may have saved her from being a mount for the king's cavalry. Soldiers use good horses hard."

"The British? The king's soldiers? The redcoat soldiers— they've come back to this colony?" Alec pushed the dogs off him and got to his feet with his rifle, his heart suddenly beating more rapidly.

Jamie nodded while he patted the sorrel's lathered neck. "Aye, Alec, they've come back to this colony, and it's taken them five years to do it. That's the devil's own long time since they last tried to seize Charles Towne from the American rebels. Did ye begin to believe that the king's army would never come back to South Carolina? Your father will be pleased to have the good news that the redcoats have come again."

"Aye, MacLeod will be pleased." Alec bit into his lower lip and added, "But knowing that the king's soldiers have come back will not please my grandparents." He looked up again at Gilchrist, "Jamie, how many soldiers came this time to Charles Towne? Did ye see them?"

After he'd stopped the nervous sidestepping mare, Jamie said, "Na, I saw no soldier myself, but I saw the king's ships that brought them in the harbor. They sailed down from New York colony. When I started home from Charles Towne, the ships were anchored offshore—so many white sails they seemed to cover the water." He leaned from the saddle. "Alec, this time, ye, too, will be old enough to fight against the American rebels here in the up-country and take the fort at Ninety-Six away from them. We'll whip the traitors to King George this time. Ye will make your father as proud of ye as he is of Duncan."

The coldness began to swell up and fill Alec's insides. "My brother Duncan is dead," he said, "and five years lying in his grave. We can thank the war for that."

Jamie scoffed, "Come now, Alec, that's the way of war. Ye should know that. Have ye been content to live under the rule of the American rebels here and be insulted by them?"

Alec shook his head. No. His father had not been at all pleased to have to swear an oath to support the American rebels against King George when the rebels had taken possession of the colony back in 1775. Not pleased at all! Like other Scottish farmers in the district, his father had been forced to swear the strong oath to keep his life and property. The rebels were stronger here now in 1780 than the king's friends.

Five years ago there had been fighting in Alec's part of the colony. With other men loyal to the king, Alec's father, Jamie, and Alec's older brother had gone to the courthouse in the village of Ninety-Six and there fought against the rebels. Twenty king's men had been killed that dark November day in 1775. One of them had been seventeen-year-old Duncan MacLeod.

And what good had that fighting done? The battle had decided nothing. A few weeks afterward a powerful rebel army had marched to Ninety-Six section and taken and garrisoned the fort. They held it still. Bold Duncan, to Alec's way of thinking, had thrown his life away!

As if Jamie could read his thoughts, he said, "Alec, I

think sometimes too on Duncan. He was my friend." He gathered up the sorrel's reins and went on speaking. "Perhaps I'll ride to your farm and tell your father that the king's ships have come back to Charles Towne."

Alec came forward to catch at the reins as Jamie started to call his hounds to him out of the thicket where they had flushed some small animal. "Jamie, did ye ride today to my grandfather's house? Did ye tell the Munns the news from Charles Towne?"

Gilchrist exploded, "By all the gods, na. Why should I? I'll leave that foul chore for ye to do. Go look upon the old traitor, Munn, not me. Ye'll be far more welcome to the witchwoman, your grandmother, than I. Ask her if we king's men will fight the American rebels again at Ninety-Six courthouse. Ask her if we shall win. That will stick in her craw." With a second call to his dogs, Jamie dug his heels into the sorrel's flank and went down into the creek where she slid and slipped on the rocks at its bottom, finally floundering across. Alec's last view of Jamie was one of him striving to stay atop Sweet Lass, yelling at the top of his lungs at her.

Alec drew in his breath in great annoyance. So—it was left to him to bring the news of the British fleet to his mother's parents! There was very bad blood between the Munns and the MacLeods. It would be clever to fetch a gift to old Munn. The pair of them were fond of rabbit, sweet and tender enough to be eaten in a stew by old people with few sound teeth remaining. A mile northward from where he had met Jamie, a fat cottontail came leaping out of some bushes into Alec's path. Startled, it bounded away, long ears laid close to its back for speed, but the rabbit could not outrun Alec's rifle ball, which brought it down in midleap.

With the rabbit dangling from his belt by its hind legs, Alec waded another icy creek and walked three miles further to the north and east before he came to his grandparents' small ill-kept farm. He didn't walk boldly up to their door. No one in the district did so foolish and dangerous a thing. He paused for a time, frowning at the log house built under winter-stripped beech trees with a dense tangle of thicket growing behind them. Smoke came wisping gray from the chimney. For a moment Alec had hoped they would be gone away, though God knows where they would go. Not visiting surely. The Munns were not well beloved in the district. People feared Andrew Munn's tongue and the scar on his cheek that told everyone he had been a traitor to the king. As for Jonet Munn, his wife, nearly everyone avoided her unless they felt a deep necessity to go to her. She was fey, as some folk who were born on Christmas Day were said to be in Scotland. She knew too much of matters common folk shied away from, matters that gave her the name of witch.

Standing where he was, Alec called out as loudly as he could, "Munn, Andrew Munn."

He saw the door of the house open very cautiously. After a moment it framed the very tall, white-bearded man, who held a musket ready. All farmers in the up-country of the colony greeted unexpected visitors in this way. The fierce and bloody wars with the Indians were not long past, and now that there was a revolution, settlers were as vigilant as ever. Who knew what man came to a person's house nowadays—friend or foe or someone who hoped to profit

by unsettled times when neighbor hated neighbor? Yet
Alec suspected that his grandfather would be quicker to
shoot a stranger than most men.

" 'Tis Alec. Alexander MacLeod," the boy shouted in
Gaelic.

"Come, Alec *dubh,*" bellowed the old man.

Alec sighed as he came over the cleared ground where
his grandmother kept her herb garden. He made his way
carefully among her low gray-green plants, noticing how
the cold weather had touched their edges with black fringes.
In the summer the Munn house blazed with color, scarlet
trumpet vines over the door and flowers covering the ground
on both sides. As Lachlan MacLeod so often said, wound-
ing Alec's mother each time, "The old hag Jonet Munn's
got green fingers as well as the black arts. She can put a
foul curse on a man or a hog with one glance of her uncanny eye."

Now, with his grandfather watching him, Alec dared not
spit three times to protect himself from his grandmother's
feyness. The Lord only knew she had never harmed him
or his family, though MacLeod hated her. Spitting would
not be wise. It could anger old Munn, who might tell his
wife. People of the section claimed the brood sows of
farmers who cursed Jonet Munn often brought forth dead
piglets at farrowing time.

Alec looked up at his grandfather, meeting the fierce
dark eyes and trying once more unsuccessfully not to let
his gaze rest fascinated on the gray-red *T* on the old man's
cheek. *T* for *traitor.* For thirty-four long years Andrew
Munn had worn the brand the king's soldiers had put on
him with a red-hot iron in Scotland.

As the old man moved aside and stepped back after lowering his musket, Alec slid past him through the narrow doorway. The Munn house was smaller and not so fine as his own home. There were only two plain wooden chairs set on the packed earth floor, a stool, a small table, and in the corner a bed, covered not with a good feather mattress, but with a moss-stuffed cloth. What his grandparents stored in the loft above, Alec didn't know for he had never been up its ladder. The boy saw that although there was a good fire of lightwood on the hearth, his grandmother was huddled in her tartan shawl in front of it on the stool. As if she were very cold, she sat close to the blaze.

Andrew Munn spoke to her in his grating voice, "Woman, Alec has come."

Jonet Munn arose. She was a tall, gaunt woman with white hair and black eyebrows that had never grayed. Her eyes were gray, even paler than the February sky outside the house. She walked to Alec, embraced him for an instant, then drew back, looking keenly into his face as she always did. It was a thing he disliked.

She said, "Each time I see ye, Alec *dubh,* Alec the black, ye grow more tall." Her strange gaze went to his belt. "Ah, I see ye have fetched us a rabbit for our supper. Ye never come to us empty-handed. But I think the rabbit is not what brings ye here, is it? Ye have news to tell us. It's been long since ye visited us."

"What news?" asked old Munn as he hung his musket over the door, then took Alec's long rifle from him and stood it in a corner out of the way.

Looking away from his grandmother's piercing eyes, Alec untied the rabbit from his belt as he said, "I fell in with

Jamie Gilchrist while I was hunting." It didn't surprise him
that she guessed he'd brought news. That was only what
could be expected of someone with second sight, a person
who could at times see into the future. Alec went on, "Jamie
has been down to Charles Towne. King George's soldiers
are there again aboard ships in the harbor. They have come
to try to capture the town from the Americans for the second
time."

Old Munn glanced at his wife, who had sat down on her
stool again staring once more into the flames, "What do ye
see now, old woman?" he asked her with his eyes on Alec's
face. To the boy's amazement, he laughed after he'd asked
the question.

"What I have seen for days, Andrew, and told ye of. The
white wings of ships, many ships, and many red soldiers
aboard them. I heard the whippoorwill last evening at dusk.
Evil news will surely come today because of that. Alec has
fetched it to us. The king's army has come here again."

Munn touched Alec's arm, warning. "Be silent now. Let
her speak," he whispered.

Alec shuddered. Her mother had told him of her own
childhood, of watching her fey mother look into the fire and
listening to her prophetic words. Very often what Jonet
Munn predicted had come to pass. And very often what she
had predicted had not been happy. Now the old woman muttered, *"Copleach, biast fionn, biast ruadh."*

Alec found her words strange. They were Gaelic but not
words men and women used every day. What would a white
beast, a *biast fionn,* or a red beast, a *biast ruadh* be? And
what did a *copleach,* a gathering of horses, have to do with
them? Horses were not usually spoken of as "beasts." Sud-

denly, while he wondered, he saw his grandmother bend over, clasping her arms around her body, "Ochone, ochone," she said softly. "Woe, woe," that is what she had said. The beasts and the gathering of horses had something then to do with woe.

Bolder than he'd ever dared be with her before, Alec went to kneel beside Jonet Munn. He asked her softly, "What do ye see for *me*, Grandmother? Will ye look into the flames for me? Will I have to go fight, too, if the redcoat soldiers come here to the north—to the up-country?" Na, he didn't have the courage to ask the one question crouching dark in the back of his mind, though he longed to know the answer. Would he be shot and killed as his brother Duncan had been?

She swung her head toward him. It seemed to him that her eyes were glazed and that she didn't see him at all. They were set somewhere in the far distance on pictures he could not see. His mother had told him once that his grandmother claimed she saw pictures in her head when she looked into the flames. She spoke to him in a croaking voice as if the words came out with great effort, "Aye, Alec *dubh,* ye will have to fight, but it will not come easy to ye."

The voice of her husband broke into her words, "Ye've looked into the fire all day. It is enough for now. Do not distress yourself, woman."

"Ochone," she keened again, bending forward, her eyes focusing on Alec. "For ye, Alec *dubh,* I see water, dark water. Ye do not know yourself now. But ye will know very soon, and then ye must make a choice. No skirling of bagpipes to lead ye into battle and no great broadsword of a Highland warrior in your hand. Dark water. That is for ye, black water, danger, and then a high place. And much death around ye."

Her husband's hand on her shoulder, she turned away once more. Alec got up, unhappy and bewildered, to hear his grandfather saying, "She may not speak again today." He shoved Alec before him to the table, pushed him down onto a chair, and said in a rasp, "She and I, we do not want the red soldiers to come to Charles Towne and besiege the city a second time. We don't want them to come marching here to the up-country. But your father MacLeod will welcome their coming because he is a true king's man—or so MacLeod calls the man who sits upon the thrones of England and Scotland now."

Alec let out a small sigh. He rested his hands on his knees, staring at the crockery plates on a shelf at one side of the hearth. Pity had led him to bring the news of the British army and ships to the old couple today, but Jonet Munn had already known it from her fire gazing. And now his grandfather was going to lecture him once more about Scotland and the reasons why he and his wife so hated the King of England and the king's soldiers. Alec knew the tale all too well. The Munns had come to the Carolinas in 1746, the year many Scots revolted against the English. The Scots had fought a great battle against the English at a place called Culloden and had lost it to the redcoat soldiers. Andrew and Jonet Munn, both Scots rebels, had been caught and transported in chains to the American colonies. They had been six weeks at sea drinking foul water and worm-ridden biscuit. If his grandmother had not had the foresight to bring a bag of raw potatoes with her from their farm when the redcoats dragged them off, she and Munn would both have died at sea. If she had not taken a pitchfork to the soldier who had come to their farm seeking her fugitive husband, she would not have been transported along with Munn. And if Munn had not fought against the king at the battle of Culloden, he would not have been branded on the face. The Munns had served for seven years as indentured servants. It had taken ten years for them to gather enough money to send for their three children left behind in Scotland. Two of the three had died on the terrible voyage. Only the youngest, Alec's mother, had survived, and she had had no memory of her parents. And in time she had married a king's man, Lachlan MacLeod.

Alec half listened to the familiar tale, but his grandfather's last sour words he caught clearly. Munn complained, "We have not seen our Margaret in five long years. Few come here to us."

"I come," flared Alec, getting up. "And I have heard that American rebels come here too—the men who shot at my father and who killed my brother. Do ye expect the loyal Scots to come?"

"Few rebels come!" said Munn somberly.

Alec asked him, "But Ellen Gilchrist comes?" He knew that Jamie's younger sister rode over to the Munns at times. Pretty golden-haired Ellen spoke to him now and then after church, seeking him out to tell him that she had visited his grandmother. Every time Ellen spoke to him, he blushed and felt very large and awkward. She was a silken poppet, far different from the freckled, thin Scottish girls who came to church in Ninety-Six village.

Munn spoke sourly, "Aye, the Gilchrist lass comes at times to see yer grandmother. She's a bold piece, that one."

Alec changed the subject, not wanting to discuss Ellen's boldness. It was true that she flirted with the boys and young men who came to church, but then so did other girls. He asked, "Why does she come here?" He wondered if she came for love philtres. Folk in Ninety-Six village whispered that Jonet Munn sold such things secretly. Whom did Ellen love? Was it—could it be Alexander MacLeod? He hoped that it was.

The old man grunted, "Who knows? They talk woman's talk in the corner. I have never heard them speak except of spinning and weaving." He gestured toward the spinning wheel in the corner next to Alec's rifle.

The boy turned his head to look over his shoulder at his grandmother. It would be pleasant and perhaps heart-warming to question her about Ellen of the long, long shining hair and rose-striped gown of taffeta that rustled when she walked up the aisle of the church to the Gilchrist pew. Whereas most girls in his district walked or rode in wagons, Ellen had a gray pony, as befitted Gilchrist importance. He wished he dared ask his grandmother why she came and if she had ever said his name or that of any other lad hereabouts.

"I'll dress your rabbit. Stay with us to supper," ordered the old man all at once.

"Na, Alec must not." Without swerving to look at him, Jonet Munn said from the fire, "There will be snow before morning, Andrew. Alec must be off with himself now."

Alec didn't wait. Delighted to be away, even without food or drink or news of Ellen, he took his rifle and went to the door. From there he said, "I promise ye I'll come to ye again if there is more news. If there is news of Charles Towne or of fighting."

His grandfather followed him to the door. He stood in it after Alec had gone outside. In his leather shirt, with one gnarled hand on each side of the frame, Munn said, "Alec, there will more than likely be fighting here, too, as well as down in the south around Charles Towne. It is not given to me to look into the flames, but I well know there will be red soldiers coming here. The red soldiers have lost battles to the Americans in the northern parts of this stranger land. They think the American rebels will be weaker here than in the north. So they have brought their many ships down here to win the war in the south."

Alec heard Jonet Munn mumbling from her stool but could not catch her words. Then suddenly, as he was about to start through her herb garden, he heard her calling after him, "Alec *dubh,* ye will know both Beasts, the White and the Red. And there will be horses. The thunder which was once far from ye comes closer to ye now."

As Alec went at a dogtrot away from the house he felt the cold clustering thick around him. He looked up into the sky. Aye, his grandmother had been right. While he'd been with her, the sky had deepened in color to a sullen gray. There would surely be snow that night. As he hastened for home he thought of her words to him. She had never looked into the fire for him before. He asked himself what "dark water" meant? There was no dark water near his home. The creeks of his countryside ran swiftly, draining out of the mist-blue mountains to the north. Who were the beasts? What did "much death" mean? Had she meant that he was going to die as Duncan had? But she had said "much death around ye." A man could only die one time. One death would not mean much death.

Running now at his Indian-style lope, he let his mind come back again to her brooding over the fire and her strange speech. What pictures had she seen in the flames?

With Lilias, his sister, Alec had lain on his stomach sometimes at night staring into the fire on their hearth. Neither of them had been able to see anything at all. Alec had been happy that he could not, though he knew well enough that men in Scotland as well as women could have second sight. His sister had seemed disappointed that she lacked her grandmother's gift. Lilias had been very young when Duncan had been killed. She couldn't recognize her grandparents if she met them at the trader's store in the village, Alec knew. Anyway, if they spoke to the Munns publicly, MacLeod would be furious. Alec secretly disobeyed his father only because he pitied the old couple, who lived such isolated lives and raised only enough food to keep them barely alive through the winters. MacLeod would let them starve if he had his way about it. Their existence was a constant embarrassment to him.

Alec made a vow to himself as he waded the fairly wide creek where he had talked with Jamie. If he got the chance to do so in secret, he would tell his mother he'd visited the Munns and told them the news from Charles Towne. Though she never spoke of them, he knew she would be pleased to learn that they fared well enough. To her they were not the "traitors" they were to her husband and the other Scots loyal to King George III. She had lived with them and understood their hatred of the British. She recalled Scotland and her dead brothers. Once wild-flower-pretty, she'd attracted the eye of big Lachlan MacLeod and had been pleased to marry him. He had been a catch as a husband for all of his bad temper. He would inherit land and livestock and a good double house. More than that, he had the fists to defy anyone who was foolish enough to say that he had married the daughter of a witchwoman.

No one insulted MacLeod's wife. But his wife obeyed him—not her parents. And that was the way of Lachlan MacLeod.

II
Gilchrist's Horse

The MacLeod farm was some five miles beyond and to the south of the village of Ninety-Six and its star-shaped fort. Alec jogged along under the fort's stockaded walls knowing that a member of its garrison watched him closely from the high catwalk, ready to raise his musket and shoot him if need be. He wondered if the American rebels were aware yet that the king's ships filled with redcoats had come back to South Carolina? If they didn't know, they would soon find out. It took weeks for the news of the war in the north, in the Middle and New England colonies, to arrive in the up-country of South Carolina. But Charles Towne was not that far away. A man riding hard from there could bring news to Ninety-Six in three days' time.

On the edge of MacLeod land a ruffed grouse rose with a rattling roar of wings out of the stubble that would be a cornfield next summer. Alec lifted his primed long rifle to his shoulder, aimed, and fired at the easy target. Mac-Leod had taught him to shoot with the long rifle as well as he had taught Duncan. A man's life could all too easily depend on his marksmanship in a countryside that had panthers and wolves. As Alec picked the bird up, the first snowflake hit the back of his hand. Aye, he had started for home just in time, thanks to his grandmother's warning. In another hour the stubble would be white with snow, and in the morning the brook he was about to cross on stepping-stones frozen solid.

The MacLeod house had been built on top of a low knoll overlooking the fields. It was a double one made of squared logs covered with clapboards. A dogtrot passage-way linked each half. Each cabin had a loft above the one main room. Behind the house lower down on the hill lay the pigsties for the sows that would farrow in the spring and a barn for the three horses and two milk cows. Lachlan Macleod, a king's man, a Tory, as he was called by the American rebels, was prospering in spite of the fact that they held the colony. His barn was stocked with hay, oats, and corn, though his cattle and hogs mostly roamed free in the woods. Alec had passed by some MacLeod cattle on his way homeward. Though MacLeod often sent cattle to market in Ninety-Six village, his real wealth lay in his pigs. Twenty stout barrels were stacked in his barn at the moment, filled with salted-down pork, good meat for sale to the highest bidder.

From a distance Alec saw something to gladden his heart and at last take his mind from his grandmother's ominous words. Some of Jamie's dogs lay in the passage-

way scratching their ears for fleas. Others were surely in
the house with their master. Alec managed a smile. He
could imagine the dog fights there would have been by now
between his father's hounds and Jamie's.

The boy went into the cabin on the right after shouting
out his name to warn his family. He pushed open the door
to find his mother in the exact posture before the fire as
Jonet Munn had been. For a moment Alec froze but then
saw that Margaret MacLeod was stirring something on a
griddle set in the coals. Thirteen-year-old Lilias, Alec's
sister, was laying the table with pewter plates, banging
them down on the naked boards.

Margaret MacLeod turned her head and smiled at her
son as he held up the grouse. She said, "God be praised,
ye've come home in time for supper, Alec *dubh*. I worried
myself over ye. We have a guest."

"Aye, Mother, Jamie. I know his dogs. I'll make ye a
guess that he's drinking rum punch with Father."

"He is," said the woman. She ordered Lilias, "Girl, take
the bird and put it into the tub outside the house. Mind
that ye put the tub high out of the reach of the dogs. Ye'll
pluck the bird tonight."

Alec's mother got up. She was tall like Jonet Munn but
not so strong-seeming and without the calm authority of
her mother. She bowed to the fierce blustering winds of
her husband's personality. MacLeod was not an easy man.
He was full of his own importance and often at odds with
his neighbors. Added to that, he was leather-lunged. When
he called to Alec over the fields or cursed out his neighbors,
be they Scots or rebels, as he rode past their houses, no one
ever failed to hear him. He had a way of taking the spirit

out of man or beast. Duncan, as Alec recalled him—and
each year the memory grew dimmer—had had something
of the same hard manner. As for himself, he was more like
his mother. MacLeod dismayed him and sometimes crushed
him. But for all of his shouting, Lachlan MacLeod could
not wither Lilias. She was no drooping flower to be cut
down by the sickle of his tongue. For days on end her long
black hair went uncombed and her feet unshod. Even now
in cold weather her feet were bare under her brown home-
spun gown made exactly like her mother's. Lilias even preferred homespun to silks and laces, though MacLeod was
willing to buy them for her. She was his despair as well
as his secret pride. No matter how he ranted at her, she
came back at him with a ready and a saucy tongue, making
him laugh and shake his head. Duncan had had something
of the same gift. Not Alec.

Lilias, who was lingering inside, gave Alec a questioning
glance over the table and asked, teasing, "Where have ye
been so long, Alec? Did ye see fair Ellen while her brother
tarries here drinking punch and getting drunk? Did Ellen
give ye the kiss ye long for?"

"Na, I did not see her." Alec hung his long rifle over
the mantel, refusing to quarrel with her. Ignoring her, he
stooped and whispered to his mother, who was bending
over the griddle again, "I took a rabbit to the Munns
today."

She gave him a startled glance, then called over her
shoulder, "Lilias, obey me. I spoke to ye about the bird.
Take it outside."

After Lilias had snatched up the grouse by its neck and
gone out, slamming the door angrily because she had been

cut out of the conversation, Margaret MacLeod asked
hastily, "Alec, how do they fare?"

"They are well enough."

"It was good of ye to go to them. I know ye pity them."
She sighed. "What did ye tell them? I think ye took them
the news of the king's ships in Charles Towne. I know ye
had it from Jamie Gilchrist. What did my father have to
say?"

"He was not surprised." Alec debated whether, now that
Lilias was out of earshot, to tell his mother the fey things
Jonet Munn had said to him. He decided not to. Instead he
said to her, "I could not stay long with them. Grandmother
said it would snow tonight and I shouldn't stay. I told them
I would come again when there was more news of the war
in this colony."

His mother put her thin hand over his, a gesture of
gratitude as well as of warning. "Do not tell your father.
It could go ill for ye. He will never forgive your grandfather for not coming with his musket to Ninety-Six courthouse, too, and fighting beside him with Duncan and the
other loyal king's men who are Scots."

"I know that," the boy said heavily. He also knew that
old Munn had not fought beside the Americans who held
the fort then either. He'd kept to his farm.

"He goes about in the village saying that he is not a
king's man and it is because of the king that he has a brand
on his face. Remember, Alec, he did not come to the
colonies of his own free will as the MacLeods did."
Margaret MacLeod might have said more, but at that
moment Lilias came back trailed by one of the MacLeod
dogs, the old red hound that was Alec's favorite. He would

have taken her hunting with him, but she'd injured one of her hind legs the week before. Now she hobbled up to Alec to sniff him and lick his hand, then lick his face because he was still bent over and she had the pure joy of reaching his cheek with her tongue.

Jamie was a very honored guest of MacLeod's. At supper the white-haired, swarthy-faced host never took his eyes off the young man who had distinguished himself at the battle of Ninety-Six courthouse and who had been a good friend to his hero son, Duncan. MacLeod drank cup after cup of rum punch with him. In high good spirits after a fine supper, he slammed his cup down on the table so hard that Alec's heavy plate rose into the air. MacLeod shouted, "So at last the king's ships have come again to Charles Towne! Long years we've waited for them, Jamie. Aye, the redcoats will seize that nest of rebels. No man can stand against a true redcoat soldier—not a true soldier trained by a king's officer."

As drunken as MacLeod, Gilchrist waggled a finger at him. "Na, ye be too hasty. The Americans stood fast against English troops at Saratoga and won. Do ye not forget that fight. And they did not so badly against us here at Ninety-Six courthouse five years past."

"Aye, Jamie, lad, but there were no redcoats there— no *true* king's soldiers! Only militia. Only king's militia, men like the two of us, against rebel militia, farmers, millers, plowmen, plain men from this colony. Ah, we are good enough marksmen but we know nothing of a soldier's discipline. Nor do the American rebels here in the up-country. Oh, I grant ye there are rebel soldiers in Charles

Towne and some hereabouts, but they will be no match at
all for the king's army come down from the north."

Gilchrist leaned back in his chair, shaking his fair head.
"Na, do not be so sure of that. The Americans ye despise so
much beat off the king's fleet in 1776 before Charles Towne
and forced the ships to sail back to the north. I do not
think that the ships will sail away a second time without
landing the soldiers aboard them. I have heard that they
have already landed men in Georgia colony, and there has
been fighting there. The rebels will give the redcoats a
fight here too, Lachlan."

"In Georgia colony, eh?" MacLeod stretched out his
thick legs under the table and called over his shoulder,
"Lilias, fetch me my pipe." When she had filled the long,
white clay pipe and lit it with a coal from the fire, Mac-
Leod took it and said, "I was born here in the colonies
as were ye, Jamie. As a lad, standing shoulder to shoulder
with my father, I shot buffalo and killed raiding Cherokee
Indians. The buffalo and the Indians are gone now from
this part of the colony. I am well content on my own land.
I have never seen the Highlands of Scotland and have no
wish to see them."

Alec nodded to himself as he got up, took down his
long rifle, and started to clean and polish it. His father
in a way was like old Munn. Now MacLeod would talk of
life in Scotland as he had had it from his own father. He
would talk of the poor soil and stone cottages and hunger
and the rule of the clan chief who had the power of life
or death over the clansmen. He would say that he was
pleased his father had decided to emigrate—and in particular pleased that he had gone with his wife *before* the

Scots rebelled in 1746 against the English. He'd tell Jamie how a MacLeod ancestor had been killed in battle against the English in 1715.

Alec heard his final words ten minutes later. "Aye, Jamie, any Highland Scot who has land from the king and who supports the rebel scum against the redcoats will lose a war against the English for the third time in one century. Na, Lachlan MacLeod does not have it in mind to lose his land. He is no traitor to King George like old Andrew Munn."

Alec saw his mother's reddening face. Then she asked quietly, "Master Gilchrist, do ye think the English redcoats will march up to Ninety-Six once they've taken Charles Towne?"

"Aye, mistress, I do. They must."

MacLeod said, "And Jamie, ye and I, we'll go join them and fight beside true redcoats and retake the fort. We'll take Alec with us. He's old enough."

Alec paused with the ramrod halfway down the barrel of the rifle. He felt a sickening weight descend on him. And his grandmother's words of "much death" came flashing back to him.

He listened now to Jamie rambling on. "Rumor had it in Charles Towne when I was there that the voyage of the fleet from New York had been a long and stormy one. Ships were wrecked on the way. Men and horses drowned. Some of the king's soldiers will be cavalry. They'll need horses once they come ashore. I got a fine bargain in my Sweet Lass in the town. Her rebel owner was eager to sell her. Much as I favor the king's army coming here I was not against getting a very fine horse out from under their noses. And I've never seen a mare like her. I'll race her soon. And wager on her, MacLeod, when I do."

Alec saw how Lilias peeped out of the corners of her green eyes at Gilchrist lolling at the table in his handsome coat. Young as she was, she was taken with him. She hung onto every word he said. Alec wondered while he polished the stock of his rifle if the Gilchrists would favor a match someday between Lilias and Jamie, though Jamie was too old for her. Or more to the point, a match between him and Ellen? They were of an age.

MacLeod was asking Jamie about the cannon on the ships and at the rebel forts set around Charles Towne, wanting to know if Jamie had heard them firing. He had.

MacLeod flung back his head and stared at his son. "Alec, *dubh,* there's a sound to stir a man's heart. Cannon fire."

Alec said nothing. Lilias entered the conversation starting with a small breathless laugh. She said while she plucked the grouse into the wooden tub filling the air with its brown feathers, "Na, Alec will not like to hear the cannon, Father. Alec hates to hear the squealing of the hogs in the autumn when ye butcher them."

The boy glowered at his sister. He guessed that she sensed he wanted to be something other than a farmer. He thought often that he would be perfectly willing to have her and her husband, whoever he might be, work the MacLeod farm someday. The trader's store in Ninety-Six fascinated him. So did the strangers who came to it passing up and down the Keowee Trail. Silent copper-skinned Indians, the Choctaws and Cherokees, who'd signed a treaty with the up-country whites giving up their land and moving their villages over the mountains. These were the Indians his father and grandfather and old Munn had fought. Who knew if they would come back seeking their old land again? If they did, they'd come with torches and scalping knives. The thought was a constant fear to folk in the district.

Other interesting men came and went at the trader's, too, Alec had noted. These were white men, tall, hard-eyed men with long rifles, long hair, and raccoon-skin caps. They brought furs with them to be sent down to Charles Towne. Mostly they were as silent as the trading Indians, but sometimes while Alec was loitering at the trader's he heard them speaking to one another. They spoke quietly of their constant struggles with the Indians in the hills. Some spoke Gaelic among themselves, but Alec had never approached them. The trader, who was friendly to him, had warned him that the "backwater men" were fiercer than the Cherokees. Certainly they looked the part.

Suddenly Jamie asked a question, a horrifying one. "Alec *dubh,* tell me, how did ye find the Munns today?"

Alec saw how Lilias sat up, dropping the grouse, and he heard his mother's soft gasp of dismay. It was followed by a great roaring from MacLeod. *"What?"*

Alec said, "I only took the Munns the news from Charles Towne." He added, hoping to stay his father's rage, "It did not please them." Was MacLeod going to take a stick to him in front of Jamie?

But the man simply asked in fury, "What more did the old devil of a traitor Munn have to say?"

"Nothing more, Father."

"What did the mad old hag say then?"

Alec told him, "She said there would be fighting in this colony."

His words made MacLeod guffaw. "To know that does not require second sight or witchcraft. Did she tell ye more? Did she tell ye something worth the hearing? Did she say *when* Charles Towne will fall to the king's forces?"

"Na." No, he would not tell anyone in the house what Jonet Munn had seen in the flames. As MacLeod and Jamie went on drinking, Alec's puzzled glance went again to the young man. He had never thought that his friend Jamie would betray his visit to the Munns to his father. After all, Jamie was the one who had sent him to the Munns in the first place. Perhaps it was the effect of the rum and too many toasts to the health of good King George. A wild strain Jamie had in him sometimes, for a fact. Sometimes he did and said things that were strange. Tonight he had enjoyed Alec's fright and humiliation. Alec had seen the pleasure in his mocking eyes and the lines of his mouth. Come to think on it, Jamie, a rich man's son, often did and said exactly as he pleased at the moment without considering anyone but himself.

Aye, Jamie would be very interested in what Jonet Munn had told Alec, but in his heart Alec knew what she had seen was for him alone.

Jamie was looking at the ceiling the next time Alec glanced at him. He pursed his lips as MacLeod asked him when Jamie thought the king's forces would take Charles Towne. Gilchrist replied, "Before the summer ends. They'll have the town in a few months' time. There are very many ships this time. Soldiers will ride north out of Georgia colony also on to Charles Towne. I think they will surround the town and starve the rebels out. It is what I would do. Then they will march here to the up-country."

MacLeod held up his cup. "And we'll march beside them on to Ninety-Six fort and take it."

Alec heard Jamie's laughter. The more he drank, the more high-pitched it became. "Na, man, *ye* may walk to the village beside the redcoats. I have something else in mind."

Offended by the refusal, which was totally unexpected, MacLeod demanded loudly, "What would that be that ye do not want me?"

Jamie leaned forward and said, "To join the king's army before it reaches this district!" He set his cup down. "I am going to raise a troop of cavalry. I plan to call it Gilchrist's Horse. I'll train my men to ride together and use a pistol well. 'Tis no good place for a long rifle—on horseback. I have the pistols for those who do not have them, and I have some horses but not enough to mount a troop. This is why I came here today, Lachlan, to ask ye for your dun gelding."

"I'll gladly ride with ye, Jamie," thundered MacLeod.

"Na, na, 'tis Alec I'm asking for—not ye." Jamie pointed a finger at MacLeod while Alec stopped cleaning the rifle, paralyzed at the words. Jamie went on, "MacLeod, ye are too heavy to ride the dun very far. I need your swiftest horse so it must be the gelding. 'Tis Alec I want. He's not got his full growth yet, but he can be taught to ride as a cavalryman, and his weight is right for the dun.

When the king's foot soldiers come against the fort, ye march out with them. They'll welcome ye and your rifle."

Alec watched his father rubbing his chin. He held his breath, hoping the man would refuse. MacLeod said slowly, "Aye, take my Alec and the dun and train them both, Jamie, once the spring plowing and planting is done. I doubt if the redcoats will be here before then. There's no reason why Alec cannot serve the king on horseback as Duncan and ye and I served him on foot five years ago." MacLeod laughed loudly. "But don't ask Alec to ride out with ye when I'm whiskey making. I'll need him. I have a plan, too. I'll meet the king's soldiers with a full barrel of whiskey and give them a good welcome. There may even be loyal Scots among 'em, men like us. They'll take up-country whiskey to gin or rum, I think. Rum is too costly for me to give to anyone but my friends." Again MacLeod lifted his cup as Alec looked on.

Ride out and seek the king's army! It was hard enough to bide on the farm hoping that it would never come.

Jamie stayed the night lying in the MacLeod's best bed on their finest feather mattress. His staying meant that Alex and Lilias climbed up into a loft to sleep rolled up in quilts because MacLeod and his wife took their children's pallets. Listening to her father snoring below, Lilias began to giggle. Alec heard her saying, "Alec *dubh,* I saw your face while they talked of Gilchrist's troop of horse. Ye don't want to ride with Jamie, do ye? Ye don't favor the coming of the redcoats to the up-country at all."

He hissed at her angrily in the darkness of the loft. "Na,

what's the bedamned war to me, girl? I'm not our brother Duncan, eager to go out to fight the rebels. I'm not a fire-eater like Gilchrist, who ye seem to favor so much that it surprises me Mother didn't catch ye making eyes at him and whip ye."

"Na," Lilias whispered, moving closer to her brother. "But ye favor Jamie's sister, Ellen. Ye'd like to eat a dumb supper with Mistress Ellen."

Alec didn't reply. She'd said truly. He wanted to eat a silent dinner of very salty corn bread with Ellen, then go to bed and hope to dream of her. If she came to him in a dream with a cup of water, it would mean that someday she would be his wife. All people young enough to think on such matters in the up-country knew that this was the best way of all to see their future bride or groom.

Still, he told Lilias fiercely, "Ye'd eat a dumb supper with Jamie in a minute if he'd do it with ye. Ye'd stand on your head if he'd take notice of ye. But ye're but a wee child yet."

Lilias spat her words at him. "Ye be a coward, Alec *dubh*. Ye hate the killing of the pigs and the branding of the calves, and ye hate the plowing and the planting, though there's no dying there. All ye care for is cooling your heels at the trader's store in the village. Ye are a plague to old Master Deckard. Ye don't want to be a farmer but a trader like him. Ye've got the look of the MacLeods but the fey spirit of the Munns."

Alec pulled his quilt up over his head and rolled over with his back to her, half stifling himself not to hear her. Why deny the truth to himself? At least now she wasn't

talking about Ellen, who had never given him one bit of
encouragement. It was less painful by far to hear the truth
said about his desire to be a trader. Na, Lilias didn't have
second sight, but all the same she saw deeply into him.
And he saw into her. No one else had seen how she looked
at Jamie.

Suddenly out of the dark the girl asked, "When will
ye go to the Munns again?"

"What makes ye think I will go there? Ye heard Father
tonight."

"I know ye, Alec *dubh*. Ye will."

"Aye, Lilias." He mumbled through the folds of the
quilt. "When there's news I'll be going."

"Will ye tell the Munns of Jamie's troop of horse?"

Alec had considered this question after Jamie had
sprung his surprise. Yes, he should tell the old couple. He
suspected Jamie might ride about visiting the farms of
known rebels in the district. Not that Jamie would harm
the rebels—only keep them "in order." But it would be wise
of the Munns not to provoke Gilchrist's uncertain temper.
"Aye, Lilias, I'll tell them."

"Ye'll visit them in secret, Alec?"

"How else can I go?" he asked her bitterly. "Am I to
ask permission of MacLeod?"

Then he felt his sister's hand on his shoulder. "Alec,
take me with ye. I can hunt with ye and travel that far on
foot, too."

When he didn't reply, she went on, "Is it true that
Grandmother Jonet is a witchwoman? Can she tell the
future and make love philtres?"

Alec wriggled Lilias's hand off him as he said, "Na, na,

she's a herb wife. She's no witch." He searched for a suitable lie. "Mother says Grandmother Munn can see the future, but if she does, she doesn't do it for me."

"Ellen Gilchrist rides to her, Alec."

"Does she then? Perhaps she talks to our grandmother of spinning or weaving?" he said, recalling old Munn's words.

"Ha!" came a soft chuckling from Lilias. "Ellen does not spin thread, and she doesn't sit at a loom as our mother does. The Gilchrists have black slaves to do that. Ellen makes tiffety-taffety puddings and sews a fine seam. Na, Alec, she goes to the Munns for love philtres. She pours the philtres into the well behind her house. That is why every lad for miles around falls in love with her. All she must do is give him the dipper from the well and offer him a drink when he comes visiting. Take me with ye to the Munns."

Alec rubbed his cheek against the quilt, annoyed with Lilias. She made him angry often, teasing and cajoling him, making him feel awkward and ill-favored. He thought of the Munns in their poverty and their loneliness. They were kinder to him than his father or his sister. They were outcasts for many reasons. He had no idea how much English they spoke. They had never used a word of it to him.

Jonet and Andrew Munn had not seen Lilias since she had been eight years old. They'd be pleased to see her again. She was comely enough and clever—too clever. Aye, he would take her to them. The visit might please them, and Lilias, he was sure, would take no harm from it. He smiled to himself, a smile hidden by the dark of the loft. His sister's wicked tongue might even meet its match in her grandmother's. That would suit him very well and would keep Lilias from demanding to go there again.

As for himself, he'd go whenever he had a notion to and hunted in their direction. Jonet Munn might have more to say to him about the things she'd seen in the fire.

Alec became drowsy thinking on the word *copleach,* a gathering of horses. How swiftly Jonet Munn's vision had come true! In less than one day's time Jamie was gathering horses for his troop of cavalry. And this gathering did concern him, too! The MacLeod dun gelding had been offered to Jamie.

Well, let him take the dun for his troop. Alexander Mac-Leod did not have to be part of the bargain! He'd talk to his father when Jamie had gone home with his dogs and the beautiful sorrel mare, Sweet Lass. Perhaps with Jamie gone and MacLeod alone and sober, he might change his father's mind.

III

A Matter of Ribbons

Alec said nothing more to his mother about his visit to the
Munns the next morning. He ate his breakfast of corn
bread and bacon and went tramping over the snow to the
barn seeking his father.

He and Lilias, who no longer attended the school taught
by the minister of their kirk in the village because she was
more than twelve years old, were both there. Lilias was
milking the black cow while MacLeod attended to a sore
on the right rear hock of the dun. The other two MacLeod
horses, the aged white mare and the dapple gray, stood
in their stalls, looking mildly at MacLeod, who was cursing
as the dun snorted and moved about uneasily.

Alec would have preferred not to have Lilias as an audi-
ence to his conversation with his father, but he knew there
was no getting rid of her. He came up to the dun and held

him by the hackamore, then said, "Father, do ye remember that last night ye gave the dun here to join Jamie's troop of horse?"

MacLeod glanced up, liniment jug and cloth in hand. "Aye, so I did."

"Ye offered me to Jamie at the same time," Alec said quietly, with a sidelong glance at Lilias, who had stopped milking.

In the silence unbroken by the whirring sound of milk into the pail, MacLeod said, "So I did, Alec. Ye'll train with Jamie and ye'll ride out with Gilchrist's Horse to find the king's soldiers before they come to Ninety-Six fort."

Alec took a deep breath and told his father, "It's one thing to take a rifle and march with the redcoats to the fort when they've arrived here. And asked for our help. 'Tis another to ride out seeking them." Staring at an old scar on the dun's withers, Alec faltered on, "I do not want to join Jamie's troop."

"What are ye saying to me?" MacLeod dropped the gelding's hoof. He stood, glaring at Alec.

The boy repeated, "I don't want to ride with Jamie!"

"The hell ye don't!" thundered the man. He set down the liniment and threw the cloth atop the jug. "*I say ye'll go.* Duncan would have gone. Ye'll be a soldier if I say ye'll be."

Alec, his heart beating faster, tried to stand his ground. "I am not Duncan, Father. I don't want to be a soldier."

"Come out of there!" shouted the man.

Aware of his sister's wide eyes and quick intake of breath, Alec came slowly out of the gelding's stall.

His hands on this thick hips, MacLeod demanded, "Who

put this daft idea into yer head? Old Munn the traitor or the witchwoman? How often do ye go to them?"

"It is my own thought, Father."

"Na, the rebel trader at the village did it. I care not which one of them is responsible. Ye'll go when Jamie calls ye out."

"Na, I will not."

"What, ye'll stay behind, a coward, and make a fool of me as well as a liar to Jamie? Na, ye will not!"

MacLeod made a sudden rush forward. Grabbing Alec by the shoulders, he shook him. Then he flung him away. The next instant the man's great first smashed into Alec's face. The boy caught at the side of the dun's stall and hung on. His father's second blow knocked him to his knees in the straw. Standing over Alec, the man bellowed, "I promised ye'd go, and so ye shall. Jamie will make something of ye more than ye are now, a milksop. Do ye think I need your rifle to defend my house and farm? Ye'll ride with Gilchrist's Horse, and ye'll make me as proud of ye as I am of Duncan." MacLeod reached down and jerked Alec to his feet by the thongs of his buckskin coat. He propped him against the stall and pulled back his fist for a third blow.

But Lilias darted between the fist and her brother. "Na, na, Alec will go with Jamie," she cried out. "Tell him ye'll go, Alec!"

"Aye, Father," the boy said between bleeding lips.

Satisfied, MacLeod let go. He gave Alec a look of savage contempt, turned on his heel, and went out of the barn, but not before he commanded, "Ye will tend to the dun from now on. He's to be your mount. See to his hock before the day's ended."

Lilias picked up the cloth, shook horse liniment out of the jug onto it, and wiped her brother's face with the sharp-scented, stinging liquid.

"Thank ye, Lilias," Alec told her. He felt so dizzy that he had to go to her milking stool and sit down.

Her laughter sounded softly through the barn. "Tush, Alec *dubh*. I saved ye to put ye in my debt. Now I think ye'll take me to visit Grandmother Jonet, will ye not?"

"Aye, Lilias." As Alec's hand went probingly to his sore jaw, he thought of the future. He must go with Jamie's troop, it seemed. His father would see to that and see further to it that he behaved creditably as a cavalryman. The only thing, short of running away, that he could do to pay out MacLeod for his brutality was to visit the Munns more often in secret. Lilias would keep the secret, too, providing Jonet Munn used her second sight for the girl's benefit.

Alec let out a deep sigh as he took blood-stained fingers away from his jaw. His grandmother was as little to be controlled as MacLeod. Who knew if she would agree to look into the fire for Lilias?

No one and nothing was to be controlled by him, it seemed. Neither Jamie nor Ellen nor the king's ships nor redcoat soldiers who had come back to besiege Charles Towne!

Like Jamie, Alec had no doubt that this time the determined royal forces would take the port city and before the summer ended, as Jamie had said.

Snowbound for a time, Alec tended faithfully to the dun, trying to keep out of his father's way. It seemed to him that MacLeod for his part did the same. Or perhaps his father simply considered the episode over and done with, because he had got his way. Jamie sent no message to the MacLeod farm about Gilchrist's Horse, and nary a word came to anyone of how things fared in Charles Towne.

Alec was not aware of the reason for his father's silence. MacLeod was thinking—thinking of Charles Towne. He'd visited the city as a boy and remembered it well enough. The king's ships blockaded the harbor while the town itself, set on a peninsula between two rivers, could soon be ringed about by redcoats who'd hold all the approaches from the north. Food might soon be very hard to come by for the rebel civilians and soldiers in Charles Towne.

MacLeod had known for some time that the trader in Ninety-Six village planned to send a shipment of cornmeal and pork-in-brine down to the city. Why not send MacLeod pork with that of other farmers in the district? He had barrels to sell.

One morning of driving, snow-melting rain a week later, while Alec was in the musty-smelling barn currycombing the dapple gray, his father came up to him through the brown dimness of the place. Alec looked up, wary of more blows, but this time MacLeod was smiling at him.

"Alec *dubh*," he said cheerfully, "it's come to me that I've got twelve barrels of salt pork to send down to Charles Towne with the trader's wagon."

Alec paused in surprise, currycomb in midair over the gray's back. "Ye plan to sell our pork to the rebels?"

"Aye, it would suit me better if the meat went to fill the bellies of King George's soldiers. But I can't get the pork out to the ships in Charles Towne harbor, can I? So I'll sell it where I can. A profit is a profit."

Turning his head away, Alec combed the gray's mane. He thought of Jamie, who'd bought Sweet Lass from a rebel in Charles Towne and then boasted that he'd saved the fleet mare from the British cavalry. His father was no better—but they called themselves king's men. They were willing to serve the king with long rifles and pistols for their own glory, but they weren't willing to lose a profit for him.

"Alec *dubh*," MacLeod went on, "ride the dun to the trader's store. Ye know old Deckard better than I. Ye have the English tongue where I have not. Tell him that I want to send my pork with him to Charles Towne."

The boy said quietly, "He's an American, a rebel. What makes ye think he'll take your meat?" He waited for his father's windy wrath.

But MacLeod only chuckled. "If Deckard's not sent off his wagons, and I saw them in the village before the snow came, he'll take my pork to the city. He'll sell it for me and have his profit—as I'll have mine."

"I'll saddle the gelding now." Then Alec asked, "When will ye be bringing the pork to the village?"

"Tomorrow." MacLeod reached into the waist pocket of his breeches, bringing out a copper coin. "While ye're there, buy a ribbon to tie back your sister's hair so I can see her bonny face sometimes. Buy her a red ribbon." He winked at Alec. "Buy a ribbon for the Gilchrist lassie as well. I know ye fancy her."

Lilias! A flood of red came pulsing up Alec's neck. Lilias had told his mother that he fancied Ellen, and his mother had told MacLeod. Damn Lilias!

MacLeod leaned his arm on the back of the gray speaking very softly, a rare thing for him. "God knows I have no objection to a match between a Gilchrist and a MacLeod."

Before Alec could catch back the words, they'd slipped out. "Then ye'd best look to Lilias and your friend, Jamie."

"Lilias? Jamie?" MacLeod's mouth fell open. He laughed louder than before and a moment later said, "So—my wee lass favors Jamie!" He slapped his palm onto the gray's flank before he started off. From a distance away, he shouted, "Na, Jamie's taken no notice of her. She's not a woman yet. I'll pin my hopes to Gilchrist's sister and to ye, Alec. She'll fetch a handsome dowry to ye. Buy a ribbon for her. Give it to her the day ye ride to the Gilchrist farm to drill with Jamie's troop. It will tell her your intentions."

And MacLeod was gone.

Alec sagged against the dapple gray. God in heaven, he'd rather face rebel muskets any day than take a ribbon to Ellen Gilchrist. In any event, he refused to do so until the cut on his lip had fully healed.

Though Alec was all too aware of the embarrassing errands that brought him to the trader's store, it was as usual a place of delight to him. He sniffed the wild odor of bales of furs from over the mountains ready for shipment. Over their rankness came far sweeter scents—nutmeg, tea, and cloves. When he'd ridden into the village, he'd spied the trader's three wagons outside the store. The shipment had not set off yet for Charles Towne. Chances were, the wagons would not go until there had been some days of sunshine to dry the mud of the old Keowee Trail, the Indian-trail wagon road, that led to the low country and to Charles Towne.

His eye on the cards of ribbon and packets of pins and

needles the trader stocked, a rain-soaked Alec loitered until
the last customer had gone out. Embarrassed by his halting
English, he wanted no listeners. True, the old rebel could
speak some Gaelic, but in a moment of folly two years past
Alec had confessed to him that he wanted to be a trader
also. From that time on the old man had refused to speak
anything to him but English as if he trained him.

"What do you want today, Alexander?" asked Deckard.
"Something for your mother—a nutmeg or a jug of mo-
lasses?"

"No, Master Deckard, I've come for two"—Alec sought
the word and found it—"ribbons." He lied, "For my sister
and my mother."

"Silk ribbons or velvet ribbons?" The trader was grin-
ning, informing Alec that he knew he lied.

"Silk or velvet—I care not. One must be red."

"Yes, see this." The trader pulled down a card of bright
red gleaming silk. "This is ha'penny a yard."

Alec nodded. "I'll have it. A yard of it."

"What's the other ribbon to be?"

"What have you?"

"For your mother, black or dark blue." Again Deckard
was smiling knowingly.

Alec shook his head. "My father woudn't like those."
He thought hard. What would please MacLeod in the matter
of a ribbon for Ellen? He would demand to see it. More
important, what might please Ellen? Suddenly he remembered her white taffeta Sunday gown. It was striped with
rose and with dark green. A yard of ribbon could tie a
bonnet onto her head and under her white chin.

"Do you have a rose?" he stammered.

"I do." And a card of rose-colored velvet appeared from the shelf onto the counter for Alec to see. He touched it with one timid finger. It was soft as a flower petal.

"It will do, Master Deckard."

Alec watched the ribbons measured, cut, and rolled into a little ball. He put them into his breeches pocket with a sigh after he'd paid out his coin.

"I trust the rose pink will please your mother, Alexander."

"It will, it will. She wants a rosebush by the doorway." Alec tried to sound more businesslike. "My father has twelve barrels of salt pork he wants to ship down to Charles Towne in your wagons." He'd rehearsed the English for this speech on the way. "He wants you to sell the pork there for him. He knows the king's ships blockade the town."

For the first time Alec saw the friendly trader turn sour. His grin faded. "A king's man like Lachlan MacLeod wants to sell food to rebels?"

"He wants to sell his pork, Master Deckard." Alec stood his ground steadily.

Deckard waggled his beard before he spoke again. "Tell your father that I'll take the pork, though it goes against my grain. There'll be great need of meat in Charles Towne before long. No belly cares where a meal comes from as long as the belly gets filled."

Alec asked, haltingly, "Do you think the king's army will take Charles Towne this time?"

The old man looked coldly at Alec. "Yes, bedamned to all of you Tories, you king's men, I think they might. They could take the town and come marching here. But before that happens, this state will know what hell is like. It will be far worse than it was in 1775 when your brother Duncan was killed."

"How will it be?" asked Alec.

"I'll tell you so you can tell your father and that wild young cockerel, James Gilchrist." The trader leaned forward over his counter. "I fought Indians twenty years ago in the district, and in 1775 I fought men who had once been my good friends. These men may not love me now, but they still trade with me. But if the king's redcoats march through this state, it will be father against son and brother against brother—not just neighbor against neighbor as it is now. If evil that time comes, what side will you choose?"

Alec told him stiffly, "The MacLeods are king's men. You favor the cause of the rebels and the Continental Congress."

"Yes, and I have some faith in a Virginian named General George Washington, who leads our armies in the north. He does well now winning battles."

Not wanting to talk about Washington, whoever he might be, Alec said, "My father will bring the barrels tomorrow in our wagon. I thank ye, Master Deckard." No, he wouldn't stay to be lectured again as he had been lectured lately by Andrew Munn and by Lachlan MacLeod.

As Alec started away, the trader called after him, "Tell your father and Gilchrist that some backwater men came here yesterday with furs. They claim that the British are stirring up the Indians over the mountains against the white settlers now."

"I'll tell them, Master Deckard."

"Only one thing more," cried the trader, as Alec stood

by the door, "if the Indians kill settlers there, what's to keep them from coming back down here? Tell me, Alexander, what does your Grandmother Munn have to say to you these days about matters hereabouts? I haven't seen her or Munn since last summer."

"Nothing." Finding more English words, Alec told him, "I don't go often to them. What would she say to me if I did go?"

"A great deal old Jonet Munn could say. She cured my gout for me. She's a very wise woman, your grandmother."

"And she's a rebel," said Alec, as he went out into the rain. Though he wouldn't tell the trader, he planned going to the Munn farm tomorrow with Lilias. The two of them would walk, hunting as they went. The dun had a hard mouth, wracking gaits, and was difficult to manage. The horse would stay in the barn in his stall.

As for worrying about MacLeod, he'd be out of the way all day. He'd be in Ninety-Six village with his wagon and pork, and after he had delivered the barrels to Deckard he'd surely linger in the tavern next door.

As Alec had guessed, MacLeod demanded to see the two ribbons the moment his son had dismounted and told him that the trader was willing to take the barrels of pork. The man looked at both ribbons, poked at the rose-colored one, lying across Alec's palm next to the scarlet and laughed. Then he took the red ribbon to wind it around his large fingers. In a slanting shaft of sunlight breaking through rain clouds, the shining ribbon to Alec's way of thinking resembled nothing so much as a spill of bright blood.

"Go to the Gilchrist farm within the week. There's no

cause to wait until Jamie sends for ye. When ye go, take this pretty with ye for the lass. Be certain to tell her 'tis a gift *ye* give her."

Alec kept his face set into hard lines. That would be a lie he told Ellen, but he would be foolish to complain to his father. Instead he said, "I spied a flock of wild turkeys on the way home. If it suits ye, I'll go out hunting them tomorrow."

"Aye, ride the dun. He's shy of rifle fire. Teach him not to fear it."

"Na, Father. I plan to go afoot. 'Tis easier for me."

MacLeod shrugged. "Suit yourself, lad, as long as ye fetch us a bird and mind ye, use no more than one ball." He went toward the house, playing with the red ribbon, leaving Alec to take the gelding into the barn and unsaddle him.

He found his sister sitting on her milking stool playing with the yellow barn cat, tickling his face with a long piece of hay while he lay on his back batting at the hay with swift paws. She jumped up so quickly at the sight of Alec that she startled the cat who streaked off into the dimness, tail straight out. Lilias came to help Alec unbuckle the dun's saddle girth while he removed the bridle and put on a hackamore. While he grunted hauling off the heavy saddle, Lilias asked him, "Alec *dubh,* will Father be going to the trader tomorrow with the pork?"

"He will. Master Deckard will send the pork to Charles Towne."

Lilias's bright green eyes were alight. "Father will take himself to the tavern after that. He'll be gone most of the day. Ye'll take me to Grandmother Munn tomorrow, Alec?"

He nodded. She had anticipated exactly what he'd been thinking. "Go to the house," he told her. "He has something for ye. I got it at the trader's."

She asked scornfully, "A poppet? A toy?"

"Na, not a poppet." Not a doll. Lilias might even like the red ribbon for a time. Not because it pleased MacLeod, but because it pleased her. And then it might be tied to the barn cat's neck or to the branch of any tree in the woods behind the house.

Who knew what Ellen Gilchrist might do with hers after he'd given it to her? Would she offer him a drink from the dipper at her bewitched well? She needn't do that. He was already smitten with her.

Though the way to the Munn house was long, the weather windy and chilly, and several icy creeks had to be waded, Lilias didn't once complain as she walked the nine miles with Alec. Wrapped in a shawl of the yellow, black, and red tartan of the MacLeods over her brown dress, she was a colorful sight. Either because it was cold, or the ground rock strewn, or because of a desire to impress her grandparents, Lilias had put on her shoes with the pewter buckles. Her curling black hair was even crowned at the top by a scarlet bow. Beside her trotted the old red hound for companionship and protection. Alec suspected that today the Munns might take very little notice of him. He had no doubt that they would be delighted to see his sister.

To his surprise Lilias put her hand into his as they halted a distance away from the Munn house. He'd killed no cottontails this time on the way, nothing but two small squirrels that hung from his belt. He looked down at her, a head shorter than he. She was trembling, something he'd never seen before.

"Is Grandmother truly a witchwoman?" she asked in a small voice very unlike her usual one.

"Na," he assured her. "She'll do no harm to ye, Lilias."

Alec cupped his hand to his mouth and called out as before. And as before, Andrew Munn came to the doorway, armed, recognized Alec, and motioned him forward with a wave of his arm. As the boy and his sister passed through Jonet Munn's herb garden, Alec heard a soft nickering. He jerked up his head, staring around him.

No, this animal wasn't Munn's old swaybacked chestnut. It was a plump gray pony, well-groomed, with a shining saddle upholstered with green velvet. It was a sidesaddle.

Alec's heart tightened in his breast at the sight of the animal tethered beside the house.

Ellen's pony!

Lilias recognized it too. She clutched at Alec's arm, hissing into his ear, "Alec *dubh*, Ellen's come here, too. She's come for more love philtres brewed of black mustard. Ye've got a rose ribbon in your breeches pocket. Give it to her now. Father told me ye bought it for her at the trader's."

Alec ground his teeth in rage. His father was full of lies and half-truths. "*I* did not buy it for her, Lilias! *He* forced me to buy it."

"Were ye so very unwilling?" she asked, laughing.

IV
Lilias

By now they were nearing the door where the old man waited. Alec called out to him, "Grandfather, I've brought Lilias with me." At his sister's soft command the red hound sat down at her side.

"Lilias?" Munn let out a roar. Then, turning his head, he shouted into the house, "Woman, Alec's come here. He's brought our granddaughter with him."

A moment later Munn stepped aside to let his wife pass through the doorway. She walked swiftly to Alec and Lilias, heedless of the red dog's growling. Her glance at Alec and the hound was only an instant's flick, but her gray eyes were intent on Lilias, not so much devouring but appraising. Finally, standing before them, she had her fill of gazing. Then she reached out and pulled both of them to her in a brief embrace. For some reason the red hound at once ceased its growling.

"Come inside. 'Tis cold here," she told them.

"Ye've got someone with ye," Alec said, hoping they could remain where they were or be sent away. He had no wish to see Ellen—not without a chance of first arranging in his mind what he would say to her.

Assured now of her welcome, Lilias went with her grandmother, but Alec hung back. As they entered the house, Munn, musket still in hand, walked up to the boy. "Do ye have news of the British from Charles Towne so soon?" The old man had a pat on the head for Alec's hound.

"Na, Grandfather." Alec jerked his head toward the door. "The Gilchrist lass is there?"

"Aye, blathering with Jonet."

Alec told him, "Jamie, her brother, plans to raise a troop of horse and ride out to meet the king's soldiers once they come to the up-country. Grandmother spoke of horses being 'gathered.' "

"I remember her words." Tall old Munn looked into the distance over Alec's head. "They will come—the red soldiers and the green. And they are gathering horses also."

"Green ones?" Alec asked in puzzlement.

"Aye, boy, there will be green soldiers, too. And Scots wearing the kilt. Jonet has seen them all in the fire three days' past. Do ye think Gilchrist will ride here to us?"

"He may," Alec faltered. "I'll shield ye if I can. I'm to ride with him—my father says. 'Tis his idea."

Munn's dark eyes bored into Alec's. "Well, if ye must, I suppose ye must," he rumbled, "but I doubt if ye will take pleasure from it. Are ye sorry because ye dislike the man who says he's king of England or because ye side with the American rebels?"

"Neither." Alec was embarrassed that his reluctance showed so clearly. "I don't want to fight. I'm not like Gilchrist or my father or"—he was tempted to add—"ye either, Grandfather."

Munn's response was a surprise to him. "Ye've got a good head on your shoulders, Alec *dubh*. Perhaps ye'll find a way out of your troubles."

"Aye," the boy told him sullenly, "I could break my neck or both of my legs."

"Ye've got more sense than that, and who knows what might take place before the soldiers get here?" Munn put his hand on Alec's arm. "Come inside now. My wife's been looking into the fire for the Gilchrist lass, but I think she's done with her."

"What did she tell Ellen?" Alec's heart beat faster as they went up to the door.

Munn grunted. "How would I be knowing that? They whispered as they always do, and I sat as far from them as I could. But I saw the sixpence the lass gave Jonet to put into her apron pocket. I'm sure the Gilchrist girl will welcome ye, too."

Angry, Alec MacLeod went into his grandparents' house, leaving the dog outside scratching. Because of Lilias he probably had to give the rose ribbon to Ellen now in front of everyone. He had hoped to have a moment alone with Ellen before she rode away. Then he could shove it at her and run off before she had a word to say.

The fire on the hearth was not so large this time, because there was no snowfall expected. Jonet Munn was standing before it talking with Lilias while Ellen was putting on her black riding cloak and getting ready to leave. Ellen looked in Alec's direction as he made an awkward bow to her. It was more of a bobbing, thanks to the cumbersome long rifle he carried. He knew it was, and it made him feel more foolish than ever.

"Alec, Jamie says ye'll ride with Gilchrist's Horse." Ellen's Gaelic was the most lilting Alec had ever heard.

"Aye." The boy fell silent, tongue-tied. He gazed at her, wondering if her apron or cloak pocket held a bottle of love philtre.

Lilias broke into the sudden silence. She reached up and pulled the scarlet ribbon through her hair and held it out as a shining loop. "See my ribbon, Ellen! Alec *dubh* bought it for me." She laughed. "Alec *dubh* fetched a ribbon home from Ninety-Six village for ye also."

All too aware of the many eyes upon him, Alec hesitated, glancing from face to face. His grandfather was looking curious, Ellen startled, and Lilias openly teasing. The look Jonet Munn gave him was unfathomable. Flushing, the boy went to a corner, set the long rifle on its butt, and came back to the fire. He reached into his breeches pocket to take out the rose ribbon, which he let dangle like a dead serpent from his hand.

With a small cry Ellen came to him. She took the ribbon, smiling. "Why, Alec, I thank ye."

"It's to tie around your bonnet at kirk." Ellen was so close to him that he could scent the lavender stalks that had been laid among her folded clothing in her chest at home.

"See it, Mistress Munn," exclaimed Ellen, showing the pretty thing to Jonet Munn. "Shall I wear it for luck in my hair or tied about my bonnet?" she asked her.

"As ye please," replied the old woman.

Ellen put up the cloak's hood. "Good day to ye, Master Munn and Mistress Munn." After that farewell she did a very saucy thing that made Alec gasp. She grabbed him by the hand and dragged him out of the house to where her pony waited. Two of the Gilchrist hounds frisked beside it. Alec supposed they'd been hunting in a thicket. As for his red hound, she had lain down to doze by the door.

There Ellen stood dimpling at him. "Alec *dubh,* I'm pleased with the ribbon and more pleased that ye will ride with Jamie." She flung out her arms. "I can scarcely wait till the king's soldiers seize Charles Towne and come marching here." She laughed. "Make me a promise, Alec. Make it now. Promise me that ye'll fetch to me the most beautiful brave young British officer ye can find. A gentleman, mind ye. An English gentleman."

Alec found the tongue to ask, "Will no Scot from the colonies suit ye, Ellen?"

"Not unless he could be a lord's son in Scotland. Now, Alec, help me mount my pony."

Gingerly Alec grasped her about the waist and lifted her onto the sidesaddle. From atop the pony she looked down on him smiling. Yet he knew she scarcely saw him for her dreams of officers, gentlemen—noblemen. In all his life he had never seen a nobleman.

To bring her back to him, he asked harshly, "What did my grandmother say to ye now? Did she promise ye an officer? Did she promise ye a lord?"

The question shocked Ellen into awareness so that her blue eyes focused on him. "Na, na, would I tell her such a thing? She is too old to understand. She's a rebel, too. She looked into the fire for me only for a moment, then said there was nothing she could see in the flames today for me at all. I think she gazes for your sister now. Has she gazed for ye also, Alec?"

Gathering his wits, Alec told her only a small portion of what Jonet Munn had said to him. "She told me that there would be a gathering of horses. She told me true. Gilchrist's Horse."

"Aye." Ellen was thoughtful.

"Ellen, when will Jamie send to me to come to him and his troop?"

"After the plowing and ye've all brought in the spring-born calves. He'll send ye a message then." Ellen leaned down laughing to brush her hand against Alec's dark cheek. "Ye grow a fierce black beard to frighten many lasses, but it does not frighten me." Taking her hand away too soon for him, she said, "Bide here outside. If the old woman looks into the blaze for Lilias, she won't want ye listening." Ellen gathered up the reins, called out to her dogs, and started away at a trot.

Alec stood staring after her. He wished she didn't ride about the countryside alone. It was dangerous. But how could she come to the Munns—except alone? He refused to believe that his grandmother had seen nothing at all in the fire for Ellen. Aye, Ellen kept her own secrets, but then so did he. But he was certain of one thing. Whatever Ellen had been told, she had not been frightened as he had. She'd ridden off happily, contented with whatever she'd got for her sixpence—whether it was a love philtre or a pleasant future to look forward to. God knows, what Jonet Munn had told him on his last visit had not been pleasant at all! "Beasts," "dark water," "much death around ye"—and "a high place!"

It seemed to Alec that he sat on the Munns' doorstep for a long time playing with the red hound's soft ears until the old man called him inside for a tankard of small beer. Clearly his grandmother and sister were finished now. Jonet Munn was stirring something in a black iron pot while Lilias sat on her grandmother's stool. Unlike Ellen, Lilias looked sour. Alec knew the sulking look from experience. Whatever she had heard had not delighted her. He wondered if the predictions made for her fitted in with those made for him. Perhaps she would tell him on the way home.

Lilias didn't wait that long. She gave Alec a hostile glance and blurted out, "She tells me that I'll never wed with Jamie. She cannot see the man that I am to marry. And she won't tell me why Jamie's not for me!"

Jonet Munn said, "Lilias, he is too old for ye, and there is something within the man that is not right." She looked over her shoulder at Alec, directing a statement not a question to him. "Ye've seen this in young Gilchrist, too, Alec."

"Aye, Grandmother." All at once Alec's heart was clutched by fright. What if Ellen were to tell Jamie that he and Lilias had come visiting the Munns, and Jamie reported the visit to MacLeod. He'd betrayed Alec once before.

"Na, na, Alec." Jonet Munn seemed to read his mind. "Ellen will say not a word of seeing ye here or of her being here today. Since the king's fleet came to this colony, she's been forbidden the company of rebels. If she tells her parents or brother that ye were here, then she tells them that she was here also."

Relieved, Alec sat down with his beer at last. After a sip he asked, "Have ye seen anything for me of late?"

Jonet Munn shook her head. "Naught but what I told ye. I see what the fire wishes to let me see—no more. At times I see what might concern ye, though, Alec—things in the lives of other people."

Lilias said angrily, "Aye, such as 'Ye'll never wed with James Gilchrist, my girl.' " She spat at Alec, "That does not say that Father will not make a match with the Gilchrists. There's fair Ellen for ye, Alec *dubh*. And I'll not give up Jamie!"

For the very first time Alec heard his grandmother sighing. "Ach, the matter of the Gilchrists could be greatly altered for ye both before this year has come to an end. I'm pleased that ye gave the ribbon to the lass, Alec. It made her happy, I think."

He shook his head. "I think ye told her things that made her happy, Grandmother—far happier than my velvet ribbon did. Ye told me nothing half so pleasant."

Her back to him, she said tonelessly, "I told the lass of this and that—the things girls like to hear."

"I got nothing half so pleasant either." Lilias got up, shaking out her skirts, and then flung her shawl about her shoulders.

Alec put down his beer and rose up from the table. Remembering the squirrels, he untied their legs from his belt and set their limp gray bodies on the tabletop.

As his sister stormed out the door, Alec went to Jonet Munn. For the first time he kissed her on the cheek. He had not expected Lilias to be so rude. He told her, "I thank ye, Grandmother. Lilias has set her heart on Jamie. Even Father says he is too old for her."

"He is." Jonet Munn's gray eyes were on a level with Alec's. "Have ye set your own heart on Gilchrist's sister?"

It was his turn to sigh. "Na, she tells me that she wants an officer, a gentleman." He didn't say an English redcoat officer was what she preferred.

Jonet Munn touched the corner of Alec's mouth with a gentle finger. "There's a new scar ye have there, Alec. Is this MacLeod's doing?"

"Aye."

"Because ye visited us?"

"Na, though that didn't please him. 'Tis because I told him I don't want to ride with Jamie's troop. But I must go."

She nodded. "So ye must—because of MacLeod."

Alec asked, "Will Jamie take me to the black water and the high place?"

"I do not think he will."

"What of the White Beast and the Red?"

"Gilchrist will know one of them. Ye, Alec *dubh,* will know them both." Jonet Munn gave Alec a small push. "Take your sister home now. And shoot a turkey along the way. Ye'll have no trouble with MacLeod. He'll be too pleased with himself for selling barrels of meat."

Alec opened his mouth in shock. She *knew* of the turkeys and of the pork!

Seeing his expression, the old woman chuckled. "Alec, Lilias told me these things. This is not second sight. Tell your mother that we send our love to her."

"I will, Grandmother." Alec picked up his rifle from the corner and went outside to join a waiting, scowling Lilias.

Old Munn walked beside Alec. Taking the boy by the arm, he led him into the bare-limbed beeches near the house. "Alec, do ye care for your grandmother?"

"I do. I care for her," he replied in surprise. "Why do ye ask that?" he added. "Ye well know I'll be beaten by my father if he hears we came here today."

"That proves something to me, Alec." Munn gripped him by the shoulders. "Lad, my heart fails me more each month that goes by. I am old. Will ye look after your grandmother when I am gone?"

Alec's mind whirled. How could he do so? MacLeod would never have her under his roof. The only way he could accomplish the charge would be to move into her house. But she was a rebel and he a king's man. And all too many people thought she was a witchwoman. "I can try, Grandfather," he said.

Munn released him. "No one can do more than that. Now go to your sister and take her home. She'll swallow her anger in time and be pleased someday that James Gilchrist was not her husband. As for the Gilchrist girl, she's a jillflirt."

"Aye." As Alec turned away he fell into step with his sister, trailed by the red hound, and thought mournfully of Ellen. She wanted an officer—not an ungainly Scots farmer. He'd been mad to think on her. He'd tell himself to pluck her from his heart. But he doubted very much if he could do so. The sweet scent of lavender in her clothing was still in his nostrils.

Lilias kept her silence until they were a mile from the Munn farm. Then all at once she halted and jabbed her fist into the air near a thicket that the hound had slunk into in search of birds. Alec knew Lilias would rather have stamped her foot, but she was too wise a hunter for that. And they wanted a turkey. She could use a long rifle near as well as he.

"I hate Grandmother Munn," Lilias hissed. "She said I was bonny and she loved me, but she said nothing that I wanted to hear."

Leaning on the rifle, Alec said, "Lilias, ye need never go back to her, though I'll take ye if ye want." He questioned himself for a moment, shrugged, and asked, "Did she say anything to ye of black water or a high place?"

"Na, na." Lilias's expression changed to one of curiosity.

"Did she speak of a White Beast or a Red Beast?"

"Aye," Lilias said with a nod. "She did speak of a Red Beast." She laughed. "What's that to me? I think she had in mind that Father will buy the neighbor's red boar after all."

Alec shook his head. "I think she was speaking of men —not of animals. She talked to me of the war when I came here last time. Did she say anything at all to ye that concerned me?"

Lilias puckered her forehead, thinking. "She did. But I did not understand it, and I may not have the right of it. She said something about your left hand but she muttered so, I was not sure I caught it." She shrugged. "And it did not concern me so I didn't listen hard."

"My left hand." Alec looked at it in the gray light of a March afternoon. It looked no different to him, long fingered, brown, and calloused in the palms from the plow handles and the axe he used to chop firewood.

Lilias flung up her hands. "Ach, who knows what she meant? Everyone knows she's fey—if not daft." After whistling the dog out of the thicket, Lilias said, "Let me have the rifle. I'll bring MacLeod a turkey."

Alec gave it to her. It was primed and loaded. She had only to aim it, cock it, and fire. If she took a second ball to bring down a bird, what of it? MacLeod would forgive Lilias for the failure where he would not forgive his son. Alec glanced up at the sky, which promised yet more rain. If the rain was a warm one, the ground would soon be ready for the plow. And later they'd ride out into the trees and thickets after their cattle.

All chores could be over and done with the first part of April. Would the rebels in Charles Towne have surrendered to the king's soldiers by that time, and the king's soldiers be on their way to the up-country?

He asked Lilias casually, "Have ye heard that there are greencoat soldiers in King George's army?"

"Na." She gave him a strange look as they walked along together. "The king's soldiers all have redcoats. That's what Father says."

Seventeen eighty was a year that was to become renowned in South Carolina for its wet weather. Lachlan MacLeod cursed the frequent March rains that forced him and Alec again and again to postpone the spring plowing. They prepared the fields for planting late that year because of the dampness of the soil.

When at last they could work, the two of them had to move more swiftly and drive the horses harder behind the plow. But they must have barley and corn to feed both them and their animals.

After a few days of frantic work in the fields, Alec and his father saddled the dun gelding and the white horse and rode out at the very end of the month to find their free-roaming cattle. It was a week's work rounding up the cows and their spring calves, catching the calves, branding them, and setting all but two beeves loose again to wander. These two steers MacLeod drove into a cowpen on his land for fattening. He'd butcher one and sell the other for beef in Ninety-Six village later. As for the sows that were to farrow, Alec and his father found them also and herded them to the pens behind the barn. This chore was one that Alec despised. The brood sows were vicious animals, quick to turn on a herder behind them and bite him with their savage jaws.

Alec found no time to go to the Munns, though at night he often lay sleepless thinking about them and his grandmother's words.

No news came from Charles Towne either to the trader or from any traveler passing the MacLeod farm. For one thing there were few travelers coming up the Keowee Trail. Thanks to the heavy rains the roads were a mire. On one of his trips to the trader's store for his father, Alec was told by Deckard to inform MacLeod that he hoped the heavily laden wagons had got through to the besieged city and weren't somewhere on the road, sunk to the tops of their wheels in mud, unmovable. This news pleased Lachlan MacLeod not at all. He stomped about the house and barn for three days, raging at the weather.

On the second day of April a bright sun broke through clouds that were blowing away in a high, cool spring wind. On that day Jamie Gilchrist came riding once more to Alec's farm. With him rode three other young men, all Scots, all men Alec knew by name. None was mounted half so finely as Jamie on the sorrel mare.

Gilchrist didn't dismount. He told MacLeod, who came out to greet him, while Alec stood in the doorway of one side of the house and Lilias smiled from the other, "Tell Alec to meet me at sunrise tomorrow at the bee tree." Jamie reached into the belt of his coat and handed MacLeod a long barreled pistol. "Give it to Alec *dubh*." The young man put his heels to the mare and bounded off followed by the other riders, all trying to look very stern and warlike. Margaret MacLeod's hens fled squawking out of their way, their feathers ruffling in outrage.

His mother came to stand behind Alec. "There do not seem to be many riders in Jamie's troop," she said.

"Na." Alec's eyes were on the horse pistol in his father's hand. They'd have to fashion a holster for it on the dun's saddle. The job would take him and his father hours to make it out of one of the cowhides in the barn. Neither of them had thought of it beforehand.

V

The Peddler from the North

The dun steamed in the sunlight of the next noon as Alec, cursing, reined him into line beside another horse. Hours of drilling under Jamie's bawled instructions had made every man fretful and every horse weary and harder to manage. Alec and the dun had suffered more than most. The nine other young Scots who'd appeared at the bee-tree rendezvous had fired pistols from horseback beforehand apparently. Their mounts were accustomed to the tug on the saddle as the long-barreled weapons were drawn out of the holsters. The noise of the cocking and firing did not make the horses dance sideways and rear up pawing the sky as the dun always did. Too, the other young men knew how to aim and shoot their pistols—not only ready them. They sometimes hit the easy targets Jamie pointed out. Not Alec, who failed to hit a target at all.

That first afternoon as he jogged homeward, Alec went with Jamie's scornful orders to cast a large number of pistol balls and spend three hours a day practicing shooting at tree trunks. As the dun stumbled crossing a creek threatening to dump Alec off into it, the boy muttered curses in English. The harsh biting words soothed him more than his native tongue at the moment.

Throughout April and the first week in May, sometimes in sunshine but more often in rain, Jamie drilled his troop. No two horses were alike and no rider had a uniform save for a band of red muslin tied around his left arm. To Alec's way of thinking, Gilchrist's Horse was of little real worth, and Alexander MacLeod the worst of the lot.

Jamie had a different opinion of his band. He took his volunteers very seriously. Sometimes at the first of a day's drilling he would command his troopers into a row and make speeches to them.

One speech, in particular, Alec recalled to himself over and over again. Jamie had said on a day late in April, "I have decided that we will not wait in idleness until the British soldiers are here. As soon as we have the news that Charles Towne has fallen, Gilchrist's Horse will ride out. We will take up as many rebels in this section of the colony as we can find. We will confine them in cowpens and keep them prisoners until the redcoats are here and have taken the fort in the village."

Jamie's eyes had flickered in Alec's direction as he spoke. There had been a glint in them that had made Alec uneasy. He guessed that Jamie was referring to Andrew and Jonet Munn. Aye, Gilchrist might round them up like cattle. Jamie had grown fiercer day by day.

If he could warn his grandparents he would, though God only knew what they would do. Alec doubted if they would leave their farm and asked himself if they were willing to leave, where they would go?

One Saturday morning mid-May, news came at last from Charles Towne to Ninety-Six district. It arrived at the MacLeod farm not from Gilchrist or one of his Scottish troopers but from enemies of the king. Lilias, who had gone to the top of the hill chasing one of the milk cows, spied the riders at a distance and came running to the barn with her skirts hiked up over her knees for speed and her shawl flapping about her shoulders. MacLeod listened to her cry, then barked an order at Alec, and all three of them headed at a run for the house. According to Lilias, the visitors were men on horseback.

The riders in the rain were only two men—certainly not any great force. Alec and his father met them with long rifles primed and ready. There was a MacLeod stationed at each door of the house. Lachlan MacLeod knew the men —villagers from Ninety-Six. He shouted at the fair-bearded man riding the roan horse, "What do ye want here, Angus? I know ye for a bedamned rebel. Do not try to draw your pistol on my son and me."

"Na, Lachlan, give us a ham and piglet and some corn, and we'll be off and give ye no trouble," the man called out to MacLeod.

"I curse ye because ye are a traitor to King George and I curse ye even more, Angus, because ye, too, are a Scot," bellowed Alec's father. "If ye want my pigs, ye'll pay me gold for them."

The man named Angus called back, "Ye sold pork to rebels in Charles Towne, Lachlan MacLeod, and ye'll make a profit! Give us what we need, and we'll ride out of the colony."

"Traitors get nothing here!" MacLeod's words rang out, and Alec tensed himself to pull the trigger of his rifle. Nausea was rising in his throat, and a mist had come over his eyes. He could scarcely see the rebel horsemen. He heard his father taunting them, "If ye're riding out, ye must be running away. Have the redcoats come to the village and chased ye rebels out of it?"

"Na," cried the second rebel, a small swarthy man Alec had seen now and then in the trader's store.

This one angry "na" made MacLeod boom with laughter. "Then I think I can tell ye what it is. Charles Towne's fallen to the king's army. That's why ye're running away? Tell me, Angus, when was the town taken?"

The bearded rebel answered sourly, "I'll tell ye then, since ye've guessed it. May the twelfth it fell. We are not running away, MacLeod. We are going to join the Patriot army that will take the colony from the British and drive them back into the sea."

"Then go to the rebels and be damned to ye, Angus." MacLeod squeezed the trigger of his rifle, sending a ball past the right side of the villager's head. "Get off my land, ye traitors," shouted Alec's father. Gritting his teeth, Alec made ready to fire, too, if need be.

Both riders jerked their horses away, put spurs to them, and rode off. The bearded man twisted in his saddle as he went to shake his fist at the MacLeod house.

MacLeod on his part shook his in defiance as he came

out of the doorway. Then, rejoicing in his easy victory, he whooped to his family, "They're coming at last. By God, the redcoats are coming." He hugged Lilias as she ran to him. "Did ye see how swiftly the rebel scum fled when I fired on them?" He turned smiling to Alec. "What kind of army will scum like that make? No army at all, I am thinking." Laughing, he told Alec, "Saddle the dun and ride to Gilchrists' now. Tell Jamie the good news."

"Aye," put in Lilias from the curve of her father's arm, "Ellen may be so glad of the news she'll give ye a kiss, Alec."

But Margaret MacLeod put her hand on her husband's arm. "Lachlan," she pleaded, "the two rebels might spy Alec riding and shoot him."

"Na, na, woman, they lack the stomach for it. They'll go to other farms seeking food and be driven off by good king's men like Alec and myself. They'll not ride to Gilchrists' at all. There are too many armed men there, and the rebels know it. Go now, Alec. Tell Jamie that I'll be making whiskey soon to greet the redcoats."

Alec gave his rifle to Lilias and ran for the barn. Moments later he was mounted and, with Jamie's pistol in the saddle holster, riding away over MacLeod land. He got as much speed as possible out of the dun. Aye, he'd carry the news of the capture of Charles Towne to the Gilchrists. But, first of all, he must tell his grandparents. He'd warn them that there could be a rounding up of rebels and that Jamie could easily be the man to come after them. He'd promise them that he'd try to stop Jamie if he could. But how he'd do so he had no idea, though he'd pondered the problem for days now.

As he rode he kept his eyes alert for the two rebels who might be just ahead of him, though they could also have taken other routes that led to North Carolina colony. In his heart he asked himself if he could have shot one of them if his father had ordered him to. God be praised, it had not come to that! The rebels had not been willing to fight for supplies. Other rebels fleeing the colony, however, might be bolder thieves and equipped with long rifles too.

Today in the afternoon Jonet Munn's herb garden was a bright green rain-washed splendor. Flowers were in bloom beside the little house. Alec had no more idea what they might be than he had of her herbs. As he reined in before the Munn cabin and cupped his hand to his mouth to call out to his grandfather, the dun suddenly let out a snort.

Wary now, Alec held back his shout. There must be other horses nearby. Perhaps the gelding only snorted at the presence of Andrew Munn's old chestnut horse, but who knew for certain? Had the fleeing rebels come here to other known rebels for food? The Munns might give it to them. Anger rose up in him. The old people had little enough for themselves.

He drew the pistol and with his knees urged his horse forward as another thought came to him—one more pleasant. Could Ellen be here again? His heart began to beat more swiftly. If she was here, he'd ride back home with her to guard her from the rebels. But, on the other hand, if she was here, how could he warn the Munns of Jamie? Well, that could be done in secret. He could take his grandfather aside and tell him.

Holding his breath, hoping for silence from his horse, Alec rode nearer the house, circling to see its right side. If the rebel raiders were there, he'd wait until they had gone. He could hide easily enough in the tall thicket behind the house. He recalled their horses well—a roan and a flea-bitten gray. Aye, there were animals beside the house. Not horses, though. They were brownish-gray mules, two of them, tethered to the fully leafed-out beeches. One, the larger, carried the telltale rubbing marks on its back of a packsaddle.

Not Ellen and not the rebels. Alec laughed suddenly. This visitor was only a peddler. Peddlers came now and then through the district carrying small things to lure pennies from up-country housewives. They brought bottles of scent, nutmegs, silver pins, copper pans, and iron pots and the like, as well as laces and ribbons. Looking into a peddler's pack was exciting, even if a person didn't buy anything. And anything that had to do with trading interested Alexander MacLeod.

Reassured, Alec boldly shouted out his name as he put the pistol back into the holster and dismounted. He stood waiting for what seemed to him an uncommonly long time before Andrew Munn came out onto the doorstep with his musket. "What brings ye here so soon again, Alec *dubh?*" he called.

"News. News from Charles Towne!" And Alec walked the gelding forward, wondering at the coolness of his reception. So soon? He had not come to the Munns in some weeks.

"What is the news?" demanded Andrew Munn.

Alec went to him before he said, "Grandfather, Charles Towne is taken. The king's army captured it on the twelfth of this month."

"Did they now?" Munn nodded. "How did ye come by the news?"

"Raiders came to our farm today. They brought the news to us, Grandfather." Alec's gaze took in the *T* on Munn's cheek, and he glanced away almost as swiftly. "My father sent me off to tell Jamie Gilchrist that Charles Towne had fallen, but I rode to ye and grandmother first of all," he faltered.

"Why would ye do that?" asked Munn, whose voice was no less harsh.

Feeling miserable, Alec told him, "Because Jamie has said that when the town fell, he means to ride out and take up known rebels as prisoners and hold them until the redcoats come."

To Alec's surprise, Andrew Munn laughed, "And ye rode first to Jonet and me? Why did ye do that?"

"Because ye be my mother's kin." Then Alec asked him, "Did ye think I rode to ye because I am not a king's man?"

"Na, na, I do not think that." Munn jerked his head toward the house. "Come inside now that ye be here. Tell the woman and Master Bean the news."

"Master Bean?"

"Aye, Donal, Donal Bean. He has the Gaelic, too. He is a peddler," Munn went on in a conversational tone. "It is a wonder to me that a man as old as Donal wanders the trails and roads still. He is as old as Jonet and myself."

Donal? Alec's mind caught at the use of the first name. His grandparents would not be quick to call anyone by his

Christian name. They must have known this man before. But there were no Beans in this part of the colony that Alec knew. Who was this man to be a friend of the Munns? Someone from Charles Towne? He must be a bold peddler or a reckless one to come riding when war had blazed forth anew.

Alec reached up onto the dun's saddle and took down the pistol, which he then put into his belt. The rain would harm it if he left it on the horse. The pistol stuck into his belt, he tethered the horse a distance from the mules, which seemed to him to have wicked looks in their eyes. Then he went into the house. Jonet Munn knelt at the hearth stirring up the fire. Beside her on her stool sat Donal. Alec eyed him dubiously. Master Bean was ill-favored: small and wizened with long gray hair. His eyes were bird sharp, though, in a face that looked to be carved out of a hickory nut. His blue coat and gray breeches were shabby and travel worn. At a glance anyone would know that he was not from the up-country because, save for his shoes, he wore no leather clothing. Even fashionable Jamie sometimes wore doeskin breeches.

Jonet Munn said, "This is our grandson, Alexander MacLeod, our small Margaret's lad, Donal." She pointed at the pistol and held out her hand for it. "Alec *dubh,* ye'll have no need of that here. 'Tis so very large and long ye could not sit down with it where it is in your belt."

Alec hesitated, staring at the peddler, then decided that there was no danger in a man so small and old. He gave the pistol to her and bowed to Bean.

The peddler spoke Gaelic in a reedy voice. "I've been told of ye, Alec. Last evening it was."

The boy asked, "Have ye been here long?"

"Na, only since yesterday. This morning I took myself and my mules and pack to some of the farms hereabouts." He smiled, showing the few teeth he had. "Now, would ye be needing shoe buckles or buttons of silver or pewter? What do ye lack?"

"Nothing at all." Then Alec asked his grandmother, who had got up by now, "While I was tending to my horse, did Grandfather tell ye the news?"

She nodded. "Aye, Charles Towne is taken!" She jerked her head toward her husband, who was on his knees reaching under their bed for the whiskey jug. "Andrew told me that men came to ye saying that the redcoats had it now and that Jamie Gilchrist might come after us."

"I'll try to stop him, Grandmother."

She laughed very softly. "I doubt ye can do that, Alec *dubh,* but we thank ye all the same for coming to us." She smiled down at the peddler, "And for coming to tell our Donal, too." Next she called to Munn, "Andrew, fetch three cups. I will drink with ye." Mystified, Alec watched her put the pistol into the basket of knitting she kept beside the hearth. "Take the basin ye'll find on the bench beside the house to the well and fill it. Then bring it inside," she ordered Alec.

He glanced at his hands before he went to do her bidding. Whatever she was cooking in the iron pot over the fire smelled very fine. He suspected he was meant to wash his hands before he joined them for supper. She had complained of the dirtiness of his hands before. Was she going to serve supper first before she talked of escaping from Jamie with her husband? Other king's men might have galloped to Jamie by now with the news. "Grandmother," Alec protested, "I told ye just now that Gilchrist might ride here."

"Ah, so ye did," said Andrew Munn, as he took three earthenware cups down from the mantel. "Gilchrist is of no great matter to us. He'll not be getting everything he wants. Go, fetch the water for us, Alec *dubh*."

Shaking his head and muttering to himself, Alec went outside. He looked up into the drizzle as he picked up the basin. Then he went to the well to haul up the heavy bucket. They were fey, both of them. He wondered what he should do now. Ride directly to Jamie with the news? Alec shook his head again. His grandparents seemed to have no fear of Jamie, but then they didn't know him well—not as they knew Ellen. He greatly doubted if Jamie had ever visited them for love philtres. The richest, cleverest young man in the section had no need of such things. Girls flung themselves at him, but he only kissed them and laughed at them and would not marry. He gave his time to drinking, cock-fighting, and horse racing. There was quicksilver in him and something else—something Alec didn't recognize because he had nothing at all of it in him. Nothing of the will-o'-the-wisp. Nothing of charm. Only the sober, trudging black Scot, the eternal frowner, admired by nobody. Yet there was a something in Jamie that Alec feared. The Munns should have fear of it, too, if they were wise.

"My God, what can I do for them now?" Alec asked the gray heavens. It seemed to him that the Munns had no intention of fleeing.

He went back to the cabin with the basin, expecting to receive a ball of soap from his grandmother along with some tart comments about the filth on his hands. But she had no soap ready. She greeted him with an odd, small smile as he sloshed water over her dirt floor. Then as he held the basin, waiting for her to tell him what she wanted him to do with it, she came forward and kissed him suddenly on the cheek. She said, "Ye know we be rebels, Andrew and I?"

Alec nodded.

"Set the basin onto the table," she ordered.

Alec did her bidding, seeing the three cups also put out on the table. The two old men and the old woman came up to it, and as Alec watched, each took a filled cup.

Andrew Munn held his and said, "Alec *dubh,* Donal and your grandmother and I came from Scotland aboard the same ship."

Alec glanced quickly at Bean's cheek. There was no brand of the traitor on it.

"Na, na," said old Munn. "He was not branded by the red soldiers—though like us he was a rebel in Scotland."

"But I was transported and indentured to the same master as your grandparents," the peddler told Alec. Suddenly he asked, "Ye have the news of the fall of Charles Towne, lad, but have ye had the news of the battle of Moncks Corner?"

"A battle? Na."

"Aye, last month it was. 'Twas a battle fought north of Charles Towne by redcoats and greencoats both against the American forces."

Alec asked eagerly, "Who won it, Master Bean?"

"The forces of the man who calls himself King George."

Alec caught at the words. So Bean was a rebel, too? Yet another traitor. He stiffened. And then he thought of the word *greencoats.* So there *were* greencoat soldiers!

"Tell him, Donal," said Jonet Munn. "Tell him why what is to happen must happen."

"Aye, Jonet." Bean grinned at Alec, a far jauntier grin than the boy would have expected. "I have been over the mountains with my mules selling needles and gathering news. The back country folk greatly fear the Indians there. Then I rode down here to your district to learn what I could from the Scottish farmers while I sold Flemish laces to their womenfolk. I learned that most of them support the cause of the British and would rather fight alongside the red soldiers and the greencoats than against them. I have the news I came to gather, and you have just informed me now that I could be hunted down by this man ye call Gilchrist. So I will ride out in a little while."

"And Alec, ye will go with Donal!" said Jonet Munn, who, still holding her cup, stooped over and took up the pistol from the basket. She cocked it and held it on him. "Alec, ye will ride away with your grandfather and Donal today. But first ye must see what we are going to do here now, because I do not think we shall meet together again, all three of us. Sit yourself down on my stool and cause us no trouble."

Stunned into instant obedience by the pistol as well as by her calm tone, Alec felt his way to her stool and sat down. He listened as the three old people held their cups high and began to sing a song he'd never heard before. It was a sad ballad and in Gaelic. When it was finished, his grandfather passed his whiskey over the water in the basin as Jonet Munn stood with the pistol trained on Alec.

"Slaint an rey," said Munn. "A health to King Charles in exile over the sea—in exile over the water. May God pre-

serve His Majesty, King Charles, rightful king of England and of Scotland and Ireland." He drained the cup.

The peddler said, as he passed his cup over the basin also, "And damnation for all time to the man who calls himself King George." He too drank.

Jonet Munn put the pistol down within swift reach on the tabletop and drank her whiskey, which she'd also passed over the basin. But she made no toast to any king. Alec sat frozen to the top of the stool. Aye, traitors all three! And Bean was more than that. He'd as much as said he was a spy. A spy for the Continental Congress for certain if he went skulking to Scottish farms trying to learn what side they favored and was dismayed that they preferred the king's army.

While Alec sat openmouthed, thunderstruck at their open treason, Munn told the peddler, "Donal, I think Alec, who hunts often, knows the trails better than I. Together we'll set ye on the one ye seek."

"Aye," agreed Bean, buttoning his coat after he set down the cup he had fondled lovingly. "Are ye certain it will lead me to the man I am sent to find? I must find him!" He grew somber. "Will the trail take me to the Pee Dee River?"

"It will. Ye'll find the man, though he is in hiding— as he must be. He'll find ye if ye ride beside the banks of the Pee Dee. He'll send ye on your way in safety with your news of the backcountry men and the Scots hereabouts."

Alec's mind sped. He had no idea who this man at the Pee Dee River might be, but surely he was a rebel, too. Who was the man Bean sought? He must be someone Bean reported to.

Old Munn turned to Alec. "Up with ye now, lad. Ye'll not be riding to Gilchrists' farm today with any news."

"Alec will have no need to ride to Gilchrist," said Jonet Munn. "If men from Ninety-Six village have the news from Charles Towne, wild Jamie will soon be told it." Her mouth twisted as Alec watched her. "No man at all James Gilchrist is! Only a thing of whims and foolish will. I have no fear of him."

"Nor I, woman," said Munn, who had taken Alec by the arm and pulled him from the stool.

Standing in front of the pistol, Jonet Munn kissed Donal Bean on the cheek as she had kissed Alec. She said, "Fare ye well, our Donal. I think ye'll reach Marion in your own time and in safety."

Marion? Alec grabbed at the name. Who was this person? Man or woman? Was it Bean's wife?

However, as Bean embraced his grandmother, he told her, "Ah, Jonet, ye grow more bonny year by year. I've envied Andrew always because ye were his wife and I had no woman of my own."

"Fah," she said, "we are old now, Donal. Ye did not tell me that ye fancied me so much when I was younger."

"Aye, but ye must take note that I never wed."

Alec saw his grandmother's smile. "And, Donal, because ye did not, some woman had a poorer life." Turning to Munn, she kissed him on the lips. "Fare ye well, my Andrew."

"Aye, Jonet." Munn gave her one long, strange look and took his black three-cornered hat down off the peg on the back of the door.

Then Jonet Munn turned to Alec. "Have a care of both

of them, Alec *dubh*. If ye can I ask ye to keep them safe
from Jamie Gilchrist."

He backed away from her, staring into her eyes. She
must have gone mad to ask him to look after the two old
traitors and send one on the proper trail to the Pee Dee
River country when she surely realized that he guessed
Bean was a spy. She expected him to aid *rebels*? He'd come
to warn the Munns—but not to help a spy escape.

"What if Jamie comes here, Grandmother?"

"I shall tell him that Andrew has gone away. I do not
think he will harm me, do ye, Alec?"

Alec looked beyond her at the pistol, but she moved to
the right blocking it from his view. No, he could not grab
at it with both old men still in the little house.

"Alec *dubh*," said Jonet Munn, "do ye know what will
happen to Donal if he is caught by Gilchrist?"

"He'll be put into a cowpen with Grandfather and held
until the British come."

"Na, na, lad," said Andrew Munn in a grating voice.
"He'll be hanged—if he is not shot. Folk may recall that
Donal has gone from farm to farm asking how the Scots
will choose when the war comes here to the up-country.
So he must ride out now! Ye must not say one word of
him unless ye'd put my neck and your grandmother's into
peril, too. What do ye say to that?"

Alec was silent for a long time. He had never had anything to do with spies before. At last he mumbled a grudg-
ing, "Aye, I will hold my tongue—for your sake."

"Good, good." Jonet Munn pointed at a cloth sack on
the bed. She said to Bean, "Donal, ye'll find corncakes and

cheese and dried venison here. I'd planned to give it to ye in the morning, but Alec's news has changed that. This food will serve ye for some days on the trail, and ye'll find good grazing for your mules."

"Thank ye, Jonet," answered the peddler. He went to a leather pack set in the corner of the house, rummaged around in it, and brought out a pair of cut-steel shoe buckles. They glittered in the light from the fire. He gave them to her gravely saying, "No one ever had feet so small. These may grace your shoes." He turned to Alec. "Lad, I am no peddler. I am a compter in a banking house in Trenton, New Jersey. When the Continental Congress and General Washington have won this war, I'll come back here mounted on a fine horse, and I'll wear a blue velvet coat and gold-laced hat."

"We like ye as ye are, Donal," said Munn, who had opened the door by now. "Come now, Donal. Take the food. The lad and I will set ye on the trail before sunset. Hasten, Alec. Bring Donal's pack with ye while I saddle my horse and the mule he rides."

Alec shot a glance at his grandmother as he passed her. She was looking after the two old men with a strange, still look on her face. She seemed not to see him at all as he hesitated for an instant in front of her, peering beyond her at the pistol. Though she did not notice him, her hand was set upon it. He could not get it from her without snatching it from her. He went to the corner, bent down, and shouldered the heavy pack. As he followed Munn and the peddler outside, he looked once more at the pistol. Her hand had not moved.

VI

The Oak in the Trail

After he'd strapped the pack onto the saddle of the larger mule, Alec stood back in an angry silence as his grandfather saddled and bridled his old chestnut mare and Bean's smaller mule. The boy noticed that the old peddler mounted the second mule with surprising agility. At a nod of command from Munn, Alec hauled himself up onto the dun and fell into line between the chestnut and the two mules. He was caught between the two old men, both of whom were armed.

Munn led the little procession for several hours until they arrived at a place in a meadow where four trails met. One they had just traveled. Another led due north to North Carolina colony. Still another went westward toward the country of the mountain men. The last wound east into underbrush. Alec's grandfather pointed to the eastern trail, which was little more than a path in the high spring grass and fringed by bushes. "Donal," he said, "this is the one that will take ye to the Pee Dee River country. Some miles from here ye'll ride into canebrakes so high ye'll not be able to see over them, even mounted as ye are on that tall gawk of a mule of yours. If ye hear riders after ye, take yourself and the mules into the cane. 'Tis so thick they'll never spy ye out and ye may spy them as they ride by."

While Alec angrily told himself that his grandfather knew the country better than he and had only employed a ruse to get him to accompany them so he couldn't ride to Jamie with the news, Bean told Andrew Munn, "Spy? Aye, that is my trade at the moment and a damnable one it is. I thank ye for your hospitality, old friend." Alec watched as the two old men clasped hands. Then Munn hauled the mare about and fixed Alec with a piercing glance as Donal Bean clucked to his mules and started off at a brisk pace.

"We'll go back now, Alec," said Munn.

"Aye, Grandfather." The boy obediently set the dun to his shattering trot. As he followed Munn, he muttered against him and everything else in his world—but chiefly against the accursed war and the wretched horse under him. Each time he saw Jamie mounted on the beautiful sorrel, Sweet Lass, he felt a small pricking of envy. No one in Gilchrist's Horse was half so well mounted. A rich man always had a superior horse, and to give Jamie full credit, he had curbed the wildness of the mare without taking from her any of her speed.

They rode homeward for some time, covering more than

half the distance in Alec's estimation, and halted in a grove of trees where there was a spring to water the horses. While they waited there under the trees they heard a shot.

Alec pulled up the dun's head and grabbed for the pistol in the saddle holster before he remembered his grandmother had taken it. Was it the raiders who had come to the Mac-Leod farm that day? Or was it simply some hunter out after a deer? The boy saw how his grandfather, too, tensed in the saddle and began to unsling his musket.

"Munn, Andrew Munn, are ye there?" came a hallooing. The cry had been in Gaelic.

"I be here," he shouted. "Who calls for me?" As he spoke he stopped his effort to get his musket ready.

"James Gilchrist."

"Na, na," Alec whispered to himself. What was Jamie doing here? This spot was miles from the Gilchrist farm. And all at once Alec guessed. Jamie was already out hunting rebels, more than likely the two rebel raiders. Someone else had fetched him the news of Charles Towne. He had gathered his troop swiftly and come out riding. But why so far from home? And why did he call out for Munn? Alec glanced at his grandfather, who had not moved.

Then he looked back to the trail and saw Jamie coming, his red armband fluttering on his arm. Behind him came six others of Gilchrist's Troop. They rode straight to Munn and surrounded him, excluding Alec from their circle of horses. Then Jamie drew his own pistol, a beautiful silver-mounted one. Alec heard his words with rising horror. "Andrew Munn, we've come seeking ye before ye, too, escape this colony to join a rebel army."

Munn replied with scorn, "Gilchrist, ye find me riding back toward my home, do ye not? Have ye no eyes in your head or the wit to see that I am not escaping?"

"Then what are ye doing here, and if ye ride back, where have ye been?" Jamie's voice was rising to a shrill fury. Alec saw how his face had changed to a dusky red at Munn's taunting. Sudden cold fear gripped Alec's heart. Jamie demanded, "And why is Alexander MacLeod with ye, ye old traitor. Alec is a true king's man."

Alec saw that his grandfather was not looking at the pistol but into Jamie's furious eyes. He said, "My grandson came with me to set an old friend of mine, a stranger to this district, on his way."

"Another rebel?" asked Gilchrist.

"Aye, but I forced the boy to come. Alec visited us today when my friend was with me, and I made Alec come with us."

Alec watched Jamie's grim nod to his troopers. "So the old witchwoman told us the truth when we rode to her. She said the two of ye guided a poor old peddler away." Without looking at Alec, Jamie asked, "Is this the truth, Alec?"

"Aye. Ye did not harm my grandmother, Jamie, did ye?"

"Na, we did not." Jamie still didn't look at Alec, but he asked, "Did ye know this old peddler to be a rebel?"

While Alec frantically searched his mind for a reply that would appease Jamie, his grandfather called out, "The boy knew it. I tell ye, I forced him to ride with us. It was none of his doing. He stands for the British. He sides with the man ye call King George. But not I! I stand for the rightful king of England, King Charles. Death and damnation to the man ye name the king. Ye be the traitor, James Gilchrist, not I. I'll aid any man at all who is against ye and the man ye call the king!"

Gilchrist turned to his troopers, waving his pistol. "Ye heard him now. Ye heard him speak treason. And ye'll all bear witness to it." Then he ordered the rider on his left, "Fetch the rope. Make a loop in it." To a second Scot of his troop, he said, "Throw the other end of the rope over the bottom limb of the big oak by the trail, Ian. Tie the old man's hands behind his back. He'll aid no more rebels!"

Alec shouted in horror, "Na, Jamie, na!"

"Hold your tongue, Alec MacLeod. I'll speak with ye later."

As his hands were being tied, Munn called out to Jamie, "Alec had no part in this, I tell ye."

His eyes filling with tears, Alec watched helplessly while a third trooper tugged on the reins of his grandfather's mare and the chestnut was led to the big oak shadowing the trail a short distance from the spring. Alec saw that the noose was ready, the other end of the rope already securely tied to a nearby stump.

"Jamie, Jamie!" Alec pushed his horse forward next to the sorrel mare. "Give him time to say his prayers."

Gilchrist came out with a wild sharp laugh. "Make his peace with God? Aye, Alec, let him do so swiftly and be damned to the old traitor. Once that's done, if ye choose ye can ride over and drag on his knees so he dies more quickly. 'Tis considered a mercy to a man who is being hanged, I'm told."

"I cannot. I cannot." Tears streamed down Alec's cheeks. This scene could not be taking place. But he saw the stern-faced riders, one on each side of his grandfather, waiting for Jamie's command. The loop of the rope was about Munn's neck. Watching him through a blur of stinging tears, Alec thought he saw the old man's lips moving in what might be prayer.

Then suddenly Andrew Munn shouted at the top of his voice, "God save King Charles!"

The moment after Jamie called out a single word. The trooper on Munn's right struck the chestnut a brutal blow on her rump. She darted forward. But her rider could not go with her. Though half-blinded by tears, Alec saw his grandfather falling into midair. He saw his long legs jerking.

And that was all he saw, for Jamie beside him reached suddenly into his boot and took out his riding crop. With it he lashed Alec's horse hard. The dun sprang forward as the chestnut had. The gelding bolted down the trail, trying to get the bit over his teeth. Uncontrollable, the horse ran with Alec clinging to his back. A mile from the oak Alec managed to stop the dun and sat atop him, trembling.

By now his grandfather was surely dead. Alec only hoped the fall had instantly broken his neck. Aloud he mumbled a prayer. Would Jamie go to Jonet Munn's house now and hang her, too, because Munn had cursed King George? Alec was tempted to run from Jamie and the other troopers, but he steeled himself to remain where he was in the trail. He might be able to save his grandmother from Jamie's further anger. Pray God that he could.

The troopers came back down the trail in single file not

long after Alec had stopped his runaway horse. Jamie, who headed his men, led Munn's chestnut by the reins. Someone had caught the old horse after her wild plunge into the underbrush—after she had given her rider to the oak and the rope. Jamie halted and passed the reins of Munn's horse to Alec.

"Take this crowbait to the old witch. 'Tis hers by right. Tell her what's happened to the traitor she wed."

"Jamie, don't harm her!" begged Alec.

"Na," said Jamie. "Gilchrist's Horse does not make war on old women. But warn her to keep her curses off me and mine or she may not be spared the next time I go hunting rebels. Now, Alec, tell me. What was the peddler's name? Ye saw the rebel at the Munns. Ye must know his name."

"He said his name was Donal Bean."

"Where did ye see him last?"

"Where the four trails meet."

"What direction did he take?"

"Northwards." Alec had guessed what would be the next question and was ready for it. He wouldn't tell Jamie the truth—not now. They weren't going to catch Bean and hang him, too, if he could help it. Not even if the old peddler was a spy. Alec asked suddenly, "Why didn't ye ask that question of my grandfather?"

"If I had, the old traitor would have lied to me." He sighed. "I think the damned peddler's got away then."

"Aye, Scot free," a listening trooper called out, then laughed at his own wit.

Alec remained silent, hoping that Jamie wouldn't ask him more questions. Looking hard at him, Jamie said, "So the peddler escapes us—but not the other old rebel. I did not relish hanging your kinsman, Alec. It is not a bonny thing to watch—a man jerking in air, dying at the end of a rope. But this is a thing ye may see again before the war is won if ye are to serve under me. And next time I doubt if ye'll weep. Ye will see other deaths before King George has won."

His face tear streaked, Alec waited beside the trail until the riders had passed. Then he fell in behind leading the chestnut. As he rode back toward his section of the colony, he wondered how he would ever find the words to tell his grandmother what had befallen.

She was working in her garden, hoeing, when he came up with Andrew Munn's mare trotting beside the dun. Leaving the hoe, she gazed up at the riderless mare for a long, long moment, then up into Alec's face. "So they caught Andrew and killed him then?"

"Aye, Grandmother. Gilchrist and his riders hanged him."

"They knew of Donal Bean's visit to us before they questioned me. I did not tell them that any more than I told them the direction he and Andrew took."

Alec nodded. "Jamie had been told of Bean, but he does not know he was a spy. I did not tell him that."

He heard her deep sigh. "What of Donal? Was he hanged too?"

"Na, he rode off before. Jamie came upon us as we were returning. He's safe enough. I told them he rode to North Carolina colony—not eastwards to the Pee Dee River."

"Where is my Andrew, Alec?"

He told her. She nodded, then said, "I have need of ye now. Get down and go to the shed for a spade while I fetch a quilt and his old plaid from the house. Ye have a knife to cut him down with, I see. We'll ride to him together now."

Alec protested, "Ye plan to bury him beside the trail? There's a graveyard next to the church in the village. They'd give him decent burial there." He almost added, even if he was a rebel, but did not.

"We'll bury him, ye and I together, in the Munn plaid he brought from Scotland with him and in a quilt from our bed."

More afraid of his fey grandmother than ever, Alec faltered, "Ye can bury him in our graveyard on the hilltop beside the two babes Mother lost to fever before I was born. MacLeod will allow that. Ye have no graveyard here."

There were no tears on her wrinkled cheeks, and her eyes were a strange stony gray. "We had no need of a graveyard, Alec *dubh*. But the Gilchrists have a very fine one, I'm told, with blooming roses and stones over their dead."

Alec shivered at her words. He must warn her. "Grandmother, Jamie told me that ye were not to cast spells upon him or his family or he would come here."

To his amazement, she laughed. "Ach, I have no need of that, lad. As for your grandfather, do not mourn him overmuch. He sought this manner of dying. In his mind he died for King Charles and for the cause of liberty from the British in this new land. I knew, too, that he would not have lived much longer. To his way of thinking Andrew found some glory at the end. Get down now, Alec, and do my bidding."

He said only one more thing before he dismounted.

"Grandfather asked me once to look after ye if he should die."

"Did he now?" Jonet Munn mused. "And how will ye do that when ye will be riding out of the up-country before the next month is finished?"

Alec asked dully, "Am I to do that?" He said nothing more about his going but told her, "I can send Mother to ye and Lilias, too, if ye'd like. We'll stand up to MacLeod, the three of us."

"Na, na." Jonet Munn put her hand on Alec's arm. "When it is time for me to see my daughter's face again, I shall see it," she told him. "Before the year is out, I shall. Until then I shall make do." She smiled in a fashion Alec found almost foxlike. "With the war drawing nearer, many folk will want to have their futures told. They'll fetch me what I need to live—king's men and Patriots both will bring me what I ask. All men fear for their future as much as they hope from it. They know the thunder grows ever nearer to them now that Charles Towne has fallen. Take your pistol while you're getting the spade. I hid it in the corn-crib in the shed."

Alec nodded, then got slowly down from his horse.

He stayed the night with his grandmother, who lay on her bed silent, her hands crossed over her breast. From time to time he'd creep to the edge of the loft where he slept on straw to look down at her. Always by candlelight and firelight her eyes were open, staring up into the dark rafters of the cabin. She gave him a breakfast of cornmeal porridge and then with a kiss sent him on his way. She said to him as he paused at the door, "Alec *dubh,* ye may be sorely beaten for helping me and for biding with me over-night."

"If I am," he told her fiercely, "my father will be sorry for it. I promise ye that. I will run away from home." As he went out to get the dun, he added, "I'll come to ye when I can."

A hand on each side of the doorway, she said, "I do not think ye will be able to come, and I'll not ask if ye'll ride with Gilchrist when the time comes and he summons ye. I know that ye must."

Alec paused in front of the house. Silent for a moment, he listened to the sounds of birds calling in the beeches before saying, "If I go with Jamie, I'll take no pleasure in it." Anger had begun to rise in him—anger against Jamie.

An hour later Alec was riding up to his own house calling out to his family. MacLeod came stomping out of the barn, glowering and armed. He put the long rifle down when he recognized Alec and bawled, "Where the devil have you been all night, boy?"

Alec stayed atop the dun. "I spent the night with Grand-mother Munn."

"Ye did that?" MacLeod came forward menacingly, and the dun, sensing his fury, stepped aside out of his way.

Alec urged the gelding back to its original place. "Jamie sent me to her with Grandfather's mare. Aye, Father, I stayed the night because it was near nightfall by the time I got her home. And before I did that, I helped bury my grandfather after Jamie had hanged him." Alec stared hard into his father's angry eyes. "Would ye have had him swinging there still beneath the oak beside the trail—bait for the crows? Would that have been a Christian thing to do, for ye to refuse to let me cut him down and give him burial when Grandmother Munn asked me to help her?" The horribly distorted and purpled face of his grandfather rose in his memory as it had again and again since Alec had climbed the oak to cut him down. He'd dug the hole beside the trail, wrapped his grandfather in the plaid and quilt, and placed him in it. He was the one who had said the Lord's Prayer over the grave—not dry-eyed, silent Jonet Munn.

Between his teeth MacLeod said, "Jamie's been here early this morning. Gilchrist told me there was a peddler there when ye rode to the Munns yesterday. He tells me ye went there *first* and never went to him at all with the news of Charles Towne. He had it from a rider from the village. He told me how the old traitor died. Why did ye ride to the Munns first of all when *I* sent ye to Jamie?" MacLeod's hand was gripping the dun's reins by now.

Alec replied simply, "To warn them." He gave his father hard glance for hard glance and said, "I am a Munn, as well as a MacLeod, Father. The Munns are my mother's people. Think on your wife." Alec leaned down to speak more softly so his mother wouldn't overhear him, though he knew MacLeod might reach up and jerk him bodily out of the saddle. "Think on her and on your great joy that her father's been hanged by a friend to ye. Did Jamie tell that I rode out with Munn and the peddler only because I was forced to it? It was not of my own free will. Did Jamie tell ye that, or did he leave it to me to tell ye?"

"Ye had a pistol, boy. Ye could have used it."

"I did not. Munn tricked me into giving it to him." Alec repeated, "Did Jamie tell ye that I was forced to go?"

MacLeod let go of the reins. "Aye, Jamie did tell me—though he likes it no more than I that ye went to the Munns before ye planned to go to him."

Alec saw that his father's rage was ebbing. He would not be beaten. In fact, in some strange way his father seemed to respect him for standing fast. And, too, for warning the Munns.

"Ah, well," MacLeod went on heavily, "Jamie caught the old traitor who cursed King George and dealt with him. There's been no harm done our cause by Andrew Munn." Then he asked, "Who was the peddler? I'm told that he was a Scot also."

"His name was Donal Bean, and he was naught but a peddler, a wee feeble man." Alec held to the lie he must always tell for the sake of his grandmother's safety. If Jamie ever learned who Bean was, her life would surely be forfeit and for that matter so might Alec's for concealing the information.

"He was a rebel?" said MacLeod.

"Aye, and a man who was transported from Scotland with the Munns and with them was indentured to the same master. An old friend to them he was."

MacLeod nodded. "So, ye and Munn set him on the road to the north. 'Tis done now, it seems, and the old witch-woman is alone. Ye'll not ride to her again. I'll not beat ye this time as ye deserve if ye'll promise me that, Alec."

As he dismounted Alec stifled a sigh. "I promise it."

Perhaps Lilias could go in his place, though he doubted it. More than likely she would be commanded to stay close to the farm for safety because of raiders moving about the countryside. Jonet Munn would understand his absence. She had said that probably he would not be able to visit her.

"Has Mother been told of her father?" Alec asked Mac-Leod, as he led the dun toward the barn.

MacLeod kept pace with him. "She has. Jamie came into the house this morning to tell me. She heard him as he spoke."

Rage washed over Alec as he envisioned the scene. Jamie and his father laughing over a stirrup cup of whiskey while his mother listened to them in an unweeping silence. Bedamned to Gilchrist, who must have a demon in him! He could have told MacLeod outside the house—but not Jamie! Alec fumed as he took the saddle and bridle off the gelding, then walked back to the house, leaving his father mending harness in the barn.

Going on into the kitchen, Alec called out to his mother. When she came toward him with her arms outstretched, he embraced her. Quietly she wept, her head on his shoulder. He told her softly, while Lilias listened, of Munn's death.

"We buried him, Grandmother and I, in his plaid beside the trail. I stayed the night with her."

"I fretted over ye, fearing a panther had got ye, Alec. How does she fare?" asked Margaret MacLeod, lifting wet eyes to his face.

"She'll fare well enough, I think." Alec went on, "She bids me tell ye when 'tis time to see ye again, she will see ye. Before the year is out, she says it is to happen."

Margaret MacLeod put her apron to her brimming eyes as she said, "Ye will never know how glad I was to see ye come riding in this morning. I would have come out to greet ye, Alec *dubh,* but I would have wept, and MacLeod has forbidden me. Thank ye for helping your grandmother. I know ye tell me truly. That is the kind of thing she would have ye tell me. We'll not speak of it again, only pray that I will see her again."

Lilias gave out a scornful sound. " 'Tis best Father doesn't put his mind too often to your warning the Munns, Alec. Ye know his temper, so we'd best not talk of this when he's about. He's set his thoughts now to the making of whiskey before the redcoat soldiers come here."

Jamie discontinued drilling with his troopers the rest of May while he rode out hunting down rebels. He did not send for Alec to join his troop, and for a time Alec dared hope that Gilchrist had discarded him because of his warning the Munns. This possibility was a comfort to Alec, though there was a sadness mixed with it—sadness that he might not even catch sight of Ellen again because he no longer rode with her brother. He could not give up all memory of her.

But he had little time to think because MacLeod kept him so busy. Each night Alec fell asleep the instant he got into bed, he was so weary. MacLeod was making whiskey. He had taken his copper tank out of the barn and set it next to the old brick furnace beside the creek. He had placed open barrels on benches near the tank. Then he'd sent Alec off to the trader's for loaf sugar and the finest leaf tobacco. Alec had had little to say at Master Deckard's store when the old trader had told him he was sorry to hear of Andrew Munn's death. He had refused to meet Deckard's gaze and hurried out as fast as he could with the sugar and tobacco.

Working together, MacLeod, Alec, and Lilias filled the barrels with a mixture of chopped corn, barley, loaf sugar, and water. While it stood fermenting, Alec gathered wood to fire the brick stove. It was Lilias's task to stir the mash in the barrels and skim off the insects and field mice that were lured by the fragrance to die, drowned in the soupy liquid.

When MacLeod guessed the mash was ripe enough, he started the runoff. Day and night Alec tended the fires under the big copper pot, which had been filled with mash. He sat in front of the flames stoking the blaze while he watched the colorless whiskey drip from copper tubing out of the tank's top into a bucket set beneath. While he tended the fire under the still, he thought often of his grandmother, wondering how she was. He wondered, too, about Donal Bean. Had he found the man he sought along the Pee Dee River? Or had he run into king's soldiers along the way there? Had he found the man named Marion? And what of Jamie Gilchrist? Had Jamie decided that he wanted nothing more to do with Alec MacLeod?

But most of all Alec asked himself where the king's army was, now that Charles Towne was secured. How close were the king's soldiers to Ninety-Six village now?

He was still wondering these things as he helped his father water down the whiskey to half-and-half proportions from the clear creek after Lilias had tossed in some pinches of tobacco to give the whiskey color and a biting flavor. Alec hoped MacLeod wouldn't make him taste the stuff.

His father's new whiskey always resembled liquid flames.

But the man insisted Alec share the first dipper with him. Down went the whiskey like a white-hot ball of lead. Alec gagged and coughed while his father beat him on the back, hooting with laughter. "Ye drink like the milksop ye used to be" he roared, "though ye've defied me and seen a man hanged and become a trooper. From the look on your face ye'd guess Lilias put poison into it instead of good tobacco. Ye'd best learn to like spirits, Alec. Ye be fifteen years now —nigh to a man full-grown. If ye can't drink whiskey with ease, you're no man and no Scot and not fit to be a king's soldier. Any day now we'll have the news of the king's army coming here. Finish the whiskey in the dipper, son."

The tenth day of June Alec awakened at dawn to the furious barking of the MacLeod hounds. His rifle ready, he joined his father in his nightshirt at one of their tiny windows. More rebels coming? There were hoofbeats in the distance. Who'd be riding to them so very early. Someone to steal their pigs?

But, no, the hoofbeats brought Jamie Gilchrist and four of his troopers through the morning mists to the front of the MacLeod house. Why was Jamie here? And in a moment Alec learned. Jamie shouted out, "MacLeod, MacLeod, *they've come*! There are king's soldiers twenty miles from here to the north. Send Alec to the bee tree as soon as ye can." No, Jamie had not forgotten Alexander MacLeod.

Whirling about, MacLeod told Alec, in wild excitement, "I'll help ye make ready to go, lad."

"Aye, Father." Alec avoided his father's eyes.

Twenty minutes later after a hasty breakfast of oatmeal he was riding to the rendezvous, his rifle, cleaned and ready to be loaded, slung across his back, and on his saddle Jamie's heavy old pistol. A leather bag of provisions hung behind the saddle. At the boy's side was his filled powder horn on a leather thong. At his hip, as always, he carried his skinning knife, the one he'd used to cut his hanged grandfather down. Armed in every respect, Alec felt nothing at all like a king's soldier in his buckskin clothing and broad-brimmed farmer's hat. Certainly he was no bold Highland warrior marching off to war with bagpipes and drums to give him courage! And he'd got none from his mother's tearful embrace. As for Lilias, she had stuck out her tongue at him because he had told her to mind her mother in his absence.

Jamie led his little company at a canter northward to country where one of his far-ranging riders, a northern scout for Gilchrist's Horse, claimed he'd spied encamped soldiers in the distance the night before. To his surprise, these men were greencoat troops, not redcoats at all. Judging from the number of horses with them, they were also cavalry. No, the scout had not ridden up to them to talk. He'd learned from a farmer that they were king's troopers. He'd galloped at once to Jamie with the news without being seen by them.

Much of that day they rode hard, through fields and wood, fording brooks, but seeing no one. And then in the distance they spotted smoke rising from a clump of trees. It was too much smoke to be coming from any chimney. Jamie ordered his men to draw their pistols and go forward at a walk to investigate. Moving slowly, they came upon a log house. It was in flames. A woman sat surrounded by her children in front of it, weeping. There were no men about that Alec could see. When the woman saw the riders, she shrieked and grabbed her nearest child, hugging him to her.

Jamie stayed in the saddle. "What's happened here?" he asked in English.

"The king's soldiers, the greencoat riders, came!" She was white-faced, terrified, her mouth working in fear. "They took our food and burned our house. What do you want from us? There's nothing left for you to take!"

Gilchrist asked, "What direction did the greencoats take?"

Getting up, she pointed northeast and shrilled at Jamie as he ordered his troop to rein away, "Kill the green devils! My man's gone to join the Continental army in North Carolina or they would have killed him today. I know it. Kill the greencoats! Kill them for me if you be good Americans!"

The woman didn't hear Jamie's wild, light laughter as they rode swiftly away. A mile further along, riding across a meadow, Alec saw another tall plume of smoke, another burning house, a rebel home. They didn't ride to this blaze, but Jamie stopped a bearded stranger walking in a lane nearby.

He asked him, speaking careful and slow English, "Have you had news of greencoat riders?"

The man nodded. "I have. They rode by me not an hour ago, but first they questioned me about known rebels in these parts. And then they told me what they did to the rebel Virginian soldiers they met north of here."

Alec listened as Jamie asked eagerly, "What's that? There are rebel troops near here, too? Will there be a battle? Where will it take place?"

The man sounded mournful. "There's *been* a battle. The greencoats chased down the Virginians and caught them at a place north of here called Waxhaw. The greencoats sliced the Virginians to bloody ribbons with their sabers, they did. They gave them no quarter, though the Virginia men begged for it. One of the greencoats boasted to me of all the killing. Bad as savage Indians, these stranger greencoats are! Their leader is the worst of them all. I say it though you may make me wish I had not." He shook his head. "I am a loyal king's man, but I do not like their leader."

Jamie cried, "Who leads them? What is his name?"

"Tarleton. Colonel Tarleton. A pure white angel he looks —but that's not what he is. He's a devil."

"Tarleton?" Jamie repeated the name. "A colonel? Where is he now?"

"Gone to burn a rebel house a distance from here. That way it lies! Look for the smoke. God help me. I told Tarleton where the house was, because he said he'd kill me if I refused to give him the names of rebels. There's a family there, small children, too. They were friends of mine. No more. No more they are." The bearded man stared up at Jamie as if he asked for comfort from him.

Gilchrist had no time for him now. He wheeled Sweet Lass about and with a yelp of joy led Alec and the others at a hard gallop in the direction the stranger had pointed.

Following at the very rear of Gilchrist's Horse, Alec reckoned that at last he was in the midst of the war. With all his heart he wished that he was not.

And even more he wished that he was not in the company of Jamie Gilchrist. He feared him now far more than he respected him. Perhaps he had done what any true king's man would do in hanging Andrew Munn, who openly cursed King George, but Alec could not get out of his mind the words Jamie had spoken when he had begged for time for his grandfather to say his prayers. "Aye, Alec, let him do so swiftly and be damned to the old traitor." The words would rankle forever.

VII

Greencoats and Purple Berries

Jamie found what he was seeking a few miles southeast: yet another pillar of smoke in the sky. He lifted his right hand as a signal for silence, then gestured toward a tree-topped hill a distance away. Leading his men, he rode to it.

From the hilltop Alec stared down on a scene far more dreadful than the one they'd just visited. A fair-haired woman lay on the ground while two small girls ran around her wailing, plucking at her hair and skirts, trying to rouse her. A third child, one perhaps two years old, sat under the large tree that shaded the house. He kept looking up in puzzlement at the swaying feet over him. A man, the father Alec guessed, had been hanged in front of his own door. Behind the house the barn was ablaze. It was the cause of the smoke.

At least twenty greencoated men were sitting in the clearing before the house. On top of a tree stump at the side of the house was a wooden keg. From its small size and its shape Alec felt it held rum. While he looked on, a greencoated trooper got up and went to it to fill the cup he carried. Then he walked back to his comrades and sat down.

Three men, in particular, caught Alec's fascinated attention. They were playing cards on a spread-out scarlet blanket. Two wore green coats. The third had removed his jacket but retained his black hat, topped with white feathers. This man, who lay on one elbow, wore a white shirt, white breeches, and black leather boots.

Alec heard the quick intake of Jamie's breath before his sharp command, "Bide here, all of ye, till I summon ye in." He spurred Sweet Lass down the hill. The moment she moved forward he started to shout in English, "Tarleton. Colonel Tarleton. I'm a king's man, too!"

From the hilltop Alec watched the man with the plumed hat get to his feet and walk to his tethered horse nearby, a magnificent black animal. He took a long, glinting dragoon pistol from the saddle holster and went back to the red blanket. Alec suspected that he must be Colonel Tarleton. His soldiers put down their cups of rum and rose up also while a sentry posted by the feet of the hanged rebel lifted his pistol and took aim on Jamie.

But no one fired. With the red cloth of Gilchrist's Horse tied proudly to his arm over his gold-colored velvet coat, Jamie walked Sweet Lass directly to the British officer and reined her in without a glance at the rebels in such distress. Tense moments went by for the riders on the hilltop while Tarleton and Gilchrist conferred. Then Alec saw Jamie wave them in, shouting "Come."

With the other men from Ninety-Six Section, Alec Mac-Leod rode down the hill to join Tarleton's force, the king's Green Dragoons. All except Alec were jubilantly happy to have joined the royal forces at last. But since old Munn had been hanged, Alec wanted even less of the Revolution than ever. The memory of the hanging and of his grandfather's horrible face haunted even his dreams.

Drawn up in a line of horsemen at Jamie's barked order, Alec had his first close view of Tarleton. He was very young, as the bearded man on the road had reported. And indeed Tarleton did look like an angel! His face was marble white, set with large, shining dark eyes. His hair was red-brown. Though the man was short, his chest, arms, and legs were abnormally strong and heavy. The British officer walked down the line of Gilchrist's Horse inspecting the troopers, glancing at their mounts, rifles, and pistols.

He said no word at all, only patted Sweet Lass and nodded to Jamie, who was beaming with joy at his approval. Jamie told Tarleton, "My lads know this part of the colony, Colonel. They'll make good scouts for you. Most have some English."

Then Tarleton spoke. His voice was a soft, slow monotone. "So they shall. My men are not Englishmen like me, Gilchrist, but American colonials like the lot of you. They come from New Jersey and Pennsylvania colonies. Your men must speak English among us to be understood."

Alec gasped. The wild greencoats were *all* colonials! He had not expected that. He had thought all would be Englishmen.

"Dismount," ordered Jamie in English. "Leave your pistols in your saddles. You'll have no need for them here."

With the others Alec got off his horse and led the dun to a tree and tethered him among the horses of the Green Dragoons.

No greencoat trooper hailed Alec. His fellows of Gilchrist's Horse went to the rum keg to join the greencoats. A couple of the men who had come with Jamie glanced uneasily at the woman and the hanged man, then averted their heads. They would not interfere with the work of the Green Dragoons, who were king's soldiers like themselves.

Alec went to sit alone beside the brook some small distance from the blazing barn. Probably because he sat so quietly, one of the small girls of the rebel family got up from her mother's side and walked over to him. He reckoned her to be around three years old, too young to understand what had happened. A pretty golden-haired child, she babbled for a while to him about her mother who was "asleep" and of her white kitten that had run away when all of the men had come. Then she fell asleep beside Alec, her hand outstretched as if unknowingly she claimed his pity. Alec swallowed hard, gazing at her. Aye, he did pity her and her family, for all that they were rebels! He suspected that her mother was dead, not simply unconscious and most certainly not asleep.

What would become of this child and the other two children? There were no farms nearby that he knew of and there were panthers and wolves in the forests.

Looking away from her, Alec watched Jamie. Gilchrist had gone back and forth to the rum, too. Now, as the very proud commander of the new force, Gilchrist's Scouts, he was sitting on the blanket with Tarleton playing cards.

Jamie's back was to Alec. Frequently Alec heard his high laughter ring out over the voices of the other men. The English colonel faced Alec. As he and Jamie and another trooper gambled, Alec noticed that Tarleton never once smiled or laughed. His face was a mask of white snow— because of its lack of life—more frightening than beautiful.

While Alec sat staring at Tarleton, he heard the child beside him whimper in her sleep. He glanced at her as she rolled over onto her side and he saw with shock that her plump fingers were within reach of a pokeweed plant. The pretty purple berries hung down over her face. Her parents must have been heedless folk to allow the weed to grow so near the house. Pokeberries were dangerous. The roots of the plant even more so. When she awoke, he'd warn her not to touch the plant and especially not to eat the berries.

While he was still looking at the berries, he heard a sudden blare of voices. Jamie's was by far the loudest. Alec looked to him once more. Gilchrist had got up and was swaying back and forth while he ranted in Gaelic. Suddenly Alec saw him fling his cards down onto the blanket at Tarleton's feet and yowl in fury. "Damn ye for a filthy cheating thief of an Englishman. You didn't win my horse fairly!"

Alec drew in his breath while Tarleton smiled up at Jamie. The smile was a melting, lazy one, dazzling in its beauty. The Englishman didn't rise to face Gilchrist. Suddenly, reaching out, the young colonel took up a pistol that lay on the blanket between him and the trooper beside him. Cocking it, without saying a word, Tarleton shot Jamie through the heart.

As Jamie pitched forward onto the blanket, Tarleton

rolled out of his way, quicker than any panther. Then he sat up next to Jamie's sprawled corpse, and Alec saw that Tarleton was still smiling.

There was a furious uproar—men bawling out in English and in Gaelic. Alec sat silent, paralyzed with fear. Would all of the men of Gilchrist's Scouts be shot down now that Jamie had quarrelled with Tarleton and been killed for it?

But the young colonel only called out sharply from where he sat, "No pistols!" and his greencoats lowered theirs. Only Jamie had provoked the leader of the Green Dragoons.

God in heaven! Horror such as he'd never known before in his life—not even when his grandfather was hanged—knifed through Alec MacLeod. This colonel, this Tarleton, had committed a deliberate murder—all the while smiling! He wanted the sorrel mare, as any man who laid eyes on Sweet Lass would want her, but unlike the others, Tarleton was willing to cheat for her and even to murder to get her. Alec recalled now how he had eyed Sweet Lass when he had inspected Jamie's troop. This killing was murder—and calculated murder at that.

True, Jamie had hanged Andrew Munn, but in all fairness Alec had had to admit to himself that his grandfather had provoked him and sought to be executed as a traitor. Alec could not truly hate Jamie for the deed.

But he could hate this man Tarleton. Was this how a king's officer went about satisfying his momentary desires? Cheating at cards? Murdering loyal men? Murdering allies? Alec's horror gave way to a sudden rage.

He reached out his arm to pull the little girl to him. The pistol shot had awakened her and made her start to cry. As he hauled her to him to stop her weeping, which might draw Tarleton's attention, Alec's left hand brushed against the pokeweed. Pokeberries. Aye, pokeberries! For a moment he looked at the pretty berries, then at the little girl nestled at his side.

In an instant he stripped off a handful of the purple fruit, one-handed, and crushed them into a pulp. Alec whispered now to the girl, trying to hide his fury from her and not alarm her. Searching desperately for the English words, he asked her, "Do you see the keg over there, sweeting? Atop the stump?"

Aye, there were no greencoats near the stump at the moment and none of Jamie's troopers. Alec opened his hand, showing her that it was filled with pulp from the berries. "Take this. Do not eat the berries. Rub the berries on your hands till your hands are purple, too, as my hand is."

Delighted with the game, she smiled as she smeared the pulp over her little hands and held them, palms up, for Alec to see. Then he told her softly, "Go to the keg on the tree stump. Wash your hands inside the keg. Don't let anyone see you wash them."

She nodded, grinned again, got up and went over to the topless keg. Holding his breath, Alec watched her wash her hands in the rum, then run over to her mother's side and sit down. The child had forgotten him and the game already. No one had seen her put her hands down into the rum because everyone in the camp had his eyes fixed on the two cursing, sweating greencoats who were hauling Jamie's body by the heels to the creek to dump him into it. Alec winced at the splashing sound.

He stayed where he was, knowing that the others would

soon return to the rum. While the hanged man swayed in the late afternoon breeze and the woman never once moved, Alec waited. While he waited, he thought about Jamie and his grandmother's words about him. Aye, Jamie would never marry Lilias. He would never marry anyone! The feyness in Gilchrist had destroyed him as Andrew Munn's long-nurtured hatred had destroyed him.

While he waited, Alec cast wary glances at Colonel Tarleton. He was the White Beast. Jonet Munn had spoken truly. He had met the White Beast. So had Jamie to his undoing. There had been a *copleach,* a gathering of horses, and a White Beast.

The Red Beast, dark water, and a high place were yet to come. Alec looked ruefully at his hand, stained dark purple with pokeberry juice. Aye, he'd used his left hand to gather the fruit. Jonet Munn had been right once more.

As the day lengthened into sunset and the Green Dragoons went back and forth into the rebel house bringing out food, Alec saw Tarleton put on his short green jacket for warmth. Would the effects of the berries *never* work? Alec's empty stomach still churned with anger, paining him. Had there been too few berries? Clearly their color and taste hadn't affected the rum, which was undoubtedly the strong-flavored brown stuff from Jamaica, the sort the up-country settlers preferred.

His stomach still taut with fury and his heart pounding unevenly, Alec sat waiting until dusk and until much more rum had been poured down the men's throats.

At last what he'd hoped for happened. First one soldier, a greencoat or one of Jamie's Scots, doubled over with cramping, then began to vomit. Alec saw with pleasure how

Tarleton, also, suddenly clasped his hands over his abdomen and retched violently.

It was time! Alec went down onto all fours, crawling. He went on his hands and knees through the bushes behind the house to the trees where the horses were tied. There he lay on his belly, hearing the sounds of groans and of men vomiting until he judged the light dim enough. Springing to his feet, he ran—not to the MacLeod dun gelding but to Sweet Lass, Jamie's horse. Na, he could not bring Jamie back, but he might be able to save his beautiful mare and riding her bring the evil news to his family.

His heart racing with fright and excitement, Alec untied Sweet Lass and mounted her. His only hope of getting away lay in surprise and swiftness. Not all of the troopers had gone near the rum. Some few would be sober and alert.

Alec kicked the mare as hard as he could. Sweet Lass came like a skyrocket out of the trees, gathering her legs under her in great bounding strides that very quickly lengthened into a gallop. A pistol ball whistled past Alec's head but in a few short moments' time he and the mare were out of sight riding into the gathering darkness.

Miles south of Tarleton's camp, Alec reined in the sorrel in a meadow under a rising moon. He flung himself along her spine, gasping for breath.

If Jamie's troopers had not been there, he would have tried to put pokeweed roots into the rum keg. The poisonous roots would have killed every man who drank. The berries were only a violent purge.

At last Alec sat up. He patted the mare's neck, grateful to her for her speed and response to his orders. Alec made a decision. He'd ride first to the Gilchrists and tell them of Jamie's death. That would be a very hard thing to do, but he could soften the blow. He could tell them that Jamie had died a soldier's death to salve their pride. No one would deny his tale for a long time.

Clearly the other men of Gilchrist's Horse would ride away with Tarleton either out of fear to attempt escape as he had and be shot or because Tarleton would convince them to scout for him. They had seemed to get on very well with the Green Dragoons, fellow colonials. Only he had not mingled with the men from Pennsylvania and New Jersey colonies. He was certain that no Scot of Jamie's command was going to tell Tarleton where Alexander MacLeod lived. Na, Tarleton would not send after him for taking the horse. The men Jamie had led would protect Alec this far, though in time they'd probably return to Ninety-Six Section and tell the fearful truth of Jamie's dying. What's more, Alec had overheard one Green Dragoon tell one of Gilchrist's troopers that Tarleton rode next to the eastern part of the colony seeking rebels to fight and farms to burn.

Alec's wild ride cross-country had made the strip of red cloth on his left arm pull loose so that it dangled in the curve of his elbow. Cursing in a spate of Gaelic, he jerked it off and let it fall to the ground. And why not? Gilchrist's Horse was no more. It was part of Tarleton's Green Dragoons—or if not yet, soon would be.

Though the Gilchrist family weren't to learn the truth from Alec, he must tell MacLeod how Jamie had died. MacLeod must know about Colonel Tarleton in case the English officer came riding to their farm. Too, Alec thought his father might be pleased to learn that he had saved

Jamie's fine sorrel mare from the Englishman to return her to Jamie's family.

As Sweet Lass took him over the miles to the Gilchrists', Alec asked himself how he would tell Jamie's family. He didn't want to wound them by telling them of Jamie's drunkenness and rash gambling and how he had staked the valuable mare. He had not had to tell Jonet Munn of her husband's death. The riderless horse had done so for him. Perhaps seeing him riding Sweet Lass would alert Jamie's parents and Ellen before Alec had to speak at all. At least, he hoped so. No one of Jamie's troop had ever ridden the mare but Jamie.

The Gilchrist house was one of the largest in the district. It had two stories and shutters to the windows. And what was more, it was whitewashed yearly. It had been built atop a hill so that it commanded a view of the cornfields and woods around it. Alec rode up to it reluctantly in the fine rain, cursing the evil fortune that made him twice within a season have to carry tidings of death. Stormcrow, that was what he was becoming.

A black maidservant of the Gilchrists was first to spy him as she drew water from the well. Leaving the bucket on its rim, she gaped at the mare, then at Alec, and ran to the house crying out. Her cries brought Jamie's father, a man as lanky as his son had been, but with powdered gray hair. He, too, stared at Sweet Lass and her strange rider while laborers came out of the barn and sheds nearby to peer at Alec. Then, recognizing Alec, Gilchrist came forward. Ellen, dressed in white muslin, with her yellow hair in ringlets, followed behind her father. Both wore puzzled expressions on their faces. Alec's heart grew heavier. Na, they did not guess. So he must tell them.

"How do ye come by Sweet Lass?" Master Gilchrist called out.

Alec took a deep breath. Ah, a great liar he was becoming as well as a bringer of evil news. "Jamie's been killed, Master Gilchrist. Killed by the damned rebels in a fight."

"Dead? He's dead?" cried Ellen, as if she could not believe him. Gilchrist himself said nothing, but his face turned grayish white with shock.

Looking at Ellen, Alec told her, "Aye, Mistress Ellen. It was but the work of a moment in time—one pistol ball did it. He did not linger in pain. We buried him where he fell after the rebels were beaten off." The vision of Jamie's body being dragged to the creek flashed through Alec's mind as he spoke. In its own way, the memory was as hideous as that of seeing old Munn hanged. Aye, Jamie had been right. He *had* seen death—Jamie's own death.

There were no tears in Master Gilchrist's faded blue eyes. "Did my son acquit himself well against the rebels?"

Alec went on with his lie. "He did. He killed two of them. One of them was their leader."

"And the man who shot him?"

"That man was killed by one of us."

"Ah." Gilchrist sighed deeply, then asked as Ellen lifted her gauze apron to her face to wipe away tears, "How did ye come by the mare, lad?"

"Because my horse was killed in the fight and I had no mount, the others decided to send me here to tell ye and to deliver Sweet Lass to ye. I'll make my way home on foot."

"Na, na." Gilchrist reached up to pat the mare on the neck and let her nuzzle at his pockets for sugar. "There'll be no need of that. Take her. I give her to ye because ye were Jamie's friend and rode with his troop. What do ye have to say to that, Ellen?"

"Aye, Father." Her pretty face crumpled in grief, Ellen came to Alec. She set one foot into his stirrup and rising up on top of his boot, put her arms around his neck to give him a salt-tasting kiss. Then she was down, running to the house, her apron to her face again. Alec had had the kiss he longed for, but there had been more pain than joy to it.

He told her father, "I do not like fetching ye such news."

"I know it, lad. Now will ye take the horse?"

"I thank ye for her. I will." His father would have wanted him to do so.

"What will ye do now?" asked Master Gilchrist.

"Ride home to tell my father. I'll bide there for a while. The others of Jamie's troop will have ridden far from where I left them by now. They are hunting down rebels. And the mare's weary from the long ride."

"Aye, lad," said the man heavily, "and ye seem weary, too. So"—he looked at his boots—"our Jamie is gone from us, and he did not find the king's redcoat soldiers at all, 'Twas the one thing he had set his heart on."

"Na." Alec said only the one word, but his thoughts were of the murderous Tarleton and his brutal greencoats. He prayed that Tarleton, the White Beast, never rode to this part of the colony.

As Master Gilchrist walked slowly to the house through the flower garden to tell his invalid wife the terrible news,

Alec turned Sweet Lass away to ride down the hill. His work was not finished. He had to tell MacLeod yet, and then he must sleep. He'd had no sleep now for more than twenty-four hours. His eyes burned with fatigue and with the rain and wind blown into them by hard riding.

MacLeod was astonished to see Alec return so soon, and even more so to see him mounted on Jamie's sorrel. So exhausted that he could hardly speak at all, Alec let his father take the saddle and bridle off the mare.

While the man rubbed Sweet Lass down in the barn, Alec told his family the real story, including why he had not told it to the Gilchrists. "I would not want to blight his memory for them."

Alec sat slumped on the milking stool while his father tended to the mare and his mother stood leaning against a manger and Lilias sat in a pile of hay weeping softly for Jamie. Alec's final words to his family were, "So Tarleton shot him and had him thrown into the creek—though that's not the story I told Jamie's family."

"Ochone," keened Margaret MacLeod.

MacLeod was long faced. Pausing with the rubbing cloth in one hand, he asked Alec, "How did ye manage to get away, my son?"

Alec's voice trailed on wearily, speaking of the rum keg and pokeberries and the escape on Sweet Lass. He looked up at his father. He had never seen MacLeod look at him before in such a manner. "I had to leave our dun behind. I thought ye'd want me to fetch Jamie's horse and his pistol home to his family." Suddenly Alec realized that Master Gilchrist had not asked him to give up the fine silver-mounted pistol or the saddle and bridle. Ah well, later he would try to return them. Perhaps Master Gilchrist had not bethought himself of them either.

MacLeod said, "Ye did well, Alec, though I could wish ye'd used a pistol on this damned murderous Englishman Tarleton instead of pokeberries. Why do ye have the mare still if ye rode first today to the Gilchrists'?"

"Master Gilchrist made me a gift of her." Alec got to his feet, feeling dizzy. "I hope to God that Tarleton never comes here," he told his father. "King's officer or not, I could shoot him down. Killing Jamie meant not a thing to him."

MacLeod shook his head. "Do not judge all of King George's officers by one man, Alec."

"Na, Father, I do not," Alec said, as he started for the barn door. He passed his mother as he did. Giving her a crooked smile, he told her, "It seems I do little but fetch news of deaths to folk nowadays. Before long everyone in this section will hate the sight of me, Mother."

She moved away from the manger. Her voice was so quiet that only he heard it. "Na, Alec. Have ye thought that the deaths ye speak of were of two men who sought to be violent? Though one of them is my own father, I must say it of him. Your father would rather ye'd killed this Colonel Tarleton with a pistol than made him ill with pokeberries so ye could redeem Jamie's horse. I am proud of ye for doing that rather than shooting the Englishman." Then she said very matter-of-factly, "Ye'll not go out seeking Gilchrist's troopers now, will ye?"

He shook his head. "Some of them were sober. They know I took the mare. They'd have to shoot me in an instant if they saw me and they were riding in company with the Green Dragoons."

She asked, "Are ye certain this Tarleton is an Englishman?"

"Aye, Mother."

Margaret MacLeod nodded. "Alec *dubh,* bide here with us. There'll be other soldiers of the king coming soon. We had more news yesterday at midday. They are marching onto Ninety-Six village now. A traveler met them on the way. Their officer, he says, is a Major Ferguson. He spoke with him. Like us, Ferguson is a Scot, and he has the Gaelic. He will not be a Tarleton!"

VIII

A Fellow Scot

Seven days spent grieving for Jamie went by while Alec waited for Ferguson's soldiers to come. During that time Alec kept the horses hidden in the woods. Tarleton's desire for Sweet Lass made him alert to her welfare and to that of the white and the gray. He'd also hidden some food and pigs and chickens there, along with Jamie's pistol. What he had seen about the country had made him uneasy when he thought of his own family and farm.

On the eighth morning as he stood keeping watch on the hilltop, scanning the countryside, Alec saw the soldiers coming. They marched in a long red file in a soft, warm rain. They were led by two officers. One rode a bay horse, the other a sorrel. The officer in the lead wore a scarlet coat with a gold epaulette on one shoulder. Ferguson? Certainly

not Colonel Tarleton—not in a red coat. It must be the
man people said was a fellow Scot.

Running down to the house, Alec called to his father,
"They're coming! They're all redcoats and two officers!"

"Major Ferguson?" asked MacLeod hopefully, getting
up and putting down his pipe.

"I do not know."

"In any case, we'll make ready to receive them as guests,
Alec *dubh*."

Together Alec and his father got the whiskey barrel out
of the barn and set it up on a bench. Next, being wary for
their safety, MacLeod sent his wife and daughter into the
woods and stood in front of his house, unarmed to show his
friendship. Alec tied the dogs behind the barn, then came
to stand beside his father.

The officer mounted on the bay was a small thin man
with his right arm in a sling of black silk. His hair beneath
his three-cornered black hat was fox red, framing a bronzed
face. The other officer was younger with fair hair and a
broad, open face. The older man rode forward slowly surrounded by his soldiers, who had their Brown Bess muskets
ready. No one was smiling in answer to Lachlan MacLeod's
wide grin. The senior officer's sharp blue eyes took in the
two MacLeods, the house, barn, and outbuildings in a cool
sweeping glance. Then he pulled a piece of paper out of
his cuff, looked at it, and asked in English in a high-pitched
voice, "MacLeod. Lachlan MacLeod, is it?"

Alec spoke for his father, "That is my father. He speaks
almost no English."

The officer had the bark of a fox for a laugh. It matched

his hair, Alec thought, with a sudden forboding. The man asked in Gaelic, "And how is his Gaelic then? How is yours, lad?"

Delighted to hear his own tongue, MacLeod called out, "As good as yours, man. I knew that true king's men would come here soon. I'm glad they be Scotsmen. Who are ye, sir?"

"Major Ferguson. I am a Scot. I am billeted at Ninety-Six village and in the fort." He jerked his head toward the second officer. "This is Cornet Ordish. He is from Virginia Colony. All of my men are colonials—not Scots. I do not speak Gaelic in front of them. Now, MacLeod, I am told that your wife is the daughter of a damned hanged rebel, Andrew Munn."

MacLeod, who'd stepped forward welcoming Ferguson, stepped backward now. "He was a rebel, but we MacLeods are all king's men. My older son, Duncan, died fighting for the king five years past at the courthouse in Ninety-Six village."

Ferguson grunted and said coldly, "I have not heard that, MacLeod. I am told that Andrew Munn was a lifelong enemy to King George and for that was branded on the face."

MacLeod protested, "Munn was, but I told ye—we are not!"

"I see." Ferguson inclined his head. "Then, if ye are loyal king's men, ye will not object if we take what we need from your farm. We have come foraging. We live off the countryside."

MacLeod spread out his big red hands. "Take what ye

will from my house and barn. I've got good whiskey for ye, too." He motioned toward the barrel.

Ferguson spoke in English to the man standing at his side. The soldier walked up to the whiskey, reversed his musket, and with the butt end beat open the barrel. The liquid cascaded over the ground, wetting Alec's and his father's shoes and scenting the air. Then Ferguson spoke again in Gaelic to MacLeod. "Though ye be a Scot, I cannot trust ye—not when your wife was the daughter of a rebel. I'll risk no scurvy rebel tricks here. A keg of rum was poisoned by one of ye colonists sometime past and drunk by the king's Green Dragoons. They could not take to their horses for some time."

Alec caught his breath. Tarleton and the pokeberries. Joy surged through him, but it mingled with a swift rising anger that Ferguson treated the MacLeods so badly.

"Lachlan MacLeod," the officer went on in Gaelic again. "We have no use for your whiskey, but have ye horses?"

"Na," Alec lied swiftly. "Raiders took them away— rebels. Traitors to the king." Though Ferguson was also a Scot, Alec found himself disliking him more violently each moment. The man was chill as winter snow. Alec disliked something else. The fact that all of Ferguson's men were like Tarleton's—all colonials. They were as hard eyed as the Green Dragoons.

Ferguson gestured to his left with his good arm, and five men ran with muskets into the MacLeod barn. Next the officer pointed to MacLeod himself and spoke in English to the soldier who had broken the whiskey barrel. "Sergeant, take Lachlan MacLeod here into custody. Bind him. He's to go to jail in the village. He attempted to give whiskey to us that may have been poisoned, and he had a notorious rebel for a father-in-law."

"What does he say?" MacLeod demanded of Alec.

"He says you're to be taken prisoner," Alec told his father in disbelief.

"Na, he will not!" MacLeod shook his fist at Ferguson. "Be damned to ye," he thundered in Gaelic. "I may not wear a red coat, but I serve King George as well as ye do, and I'm a Scot like yourself. I've driven rebel raiders off, and I'll send ye packing, too. I had naught to do with old Munn or poisoned rum. Curse Munn's soul to a black hell. I gave one fine son to die for the king, and I'll give my pigs and corn. But ye'll never make a prisoner of Lachlan MacLeod. I'll not lie in jail with rebels."

Suddenly before Alec could do anything, MacLeod had spun about striding rapidly for the house. Alec watched helplessly as at Ferguson's nod the sergeant came running forward with his musket. Swinging the weapon high, the redcoat brought it down on the back of MacLeod's head. Alec heard his father groan, then saw him sink to his knees and fall face downward in the mud. Another soldier had his musket trained on Alec.

Major Ferguson told Alec, who stood frozen to the spot, "Ye be but a lad. It's my guess your women are hiding in the woods. We shall not hunt them down. I do not make war on women. I want ye to come to Ninety-Six village and volunteer for the king's service. Other lads your age are coming in and being made into soldiers for the king. Because ye are a fellow Scot and did not try to get a rifle from the house, as I know your father meant to do, I'll spare ye today. And I'll not burn your house. Bury your father, or if he's still alive, fetch the fool to the village with ye if he can travel. Get your womenfolk settled and come to the fort in three days' time. If ye do not come, I'll send men here after ye—and after your father." Ferguson turned his head to look behind him. "Cornet Ordish, ye are to come after this lad to impress him into my forces if he has not come to the fort in three days' time." These words were in English.

Alec said nothing. He looked up into Ferguson's stern face, then looked away at his father, who had not moved.

Afraid to go to him, the boy looked on as the soldiers who had gone into the barn came out with sacks filled with corn and squirming with live chickens. Still other men, now led by Cornet Ordish, came out of the house with the MacLeod long rifles and most of the family quilts. As he passed Alec, the young cornet gave him a strange glance, one almost of understanding. Satisfied, Major Ferguson gave a sharp command and the laden soldiers went to the wagon that had brought up the rear of their march. They piled what they had foraged inside it, then stood waiting for Ferguson's command. He consulted the paper he had in his cuff while Alec watched him, then swung his horse about to go to the next farm.

When they had gone down the lane, Alec ran to his father to turn him over and wash the bloodstained mud from his face. MacLeod was breathing very heavily, gasping and snorting. The back of his head was soaked with his blood, and his hair matted with it. Leaving him, Alec raced into the woods after his mother and sister. Thanks to his foresight, the redcoats had not got the horses and all of the pigs and chickens. The rifles were another matter, but Jamie's silver-mounted pistol he had still. The MacLeods were not totally weaponless. He had hidden the pistol in the hollow of a tree, wrapped in a cloth to keep it dry. Alec made a fierce promise to himself as he ran through the trees. He would never go to Ninety-Six fort and join Major Ferguson. But he couldn't stay on the farm either. This "fellow Scot" had meant what he said. Cornet Ordish would come after him and his father soon. Alec decided once he'd told the evil news to his mother and Lilias he'd hie himself to Jonet Munn at once. God forbid that Ferguson's next destination of the day should be there. Still, he had been especially interested in her husband, the "traitor."

Aye, he'd ask her advice as to what he should do. While he was talking with her, he'd tell her he'd met both of her beasts now—the red and the white. They were both officers of the king. Ferguson not only wore a red coat, he had red hair.

Alec cupped his hands to his mouth to call his mother and sister, who came running to him an instant later from out of a thicket and stood together facing him while the words stumbled out about Ferguson's visit.

His mother spoke as if in a dream. "Do ye say they refused your father's whiskey and they sore hurt him? They were not Scots at all?" She shook her head.

"Only one man was—the major."

"It is difficult to believe. Alec, ride to your grandmother and bring her to our house. Tell her that I have need of her if your father's been hurt."

"Aye."

Lilias, who'd gone to sit nearby on a tree stump, asked Alec, "Why didn't ye kill the redcoat soldiers?" Her eyes were green black with fury.

"Our long rifles were inside the house. The redcoat soldiers took them away with them."

"Then how are we to defend ourselves from anyone?" Her lip twisted in scorn.

He didn't reply to her. He went to the tree where Sweet Lass was tethered. Reaching inside the hollow in the trunk, he took out Jamie's pistol and removed the cloth around it. Walking to her, he gave it to her with the words. "Keep this until I come back. I do not think Ferguson will return until the three days are up. Then someone will come for Father and me."

The three of them had a hard time dragging MacLeod's heavy body into the house and putting him on a bed whose quilts had been stripped by the redcoats. He was breathing less noisily now, but he was still alive, with his wife weeping over him.

Alec, who had brought Sweet Lass out of the woods with him, saddled her and set off for the Munn house. He had no doubt that his grandmother would come with him. His thoughts while he rode were filled with hatred toward the king's soldiers. He'd left his mother and sister putting cold cloths on his father's head. Would MacLeod die, too, as Duncan and Andrew Munn had? Would Ferguson also go today to the Gilchrists? He hoped Master Gilchrist would have the good sense not to provoke the Scottish major. At the thought of Ferguson, Alec's heels dug into the mare's flanks urging speed.

To his great relief, there were no redcoats gathered

around the Munn house. His grandmother was sitting on the step outside as if she waited for someone. Behind her, visible through the open door, was a large bundle. When she spied him, she got up, letting her tartan shawl fall back from her head. Munn's old chestnut horse was saddled and bridled beside the doorstep as if it waited too.

Alec reined in and let his grandmother speak first. "Ye've come for me, Alec *dubh*?"

"Yes, to get ye away before the redcoats arrive. Mother has need of ye. Father's been hurt. Are ye ready to go?"

"Aye."

He was not surprised to find her ready to leave. Either her second sight had prepared her, or she might easily have learned that the redcoats were foraging and expected Alec to take her somewhere into the woods and hide her. She could have many rebel friends who would bring her secret warnings.

She asked, "Will ye take the bundle on your mare?"

"I will. Do ye have a musket or a pistol?" Alec was hoping that Jamie's troopers might have overlooked a weapon when they came to her weeks before, asking where Munn and Donal Bean were.

"Na, I do not. Andrew's musket was not returned to me with the horse. Do ye not remember?"

Alec nodded. "Redcoat soldiers came to our house today and took our long rifles. We thought they came in friendship." He paused, then added swiftly, "They have hit my father on the head with a musket butt. He welcomed them with whiskey he'd made for them, but they may have murdered him."

"Ochone, ochone," Jonet Munn muttered, looking up

into the sky that promised more rain. "So now that he is ill I can see my daughter again? Am I to nurse Lachlan MacLeod, who hates me?"

"That is what Mother is asking. Aye." Alec got down from Sweet Lass, handing her reins to Jonet Munn. "There's been another death. Has no one told ye of Jamie Gilchrist's dying?"

"I have heard. His sister came to tell me yesterday and to buy valerian leaves from me to make tea for her mother. Valerian soothes grief. I did not tell Mistress Ellen that her brother was marked out from his birth to die young."

Alec sighed as he picked up her bundle. She had thought of everything. There were cords lying next to it to bind it onto the mare. As he carried it to Sweet Lass and tied it to her saddle, he asked, "Grandmother, I have seen the Red Beast and the White now. Have ye looked recently into the flames for me?"

"I have, but I have seen nothing else. I can see only what is shown to me to see."

He demanded harshly, pressing her for an answer, "Am I to die also? Tell me truly."

"I do not know, but I do not think ye will. There's still the dark water and the high place ahead for ye and somewhat to do with your hand, your left hand."

Alec smiled grimly. Aye, he'd crushed the pokeberries in his left hand!

"What of the two Beasts that serve King George?"

"One will die. The other not. I do not know which one will die."

Alec jerked savagely on the last cord, making the startled mare jump sideways. Through his teeth he said, "What ye say only pleases me by half, Grandmother. I wish to God both would die." Going to her, Alec helped her mount the chestnut. As he set her into the saddle, he told her, "The Scots officer who came today warned me if I do not join the king's army in the village, he'll send men to bring me there, and he plans to put Father into jail."

She looked down at his upturned face and touched his cheek. "Could ye serve under men who have done what has been done to us, Alec *dubh,* though ye say ye give your loyalty to the man who says he is King George?"

"Na, na!" Alec shook his head violently. And now hurriedly he told her of his afternoon with Colonel Tarleton and the pokeberries.

She listened gravely, then said, "Ah, ye must go away and quickly, too. Do not fret yourself over Lilias and your mother and father and myself. Have ye thought where ye will go?"

"Over the mountains—or into North Carolina Colony."

"Alec"—her strange eyes fixed him—"I know where ye would find a friend."

"Where is that? Who is it?" He knew no one except in his section of the colony.

"Donal Bean. Go to Donal Bean."

"Where would I find him?"

"Have ye forgotten what ye overheard so soon?" She was chuckling gently. "Why—Donal Bean's with Francis Marion. The red soldiers will never get their hands on Marion. He is a will-o'-the-wisp. Ye cannot find him. He finds ye. Do ye not know what the red soldiers are calling Colonel Marion? They name him Swamp Fox. Now let us go. I have what I need from here. I'll help my poor Margaret with her husband as well as I may. When ye've got me safely there, ye should think of riding to Francis Marion, where ye'll find Donal. Tell Donal of my Andrew's death. Tell him that Andrew died as he saw fit—that he greatly feared to die in his bed. Tell him not to mourn for him. Take a message to old Donal from me, Alec *dubh*."

Alec's mind had been busy while Jonet Munn had been talking. Aye, it could be wise to find the peddler. Alec knew not a soul over the mountains, and many Indians were there—hostile Indians. He nodded after he mounted Sweet Lass. "When I've fetched ye to our farm and settled some matters, I'll go where ye tell me to go."

Sadly the boy started toward his home, with his grandmother riding behind him. Drops of rain beat down on them. They ran over the brim of his hat and fell onto his hands. He looked at his left hand, slick with the rain. Somehow he felt that his grandmother had seen more in the fire regarding his hand than she was telling him. She had not said that the crushing of the pokeberries had been the remarkable deed of his left hand. What would riding to the rebel, Colonel Marion, have to do with his future? How strangely his life had fallen out. He was no more a king's man, but he was certainly not a rebel either. He didn't know what he was anymore. The uncertainty was a very uncomfortable feeling.

Lachlan MacLeod never truly "came back to himself," as Jonet Munn put it. Some hours after he'd been hit by Ferguson's sergeant, he regained consciousness, but he was no longer the loud, harsh, overbearing man his family had known. He was childlike, whimpering, unable to recognize his wife and children or Jonet Munn, whom he had once hated. He lay abed and was fed from a papboat, as a small child would be. His hounds were let into the room where he lay. The oldest of them fell onto her belly beside the bed and refused to be led out. When she yelped in Alec's grasp and MacLeod muttered something from the bed, Jonet Munn told him, "Let that dog stay. She comforts him."

Alec bowed to her wisdom here, as he had bowed to it the night before when she suggested that he ride away the next day.

As he saddled Sweet Lass preparatory to riding off for what he knew might be the last time, she came out to the barn before he made his final farewells to his mother and Lilias. "Grandmother, I do not like to leave ye alone and unarmed," he told her. He had Jamie's pistol in the saddle holster once more. She had insisted he take it with him.

"We have pitchforks, and neighbors will bring your mother a long rifle or musket if she asks them, Alec *dubh*."

"Na, do not ask the neighbors. We have money enough to buy a long rifle from Master Deckard in the village. He will sell one in secret to ye. I guess he has hidden one or two away for Patriots who need a rifle." Deckard had sent MacLeod his profit from the sale of the goods in Charles Towne four days before Major Ferguson had come to the MacLeod farm. The gold coins were hidden under the floor of the smokehouse. His mother knew where they were. He asked, "Grandmother, what will ye say to the man Ferguson is going to send after me and Father?"

The old woman smiled. "I do not think ye'll fancy hearing my words. I plan to tell him that ye be a coward and ye ran off rather than serve in any army. Ye fled in the middle of the night."

"God. Can ye think of nothing better than that?"

"Shall I tell them that ye near killed a troop of king's dragoons with pokeberries? Ye are no coward."

As Alec tightened the mare's girth, then tied the sack of provisions to her saddle, he asked, "What will ye tell them about Father?"

"That they have made him witless as a babe. That he is of no harm to them and in jail would be only a burden to his keepers."

Not looking at her, Alec asked, "Will Father die?"

"I do not know. They will not take him away with them. I can promise ye that. They will not hang an idiot."

Alec's eyes met hers. "What of ye, Grandmother?"

Her laughter was the same young sound Alec had heard once before. "Ach, they'd hang your grandfather but not me, an old half-mad hag. Na, Major Ferguson would not do that. He would not hang a woman, I think." Jonet Munn reached into the pocket of her apron and took out what Alec recognized immediately as a piece of her shawl. "Donal Bean will know the tartan. From it he will realize that I have sent ye to him. Now, Alec *dubh,* listen closely to me. If ye are met by Colonel Marion's men on the way to his camp on the Pee Dee River, do not fire on them. Call out to them in English. Call out the name of Donal Bean. Tell them that ye seek the peddler." She patted Sweet Lass as Alec led her outside, then added as she walked along beside him, "If Donal and Colonel Marion are not clever enough to see it with their own eyes, tell them that ye have the swiftest horse in the colony. Let no man take her from ye!"

Outside the barn she stopped to say, "Did ye know that Andrew once saw the king he fought for? With his hand your grandfather could have reached out and touched Bonnie Prince Charlie as he rode by him in Scotland. Your father MacLeod never once set eyes on this man he falsely called King George."

"I've thought on that, Grandmother. King George is not here in South Carolina with his armies."

"Na, he is not. Ye've never seen his face, nor did your father or his father before him." Jonet Munn touched Alec's arm. "Ye have the English enough to make your way in life wherever ye want to go. And ye have wits. And this rich land is yours."

For the first time Alec spoke his soul to her about his ambitions. He said fiercely but softly, because he could see Margaret MacLeod and Lilias waiting in the kitchen doorway of the house, "My land? Ay, this is my land. I don't choose to be a farmer, though. I wish to be a trader."

Jonet Munn gave him a look that told him she understood, but her words were not what he expected. "Alec *dubh,* I was not speaking of this land beneath our shoes at this moment. I was speaking of this country, always strange to your grandfather and myself, because we did not want to come here. We are Scots—he and I. Your father thought of himself as a landholding colonist first, then as a Scot. As for yourself, ye need not hold to the idea that ye are a Scot at all, though ye have the Gaelic ready-to-mouth to

pass for one in Scotland or anywhere else. Ye have no
MacLeod clan chief to command ye into battle and ye owe
nothing at all to the man your father called King George.
Ye've all paid for the land here in full with your brother's
life five years past. If ye do not want this farm, there's good
land aplenty elsewhere. Sell this farm if ye choose when the
war is ended."

"Na, it is for Lilias and Mother." And Alec went forward with Jamie Gilchrist's horse and Jamie's pistol to take
a tearful farewell of his mother and receive a fierce, smother-
ing embrace from Lilias.

Because he had money from the hoard in the smokehouse, Alec had made a secret decision as he lay the night
before in the loft listening to his father's labored breathing.
He'd return Jamie's pistol to the Gilchrists before he went
riding toward the Pee Dee River country. He'd buy himself
another somewhere if he could. Master Gilchrist had given
the mare to him in so many words but had said nothing
about the pistol. He might have overlooked it. So he'd return the weapon, but he would not tell the Gilchrists that
he was leaving this section of the colony and certainly not
that he was hunting for a rebel spy and a rebel colonel.
That information could get him hanged if Gilchrist or one
of their laborers sent word to Major Ferguson at the fort
that Alec was on his way.

He never saw Jamie's father, the man he sought. As
Alec rode past the Gilchrist graveyard, he saw a white
flicker of movement among the headstones. He reined in the
mare so suddenly that she reared and nickered. A ghost?
In the late afternoon, a ghost? But now Alec saw something

else, Ellen's fat gray pony grazing at the edges of the nearby grove of trees that sheltered some of the graves. He called out, "Who's there?"

At his cry Ellen herself rose up. She had flowers in her hands, pink briar roses that she obviously was putting on the graves. Mistress Gilchrist, her mother, had borne eleven children. Alec knew the pitiful history. Four had died of the smallpox before Jamie had been born, and three others had died in their cradles before Ellen had come, and two died after her birth. There were other Gilchrists there— Ellen's grandparents, an uncle killed by marauding Indians years ago, and two of her father's sisters. But not her brother. Not bold, wild Jamie! The Gilchrists had grown rich in South Carolina, but their line had not flourished.

"Alec!" Ellen cried. She came through the high summer grass toward him, her hands filled with roses.

His heart tightened as she stepped beside Sweet Lass. She patted the mare affectionately, then looked up at Alec. "I am sorry to hear what happened to your father. How does he fare?"

"He has lost his wits, Mistress Ellen." Alec added, "We can thank our fellow Scot, Major Ferguson, for that. Has he come to your farm?"

Ellen bobbed her head. "He came. He is a fine soldier of the king, my father says."

"Others I know might not agree," Alec told her sourly.

"Cornet Spencer Ordish says that Major Ferguson is a very brave soldier."

"I see you know Cornet Ordish, too." Alec fixed his eyes on Ellen's face, watching her turn as pink as the roses she had in her hands.

"Aye, he's ridden twice to visit us since he first came with Major Ferguson for corn and horses. Three of our laborers went to the fort to join Ferguson's men. I had to talk to Master Ordish through one of our laborers who speaks finer English than I." Her eyes lowered, Ellen said very softly, "Cornet Ordish asked me to study English with him."

Alec curbed bitter words rising to his lips. The Gilchrists had no dislike of Ferguson and Ordish, but then they had no cause to hate as he did. They had not been told the true facts of Jamie's death, and even now he wouldn't tell them. And they had not suffered the mishap of having a rebel kinsman! Ellen's behavior had given her away. She fancied Ferguson's young Virginian officer. Alec reflected on his one and only view of Ordish. He had been tall and very handsome in his gold-laced hat. The scarlet coat had not harmed his appearance in the slightest. Alec glanced down at his own dingy buckskin. What a strange picture he must make astride the beautiful mare and with such a fine pistol in his saddle holster. No wonder she preferred the dazzling Cornet to him.

He took the pistol out now and handed it down to her, butt first. "It was your brother's, Ellen."

The girl didn't take it. She stepped away and stood motionless with her full-skirted white muslin gown blowing about her ankles. "Na, na, Alec. It's for ye to keep."

He said in a croaking voice that surprised him, "When I fetched the mare to your father, mistress, he told me I was to keep her for my own. I did not remember to give the pistol to him then. It is a very fine pistol, too fine for the likes of me."

"Ach, Alec *dubh*!" There were tears in Ellen's eyes. "Do

not take it to my father. He gave ye Sweet Lass and the saddle. He knew ye had Jamie's pistol, too. He gave it to ye at the same moment, though he may not have said so. I heard him tell Mother that he wanted ye to have all that belonged to Jamie. Because ye loved him, too. If ye take the pistol to him, ye'll wound him more. And I will not have it from your hand."

"Perhaps ye can give it to Cornet Ordish. And give him the mare as well."

"He was never a friend to Jamie as ye were, Alec. Ye saved his horse and pistol from the rebels. Ye were a very great friend to my brother—the best he had."

Alec looked away to the headstones. A great friend? A very great liar. As he put the pistol back into the holster, knowing she would not take it and would let it lie rusting in the grass if he dropped it, he told her, "I thank ye. Tell your father that I thank him also."

Ellen wiped her face with the back of her hand. "Alec, will ye join Major Ferguson's American Volunteers at the fort soon? Most of the young men here are going to him. And ye did ride with Gilchrist's Horse."

Her last words gave Alec the opening he had been frantically searching for. She'd hear soon enough that he'd run away to escape serving under Ferguson, but he could save his pride at the moment. "What—be a foot soldier?" he scoffed. "Not when I have a horse such as Sweet Lass. Na, I ride out today to seek someone who can use both the mare and myself."

"May luck go with ye, Alec *dubh*." This time Ellen didn't put her foot into his stirrup to kiss him good-bye. Alec suspected she saved her kisses for Cornet Ordish, who was teaching her more than English. Welladay, she'd yearned for a fine king's officer to come riding, and one had come. Alec's thoughts were savage as they raced to the memory of Colonel Tarleton. At least this Virginian she fancied was not the White Beast, although he served under the Red Beast. Pray to God that Tarleton never came to Ninety-Six Section.

"Fare ye well, Ellen. May God keep ye, too," were Alec's final words, as he sent Sweet Lass into a trot.

Ellen was lost to him. He had no reason anymore to stay in this part of the colony. He hoped that the Gilchrists would still befriend the MacLeod family, even if Jonet Munn was with them now. For Jamie's sake and Lachlan MacLeod's sake they might do that—certainly not for Alec's once the news reached them that he had fled the service of the king.

"I will never wear a red coat!" Alec vowed to the mare, as they rode away from Jamie's sister.

Alec MacLeod rode northeast for three days, sleeping in the heat of the afternoon hidden in trees or in a thicket. The miles he journeyed on the sorrel were made in the very early morning or toward nightfall while he could still see the countryside. Although he spied smoke rising from burning houses in the distance a number of times, he didn't ride to them. Alone, armed only with a pistol, he feared to fall in with either king's soldiers or rebels out raiding and foraging.

He didn't know this part of the colony or the names of the rivers and brooks he had crossed after he'd left the countryside he recalled from his traveling with Jamie and his troopers earlier that month. He had the money his mother had given him, but he didn't use it to pay ferrymen to take him and the mare across rivers in their flatboats. Ferrymen gleaned much news, but they also often had wagging tongues. When Alec saw a ferry from a distance, he avoided it and rode downstream where there was a bend in the stream or a ford shallow enough. When he found a suitable narrow place, even though it might be deep, he swam Sweet Lass across, holding to her tail. And always he followed his grandmother's instructions. He rode northeast.

In the afternoon of the fourth day Alec was forced to hire a flatboat. The almost constant June rains had swollen one river into a swiftness he was afraid to attempt on the mare. The ferryman was a little man with a white cockade in his hat. He looked Alec and Sweet Lass over with sharp eyes, though asking nary a word about what brought a lone young stranger to his ferry point.

Alec asked him casually, as they reached the opposite bank, "Are there soldiers hereabouts?"

The ferryman nodded. "There have been soldiers not long past, I've heard. They are seen sometimes along the Pee Dee."

As Alec paid him a small coin and mounted, he asked, "What lies downstream?" His heart had begun to beat faster. He'd already learned one thing. This was the Pee Dee, the river he had been seeking, Marion's river.

"Swamps," came the answer. "And whatever things a man finds in a swamp." He laughed. Then he turned his back on Alec and began to push his boat across the Pee Dee, walking from one end of the boat to the other with the long pole. As he poled the flatboat over, he started to whistle. Alec had thought he could whistle loudly, but this man's was the loudest as well as the most tuneless whistle he had ever heard.

Some miles downstream Alec heard whistling again. It was no birdsong and as tuneless as the ferryman's. The boy halted Sweet Lass and shakily drew out Jamie's pistol, waiting. Was it a signaling? A sweat of fright broke out on his body, adding to the streams of perspiration the hot, muggy day had already created. He stayed quiet where he was, praying that the mare wouldn't snort. Her ears pricked forward; she was uneasy too.

The two of them didn't have long to wait. Men came silently out of the thickets on each side of the trail that wound along the Pee Dee. Two came from the direction of the river, three from the roadside. Four of the men Alec saw in the failing light had white cockades in their hats. The fifth man wore a strange-looking round hat of leather.

All five, though they were mud-stained and ragged, were armed. Two had long rifles leveled at his breast.

He cried out in English, "Donal Bean! I seek Donal Bean!"

"Put the pistol into the holster. Then tell us who you are," the man in the round hat demanded in a soft bass voice. He was black, a large, thick-bodied man.

"I am Alexander MacLeod of Ninety-Six Section," Alec told him in English, as he put the pistol back into the holster.

"What are you? A king's man or a Patriot?" the Negro demanded.

Alec shook his head. "I am not a king's man. I've come

seeking Donal Bean, a peddler, who is a friend to my mother's family."

The bass voice rumbled. "Tell of this peddler, boy."

The long rifles were still at his breast as Alec struggled with the English. "An old man he is, with long gray hair. He speaks Gaelic because he was born in Scotland."

"Is this Bean a king's man?" asked the Negro.

"I do not think he is." Alec spoke with great care. "Bean would know who I am. I've brought something to him from the Munns, who were his friends. Jonet Munn, my grandmother, told me where to hunt for Master Bean." Alec sought the complicated English words in his mind and came out with what he hoped meant, "She said to me that I would not find the peddler but that his friends would find me on the way to him."

The black man understood him. "Who would the friends of this old peddler be? Did she tell you that?"

"Colonel Francis Marion, she said. She sent me to join Colonel Marion. I do not want to join the king's army at Ninety-Six fort, so I left my part of the colony."

A second voice, a harsh, angry one, asked Alec, "Why not serve under the king? Many of you damned wild Scots do. In North Carolina you Scots fought a battle for him in 1775."

"King's soldiers hanged my grandfather, shot my friend, and wounded my father."

Alec's words surprised the Negro, who said, "So, old Andrew Munn's been hanged! Damn the man who did that!" Then he asked, "How do you come by so fine a horse, boy?"

His head spinning from the effort of finding the right

English words, Alec told him slowly, "The mare was given to me after one of Tarleton's greencoat soldiers killed my friend, her master. I didn't steal her." He knew all too well what these men were thinking.

One of the white cockades laughed and said, "Oscar, shall we fetch this boy to the peddler or shall we fetch the peddler to him?"

There was silence for a time except for the rushing sound of the Pee Dee and the hum of swarms of insects attacking Alec and the mare and the men on foot alike. Then deep-voiced Oscar said, "We'll take him with us. He might have news from the up-country. Get down, boy, and put your hands behind your back."

IX

Dark Waters

Alec dismounted and put his hands behind him as ordered while the men came up to surround him. One tied his hands behind his back. Another took the mare's reins. "Shall I blindfold him?" asked the man who had tied his hands. This man was also a Negro, but unlike Oscar, was thin and tall.

"No," said Oscar, who seemed to be the leader of the five. "If the boy lies to us, the old peddler will tell us so, and we'll shoot the lad. He'll not leave us alive until we are sure of him."

Walking awkwardly among the men as night came on, Alec was certain that he was with Marion's men. The whistling ferryman was also a rebel. His white cockade proved that, Alec suspected. The same tune whistled had surely been a signal to a concealed sentinel, who had relayed it. His grandmother had been right. He had not had to find Colonel Marion. Instead, *he* had been found, as she'd predicted.

Marion's soldiers went into a dense thicket a half mile or so down the road. Threading their way through it, they came next to a patch of briars that tore at Alec's stockings as he stumbled through them. Beyond the briars was a shallow creek draining out of the Pee Dee. Marion's men waded through it, moving silently, and Sweet Lass snuffling her displeasure at the water, followed splashing through. A tall tree loomed ahead of them. Bark had been ripped from its trunk, which shone white in the gloom. It stood alone on a mound covered with a low tangle of brush. On the other side of it was more shallow water, which the soldiers again waded.

Now Alec felt something other than slippery, foot-catching mire under his feet. He was walking over boards laid alongside one another as a sort of causeway. On each side of the causeway lay water. Great trees, totally unfamiliar to him, stood in the water on its brink. They were like enormous phantoms rising over lesser trees, threatening them. A foul smell came from this black water, which was even darker than the shadows of the coming night. Through one gap among two giant trees, Alec could see a glow in the distance—not the cheery red of fires but a fearful white-green phosphorus of a stagnant pool. Dark waters, aye! Alec thought of his grandmother's words as he slid on the uneven logs and was jerked upright by the man walking behind him.

The five never spoke, though at times they would whistle and have their whistling answered from somewhere in the distance. The swamp was silent in the hot night air. No bird-calls, no cricket sounds, though Alec had heard them earlier in the day as he rode along the Pee Dee. Only once did he hear something—a dull wail, then a splashing, bubbling sound on his right.

"Alligator," the man behind him told him softly. Then he added, "We feed King George's spies to 'em."

At the end of the causeway the soldiers halted. The deep-voiced black man asked Alec, "Do you swim? There's a wide, deep creek ahead."

All too aware of the nearby alligator, Alec said, "No, the mare took me across rivers."

"She must swim behind us. Wait here." Oscar went into some brush, leaving Alec with the other four men. A few moments later Oscar was back in a cypress-log canoe, propelled by a pole instead of paddles. Alec was shoved into its bottom, and then two other men entered it. Oscar gave his pole to another and went to Sweet Lass, pulling the pistol from her holster. He put it into his belt. Taking her reins, he pulled her down into the water and got into the canoe with the others. Holding fast to her reins, Oscar hauled the mare along as she swam beside the canoe, while the last man poled the craft over the water.

"The alligators will not attack the mare. The horse is too large," Oscar told the anxious Alec in a deep rumble half-way across the water.

By the time they had crossed the stream, night had fallen. The red dots of campfires shone in the near distance.

They were approaching land. Alec was dragged out of the canoe and up a bank, and then was shoved forward as Sweet Lass was urged up out of the water by Oscar. Oscar didn't whistle now. He called out two words, "Tarleton's Quarter."

"Tarleton's Quarter. Come in," came a welcoming call from somewhere above Alec. He looked up. There surely was a sentry high in a tree not far from him.

Oscar told Alec, "You'll find the peddler here. God help you if he does not know who you are."

"Where am I?" asked Alec, frightened by the threat.

"On an island. In Colonel Marion's camp. This place has a name, but you do not need to know what it is."

The big Negro took Alec with him over very solid ground, passing several little fires where ragged men sat or lay silent on the earth. They looked up as Oscar, Alec, and Sweet Lass, led by another man, passed. A moment later most of these men got up and followed Oscar and the newcomers. By the time Alec and the mare and their captors had arrived at the central fire that blazed in front of a lean-to made of brush and logs, there were eighteen men behind them. Alec glanced over his shoulder at them once. They were scarecrows of men with faces so soot blackened that he could not tell if they were white or black men.

"Colonel Marion," Oscar called out, "a boy's here hunting for the peddler."

Alec watched as the man Donal Bean had been sent to by George Washington came out of the lean-to. Francis Marion, to his shock, wore a red coat like that of a king's soldier—though on second glance it was not cut in the same way, and the color was a deeper red. The American colonel was a thin, small-sized man somewhat resembling Ferguson in build, but the Scot had reddish hair and a bronzed face, while Marion was black haired and yellow skinned. His nose was large, his eyes very black, large, and somewhat bulging. He looked hard at Alec, then at Sweet Lass still dripping water from her swim.

In a warm and gentle voice, Marion asked, "What peddler do you seek here in the swamp?"

"His name is Donal Bean."

"Old Munn's been hanged, he says," Oscar explained to the colonel.

A flicker of feeling crossed Marion's face for an instant, then was gone. "Who hanged the old man, boy?"

Alec replied, "King's troopers in Ninety-Six Section. Munn was my grandfather, sir."

Marion nodded. "I did not know Andrew Munn, but I had heard of him. So he is caught and hanged too. Yes, the British and the American Loyalists are hanging Patriots now in Camden Town too. They are being hanged from the rafters of their own houses." He ordered one of the men beside him, "Fetch the old peddler here to me. Does he know you, lad?"

"I have met him. There's something in the cuff of my coat for him."

Marion inclined his head at Oscar. The enormous Negro, who was Marion's servant as well as his friend, reached behind Alec and felt in his cuffs, one after the other. Then he brought out the blue, green, and red piece of shawl and handed it to the colonel.

Marion held it, looking at it doubtfully. Then he asked, "What is this?"

Alec told him, "The tartan of the Munns. Bean's a Highland Scot. He'll know it." He started to say that he, too, was a Scot but stopped himself, remembering his grandmother's words that *he* must choose his own identity now. Instead, he told Marion, "He'll know it comes from my grandmother's shawl and that she sent me here. She cut it off for me."

The soldier Marion had dispatched returned soon with Donal Bean in tow, stumbling over the rough ground. Bean stared first at Alec, clearly surprised, then at Marion, but he said not a word.

"Do you know this boy?" asked Marion.

Bean nodded. "Alexander MacLeod of Ninety-Six Section."

"Who are his grandparents?"

"Andrew Munn and his wife, Jonet. You know of old Munn, our friend in the up-country." When Marion held out the piece of shawl, Bean took it and went to the fire to examine it. "It is the Munn tartan," he said. Then he asked Alec in Gaelic, "Did you fetch it here from your grandparents?"

In Gaelic Alec replied, "Na, from my grandmother. King's troopers rode out the day ye left us on the trail, sir, and gathered up some of the rebels in our section. They caught my grandfather as we were riding home. He cursed King George, so they hanged him from a tree in the trail. Grandmother said he sought his death."

"Aye, so Andrew could." The peddler spoke very gently as he held the piece of cloth.

Francis Marion's voice broke in roughly. "Speak English in my camp, Master Bean. I do not permit anything but English to be spoken here." He pointed to a heap of boughs and leaves in front of his lean-to. Bean sat down on them. Then, as Marion gestured again, so did Alec after Oscar, without waiting for a command, had untied his hands.

The colonel's first question was for Bean while Alec rubbed his wrists. "This boy who came seeking you rides a very fine horse—easily the best in this camp. Have you seen that mare before?"

"No, Colonel."

Marion's black gaze dwelt on Alec's face. "How did you come by such a fine animal?"

Alec chose his English words with great care as he told his tale of Jamie and Tarleton, carefully not mentioning the pokeberries in the rum. For all of his calm and soft-spoken ways this American colonel was to be feared. His dark eyes missed not a trace of expression on a man's face.

When Alec had finished, Marion said dryly, "I have heard that young Tarleton does not like to lose at cards or at anything else. We must teach him how to lose battles." Then Marion asked Donal Bean, "Do you believe this boy who rode out to join Colonel Tarleton but did not remain with the Green Dragoons and who now has such a fine horse? It seems a very strange tale to me, Master Bean."

To his immense relief Alec saw Bean's nod. "Yes, Colonel Marion. I have heard of this James Gilchrist before. At the house of Andrew Munn, it was. Alexander brought the news to us that Gilchrist was riding out after rebels. I believe that Alexander may have saved my life by doing so."

Alec said, "I came there to warn my grandparents of Jamie and his troopers."

The colonel nodded. He settled himself on the boughs

and said, "I am going to test you now. What king's soldier not long ago took charge in the Ninety-Six Section? I know his name. Do you?"

"Major Patrick Ferguson, sir," Alec faltered. "Sir, it is because of Ferguson that I've been sent here to you and to Master Bean."

Marion's heavy dark brows rose slightly. "Ferguson *also?* First Tarleton, *then* Ferguson?"

Aided by Bean's supplied English words, Alec told Marion of the encounter between Ferguson and his father. He finished by saying, "Major Ferguson promised he would come seeking me soon to force me into the army he gathers at the fort. Many men from my section are joining him."

"How old are you?" Marion asked suddenly.

"Nigh to fifteen, sir."

"Old enough to fight—and a marksman, too, I suspect. Did you know that Tarleton is now in Charles Towne? Do you know the numbers of the king's forces there or in Camden Town? I know them as of the moment. Tell me if you do, and we shall match numbers."

"I do not know that, sir."

Marion's words were chilling. "I would have ordered your father stopped also if he had run away from me to get his rifle when I came foraging. We here forage, too. The only point I can see in your favor is that you ran off two times rather than serve in the king's force. But if you are strong against fighting, why have you come here to me?"

Alec hesitated for a long moment. Then because he could hold back no longer, he said, "The things I did to avenge my friend Jamie were not enough. I want to do more, sir.

By joining Ferguson I wouldn't avenge Jamie or my father, would I? I'd be—"

Donal Bean broke in then. "Alexander, I believe you are saying that you did something *more* than stealing the mare from Tarleton. What was this?"

Embarrassed, Alec said, "It is not worth the telling."

"Let me be the judge of that," commanded Marion.

"I saw Tarleton shoot Jamie." Alec stopped, his face turning crimson as he took a deep breath. He went on then in broken English, telling his listeners of the pokeberries and of the little girl who'd washed her hands in the rum at his suggestion. "It was not of any importance."

As he looked from Marion's to Bean's faces, he saw that both men were smiling. Smiles suited neither face very well. Marion told Alec, "So that is how Tarleton came by the poisoned rum! His greencoat devils couldn't ride for three full days. Few men twice your age have accomplished that much where Ban Tarleton is concerned." Unsmiling now, Marion went on, "You think very quickly. You kept your head, and you bested Tarleton. Perhaps it has not occurred to you that those three days meant that families in the area could be warned by kindly neighbors of Tarleton's coming and given time to flee to safety."

"No, sir," Alec said wearily, thinking that having Sweet Lass still mattered more to him. She had been led off by Oscar and greeted somewhere on the island by stampings and snortings in the darkness. Marion had horses then.

The colonel got up with effort, and Alec saw that he limped badly as he stepped off the boughs. He spoke to Bean, "Master Bean, you brought me the news not long

ago that the Scots in the up-country will not fight for the
American cause. Yet here is a Scot with a horse beyond
compare. What do you say? Shall I have him shot as a possible spy and keep his horse, or shall I use both him and
the mare?"

"Use the lad, Colonel."

Francis Marion turned to Alec. "You will serve me
then?"

"Yes, sir, if you will have me."

Marion smiled thinly. "Do not try to poison my men with
plants."

"No, sir." Alec got up too. He asked Marion, "Do you
know what the British call you, sir?"

The American colonel shook his head. He smiled. "I do
not permit cursing in my camp—at least within my hearing."

"It is the Swamp Fox, sir."

Marion paused, then said soberly, "I do not dislike the
name." And he went into his lean-to.

Alec spent that night in Donal Bean's shelter, wrapped in
a damp blanket taken by Oscar from behind Sweet Lass's
saddle and given to him with a warning about sentries
posted on the island in case Alec thought of escape.

In the morning Bean, who'd talked half the night, shook
Alec awake after pulling the blanket from his head where
he had drawn it high to keep the mosquitoes off his face.
Alec wondered about the old man. Why hadn't he ridden
north to General Washington after he'd had the news that
most of his fellow Scots would choose for King George?

Whatever the reasons might be for his lingering in the swamp, Alec was grateful that Bean had been present to vouch for him. Aye, Colonel Marion might indeed have ordered Alec shot.

The boy followed Bean out of the lean-to and stared at a dismal world such as he'd never seen before. It was a place of dim, murky greenness. He recognized the oaks and pines on Marion's island, but then he pointed wordlessly to an unfamiliar tree. It was an enormous one with its roots submerged in the water. Bean said one word, "Cypress." Alec shuddered. Trees, like sinister watchers, festooned with trailing vines, overhung the black water in every direction.

As he looked toward the north he saw men in a canoe moving silently toward the island. They weren't using poles but very long forked sticks, which they pushed against overhanging tree limbs to propel them to the island in absolute silence.

Bean told Alec before he went off to meet the canoe, "There's food by the fire, lad."

Alec went to the blaze, where a Negro boy in a tattered shirt was busy with a fire-blackened skillet. Without a word the boy gave him a piece of cold, greasy bacon and some hot hoecake from the skillet. Then, as he rose to go to the canoe also, he said, "Mebbe roast pig tonight for supper. There's fierce wild pigs in this swamp. Watch out they don't getcha."

Alec sat pondering this information until he heard a whistling signal and saw Colonel Marion come out of his lean-to and limp down to the water's edge. He watched the American greet the canoe and saw the four men in the canoe come up onto the island. Three of them wore shabby jackets of different colors and white cockades in their hats. The fourth man seemed naked, yet not naked. He was covered from head to foot with a black substance that bristled with flecks of white and gray. Tar and feathers! Alec had heard of that punishment. His father had often said in his hearing that Andrew Munn deserved it.

Alec put down the bacon, wanting to retch. This man had been stripped, had had hot tar poured over him, and feathers sprinkled over the tar. Alec wondered if his skin would come off when the tar was peeled away. The man, supported under each arm by one of Marion's men, had suffered even more. There was clotted blood on his forehead and cheeks.

With the hoecake in his pocket, Alec walked behind the newcomers to Marion's shelter. The tarred and feathered man was laid down outside it on a blanket. Marion knelt beside him and asked, "Who are you? Who did this to you?" His voice was soft as a woman's with sympathy. At its sound of caring, Alec felt his heart flowing suddenly out to the American leader.

The tarred man gasped out, "King George's men, my neighbors." He mumbled his name. "They tarred and feathered me and beat me with a rope." He drank from a flask Oscar handed him and went on, "They set me adrift in the swamp in a little canoe after they'd branded me."

"We found him and took him into our canoe," one of Marion's men told the Swamp Fox. Alec stood peering over this man's shoulder, watching Oscar, who was gently wiping off the tar and blood. Under the blood lay the letters *G.R.* Aye, *Georgius Rex*—King George. Alec trembled, recalling the ugly *T* on his grandfather's face. Redcoat soldiers in Scotland had marked him, but this man had been tortured and disfigured by his neighbors, Loyalist Americans!

"Ochone, so much sorrow. So much pain!" he heard Donal Bean saying behind him. Alec knew what the old man meant: not just the brutality the Loyalists showed to the Patriots, but the cruelty meted out to the king's followers by the Americans. The night before Master Bean had told him dreadful tales of events in the northern colonies. Patriots tarred and feathered, hanged, burned and looted, too.

Half sick, Alec went off to seek Sweet Lass. He comforted her while she pricked her ears forward and moved nervously about as the agonized cries of the tortured man rose up from time to time. Yellow jackets darted about Alec, and gray squirrels played in the branches of the tree over his head as he stared at the quiet water nearby. It was dark water, indeed, by day as well as by night, stained almost black by the roots of the cypresses. Alec had already seen that Jamie's pistol was gone from the saddle holster. He leaned his face against the mare's warm neck, thinking of his family. Ferguson's three days were past. Had his grandmother dealt successfully with Ellen's Cornet Ordish? And what had Francis Marion and Donal Bean meant when they had spoken of "using him and the mare"?

Leaving Sweet Lass on the island, Alec was sent off that same morning with Oscar and six others. Their mission was one of foraging, which they meant to do by ambush.

Oscar gave Alec a knife only, though the others had pistols and rifles. So Marion still put no real trust in him, though Bean had. He had to prove his loyalty.

And prove it indeed Alec MacLeod did that day! When a laden farm wagon approached on the road, he sprang out and stood ready behind Oscar while Marion's very large lieutenant explored the wagon of the Loyalist farmer bound for Charles Towne to trade with the British. Though Alec's heart raced with fright, his part had not been such a hard thing to do—not sheltered by Oscar's great comforting bulk. But Oscar knew that he had been there behind him. That should prove both loyalty and courage.

Oscar took jerked venison, a keg of ships' biscuit, and a small barrel of ale, and let the terrified Loyalist go on his way lashing his horse to a wild canter down the road. Then Oscar forced the lid off the ale and invited his comrades to drink. They dipped Alec's hat into the brew and took turns drinking from it, laughing. Later in the hot summer sunshine the evaporating ale cooled Alec's head as he went back into the swamp with the others, carrying a sack of dried deer meat on his back.

He heard the men with him talking as they went along through the mire toward the secret island. One called out, "Oscar, the lad had his blade ready behind you."

A second man asked with a whinny of laughter, "Yes, but would he have used it against a Loyalist or a redcoat?"

Oscar's rumbling voice floated back from the lead as Alec stepped high over a tree root in his path. "I think he would have used the knife. You do not know yet who this boy is."

"He's a scurvy Scotsman from the up-country!"

Again came the bass voice, "This one, though he seems nothing at all, was the man who nigh killed Tarleton with rum he poisoned with pokeberries."

Alec said nothing, though his spirits lifted with happiness. What he had done might easily have saved lives. Marion had convinced him. Alec lurched along the swaying plank of the swamp road. He had been accepted, though he was a "scurvy Scotsman."

Aye, these men of Francis Marion's were his people! Alec knew in his heart that he would never lose the memory of his colonel's gentle words to the man who had been tarred and feathered.

As he went along the causeway, attacked by clouds of vicious mosquitoes, Alec conjured up the White Beast and the Red Beast in his mind. Milk-white Tarleton, and Ferguson, red as a fox, hot as flame, and almost as quick to burn as Tarleton perhaps? In the very brief time Alec had seen Ferguson he'd sensed a feyness in him, too—not the same quicksilver sort that he felt in Jamie, but a feyness all the same. There was no blustering in Ferguson. He was a deliberate man and one who would accomplish what he set out to do—no matter the odds. Aye, Ferguson would surely send Ellen's Cornet after Alexander Mac-Leod in three days' time.

Alec's thoughts turned to Francis Marion as he waded through shallow water. He was a deliberate man also, but there was no wild, odd streak in his makeup. Marion was a plain man, sober and somber, and greatly beloved by the men who followed him. The reason, Alec knew, lay in Marion's character. Another lay outside the man. Tarleton's greencoat cavalry and Ferguson's redcoat infantry had one thing in common. All of them were colonials, all American Loyalists. But they served under an Englishman and a Scot. Marion's shabby, swamp-smelling scarecrows were Americans serving a leader who was also an American. They gave their love to one of their own!

"And so do I," vowed Alec, as he shifted the venison to his other shoulder. With these words he put behind him the lecturing and speeches of his father and Jamie—and even of Andrew Munn.

That night Alec told Donal Bean of his decision to serve Colonel Marion for "reasons of affection"—not so much out of approval for the Patriot cause. Bean heard him out, then chuckled softly into the darkness as he lay next to Alec in the lean-to. He told Alec in Gaelic, "Aye, laddie, Marion's a man to give your heart and your hand to. Did ye find it so hard to change your loyalty?"

The boy rolled over onto his side and looked out into the hot night toward the colonel's lean-to. "Master Bean, I do not think I was ever King George's man as much as my father was." Alec paused wondering how his next words would be received, but he went on all the same. "That doesn't say that I am King Charles's man either as Grandfather Munn was. And I am not sure that I am a man for General Washington or the Continental Congress either."

Alec had expected an explosion of anger, but again there was only a chuckle. Bean waved off night insects and said, "Na, I think ye simply be Francis Marion's man. As for me, I am simply General Washington's man. A person gives his loyalty where his heart leads him."

Alec sat up suddenly. "But I thought, master, that ye supported King Charles over-the-sea?"

Bean let out a long sigh. "Ach, laddie, I gave up that dream years past. I drank to the health of King Charles only to please Jonet and Andrew. I did not suffer in this new land as they did. I had no children. It was not difficult for me to come to think of myself as an American." He reached out to touch Alec's hand as Alec told himself that he wished this wise and easy man could have been his grandfather. "Alec, I think ye will become an American in time, though ye call yourself a colonial yet."

Alec fell back onto his elbows. "If the war is not won by Washington and Marion, will all men who fight under them be hanged or shot by the British?"

"Na, na, Alec, that is not the way of war. Defeated soldiers are not shot by their conquerors. Only a few might be hanged—leaders such as Colonel Marion, myself, and yourself, of course."

"What?" Alec surged up once more.

"Ye foraged today with Oscar, but Marion has other plans for ye. To use ye as a courier to carry messages for him and to gather information. A courier reports what he sees as he goes about the countryside as a common traveler or as a poor peddler. In a sense he is a spy, ye know. Hanging is the penalty for spying."

Alec said angrily, "I will not take easily to spying, Master Bean."

"Nor did I, Alec. But the two of us have an advantage as spies."

The boy asked sourly, "What might that be?"

"Most folk think I am old, foolish, and harmless. They'll

think, unless ye foolishly give them reason to think otherwise, that ye be young, foolish, and harmless."

Alec sighed. "Master, everyone takes note of Sweet Lass."

"Aye, lad, there lies your danger, but in your light weight and her fleetness lie your safety. If ye wrested her from Colonel Tarleton, Colonel Marion thinks ye can keep yourself and herself safe from any man."

As a night-hunting alligator boomed, then splashed down somewhere near the island, Alec asked, "Have you been in many battles, Master Bean?"

"Only one—at Brandywine Creek in Pennsylvania, where Major Ferguson was shot in the arm by a musket ball. Old as I am, I can take up a musket if need be. I did there—though I do not think it was my ball that hit Ferguson." Bean coughed. "I was not aiming at him in any event. I am no marksman, mind ye."

"I wonder if I will fight, too." Alec's voice was gloomy.

"Ye be old enough and tall enough. Perhaps ye will go into battle under Colonel Marion. But perhaps some other soldier will lead ye, Alec *dubh*. Francis Marion is not the only Patriot commander in this part of the South."

"Who are the others?"

"I do not know the names of all of them, and others may arise besides. I think before long there will be hot fighting in many parts of this state. I know of a Colonel Sumter in the north. I think you will find that all of the American commanders will have seen service as Indian fighters and some will be veterans of the French and Indian War of twenty years past. They know how to fight."

Alec sank back into his blanket, then began scratching the insect bites on his face. Pray to God, Francis Marion would leave the hateful swamp soon. Camping here was a torture to his men and their horses and mules. As far as he could see, the only good thing about becoming a courier for the Swamp Fox was that his duties would surely take him out of the swamp.

Two days later Alec and Oscar led Sweet Lass out onto the road beside the Pee Dee, and on Marion's orders Alec rode alone to a tavern on the outskirts of a hamlet held by a garrison of king's soldiers. The little village was a half day's ride from Marion's island. Waiting, hidden in a grove of trees outside it at twilight, Alec felt in his pocket for the tarnished silver button that had been cut off Marion's uniform coat. It bore the insignia of the colonel's old militia regiment, the 2nd South Carolina. Oscar had given it to him with instructions.

At nightfall Alec dismounted and tethered the mare to a tree, then made his way on foot to the rear door of the tavern. It was made of whitewashed clapboard and named the Rose and Crown. He rapped on the stout door, and when it opened into pitch blackness, he murmured in a trembling voice, "Tarleton's Quarter."

Donal Bean had told him the meaning of the words he had been instructed to use and had heard when he first came to Marion's Island. They referred to Tarleton's butchery of the Americans he'd overtaken on the road to North Carolina last spring. Though the American had asked for quarter, for mercy, they had been refused by Tarleton. Tarleton's Quarter meant no quarter at all.

Listening to Donal Bean telling him this story, Alec had remembered the sorrowful words of the man he'd met on the road with Jamie just before Jamie fell in with Tarleton and his Green Dragoons.

Still thinking of Jamie, Alec sniffed the air of the Rose and Crown. By its heat and scent of food he thought he had surely come to the kitchen.

And then a soft laughing voice whispered out of the darkness. "Give me the token." Alec felt a hand poking at his breast. He caught it, disturbed. It was small and very soft, a woman's hand. She wrenched it away and said in return, "Tarleton's Quarter." Then she repeated, "The token. Give me the token."

Alec fumbled for Colonel Marion's button and gave it to her. She returned it in a moment, after her fingers had made out its markings. "Tell the man you serve that General Gates is on the march for the Continental Congress," she said to Alec. "He will march down through North Carolina. Now give me your hand."

When Alec extended it, wondering what sort of token he was to take back to Colonel Marion, the woman drew him to her and kissed him on the mouth. She tasted of brown sugar sweetmeats. Then before he could even gasp, she shoved something hot and sticky into the hand she had just let go of. What she had given him was a leg of roast fowl, he learned later, though the touch of it alarmed him at first. Before he mounted Sweet Lass, he devoured the chicken leg.

Alec rode off, somewhat less worried about his role as a courier than before. He had not seen the woman's face nor had she seen his. He had not expected both food and a kiss, but he had to admit to himself that visiting the Rose and Crown again would not be too much of a burden. The only thing that concerned him was whether to tell Colonel Marion what sort of reception his couriers received. He doubted if the Swamp Fox would approve of this encounter.

But the next two visits to the tavern by night disappointed him. He got neither a kiss nor food, and the woman he spoke to in the darkness had a different whisper and no laughter. He missed the first woman spy. He sensed that the second woman was the mother of the first and that she was not half so generous. But she sent messages to the Swamp Fox that General Gates was still marching toward the colony from the north with an army. Alec knew from talk in Marion's camp who Gates was. He was the hero of the Battle of Saratoga, the man who had defeated the British soldiers in New York. On his third visit the woman hissed to him that the king's army was very strong in Camden Town and that folk believed that there would be a battle ere long between Gates's army and the British in garrison at Camden under Lord Cornwallis.

That next morning, after riding half the night on Sweet Lass and being guided through the swamp by Oscar, who had waited for him beside the road, Alec spoke to Donal Bean as they breakfasted on dried venison and hoecake. Always careful to speak English where he might be overheard, Alec asked the peddler, "Have you ever been to Camden Town, Master Bean?"

"Yes."

"Is it a high place?"

Bean spat out a bit of hoecake that was charred and

said, "It is higher than a swamp, but I would not say it was a high place, no."

Alec gazed into the smoking campfire as he chewed, wishing he could see into the flames as his grandmother could. Just about any place in the colony would be a high place compared to Francis Marion's lair in the swamps.

X

The Gamecock

It rained in early and mid-July—so much so that the dark
waters rose higher about Marion's island, shrinking its
surface. The camp was becoming crowded, not solely because of the decreasing solid ground but because more
men were coming in from both sides of the Pee Dee River.

Some of them brought news to Colonel Marion, though,
to Alec's disappointment, none of them could relieve his
fears for his family by telling what transpired in distant
Ninety-Six Section. He ached to know how they were and
how Jonet Munn had fared with the redcoats who had
come seeking him. He wondered, too, how Ellen felt now
about Cornet Ordish, who might have been sent to take
Alec in and force him to enlist.

But under the cool gaze of Donal Bean, with whom he
was now firm friends, Alec kept his worries to himself.

They were personal. There was scarcely a man in the camp —except possibly for the bachelor Bean—who had not left family behind to the mercies of the Loyalists and the king's armies. The constant sight of the man who'd been tarred, feathered, and branded made Alec's own anxieties seem selfish. The Patriot had entirely lost his mind. Bald-headed, with his skin raw, pink, and glistening, he had to be tied to a tree on the island day and night so he wouldn't throw himself into the swamp water to drown. Sometimes he crooned to himself, and often during the night he moaned. Marion refused to send him home by stealth, though he could have done so, he knew so many secret ways about the river country. If he sent him to his family, the Loyalists might murder him, and there was always a chance that he might regain his wits. All this trouble made Alec reflect on his own father and on his mother's saying that those who sought violence found it. He had learned that the tarred and feathered stranger had publicly cursed King George in a tavern in Kingstree Town.

The realization that now he, too, sought violence— —though not with the same passion that Jamie and his father and grandfather had—disturbed Alec. He would be glad if the war ended at any moment.

Alec came to the campfire each time a new man joined Marion to hear what the newcomer might say after he'd gone into the colonel's lean-to to report. The news was almost always the same. The king's redcoats were strong in Camden Town. Tarleton, whose headquarters were south of Marion's island, in Charles Towne, had left that city and was scouring the country, killing, looting, and burning. And General Gates was rumored still to be marching down from the north. Colonel Sumter, the man Donal Bean had spoken of, was also in the north now, over the border in North Carolina.

Alec heard Oscar questioning the latest newcomer one afternoon. He had been brought into the swamp as Alec had, but this man had come blindfolded as well as bound. He was a squinting, long-shanked man in a threadbare black coat. Oscar asked him, "Where is your home?"

The stranger jerked up his head. "Why do you ask? Your colonel is satisfied that I am who I am."

"And who would that be?" Oscar demanded.

"My name is Marcus. My home is in North Carolina. I serve Colonel Sumter."

"He sent you here to Marion?" asked Donal Bean.

"Yes, with a message from General Gates." Marcus took the mug of ale Oscar gave him while Alec listened to the hated swamp noises: the croaking of frogs, distant booming of alligators, and now and then the hideous screeching of an owl. A soft splashing arose as Sumter's messenger drank a second cup in unhurried silence. Alec knew the splashing was a surfacing alligator. It would sink silently in a moment into the dreadful dark water.

"How did you prove to Colonel Marion that you came from Sumter?" Oscar asked.

The stranger put down the ale, scratched himself, and stuck his hand into his coat pocket. "I see you favor the white cockade down here in the bogs," he said. "Colonel Sumter favors another token. I like it better too." Out came the hand with a long bronze and black feather that had been doubled over in the deep pocket. The man took off his three-cornered hat and stuck the fighting cock's tail

feather in and out of two of the holes in the hat's crown.
"I'm the Gamecock's man," he told Oscar proudly. "That's
what the British in Camden Town call Sumter these days.
People there say that Tarleton, the devil, gave him the
name as he named your colonel Swamp Fox. But I don't
know if there's any truth in it."

Oscar's laugh was deep and hearty as the man donned
his hat again. "I believe that, man. Take more ale." And
he refilled the mug from a foraged keg beside the fire.
"Can you tell us your news, or did Colonel Marion bid
you be quiet?"

Over a piece of roasted swamp pig, Marcus looked at
Oscar, Alec, Donal Bean, and the others. Clearly Sumter's
courier was enjoying the attention he was getting. He replied when he was ready, after more pig and more ale.
"General Gates has asked Colonel Sumter to send out his
people to convince loyal American men all over this state
to join him in North Carolina. And then Gates will give
battle to the king's army."

"When shall that be?" asked Donal Bean.

Marcus put down the meat to slap at a mosquito that
had landed on his other hand. "Soon, I think. You won't
stay much longer in this accursed bog."

Sumter's messenger didn't stay long. He went off to the
north the next morning, carrying the numbers of Marion's
soldiers in his head and whatever secret messages Marion
might have given him to convey to Sumter and Gates.

Keeping out of sight by day as usual, Alec rode twice
more to the Rose and Crown in the village to learn what
the tavern woman had to tell him of events in the colony.
Although he still hoped for food and a kiss, they were

never forthcoming. The second time he heard that Colonel Tarleton was rumored to be in Camden Town with his Green Dragoons. Aye, there surely was a battle in the offing if the White Beast had gone there to join Lord Cornwallis, the commander in chief of the king's army.

The day after his fifth trip to the tavern, Alec saw another courier from Colonel Sumter at Marion's camp. This one wasn't a man but a woman old enough to be Alec's mother. She was plump, with pink cheeks and glossy dark hair. Her mire-stained gown was of bright green silk and her long black cloak of fine velvet, making her strangely out of place among Marion's sooty swamp men. She did not sit by the fire once she'd dredged a gamecock's feather out of the pocket of her cloak with the laughing words for everyone to hear. "It comes from the tail of Colonel Sumter's fiercest cock. Poor little bird, he's got no tail feathers at all anymore. They've all been plucked to serve the cause of liberty." She laughed again loudly, then turned about to shake a finger at Oscar. "Fie on you. You drop me into a canoe as if I were a sack of cornmeal. Take more care of me or I shall tell the man I serve what sort of wild men you are here in the swamp."

Oscar grinned at her and said, "Mistress Sampson, you weigh somewhat more than a sack of cornmeal."

Marion limped out of his lean-to and bowed with a grave courtesy to the woman, who was clearly preparing a saucy answer to what Oscar had said. Marion told her, "Mistress Sampson, I am glad to see you again. Will it please you to enter?"

"Who is she?" Alec asked Oscar, as the woman went inside with the colonel.

Oscar chuckled. "The wife of a rich merchant in Charlotte in North Carolina. She travels much on her husband's business. He is a king's man."

Alec asked, astonished, "And *she* serves Sumter?"

"She does. Her husband does not know that she and her coachman are Patriots and that she visits us here with word from Sumter while her coachman waits on the road for her. She is very clever." Then Oscar asked all at once, catching Alec off guard, "I have been told by Master Bean that your father is a king's man, too."

"He is a king's man, yes." What more could Alec say?

Somewhat later Alec watched Mistress Sampson being put into a waiting canoe by Oscar, who waded out to it carrying the woman in his arms. Both were laughing. Alec's last sight of her was of her frantically chasing off mosquitoes with both hands as she sat in the dugout that was being poled away from the bank. She would go on to Charles Towne with her coachman, a fellow patriot, with no one being the wiser that she had brought information to the Swamp Fox.

An hour after she had gone, Francis Marion came out of his shelter and called his men to assemble. He got up onto a low stump, then began addressing them in his calm, soft voice. "General Gates and Colonel Sumter have made camp at Deep River in North Carolina. I have been summoned there. I break camp tomorrow morning and ride north. I will take nineteen men only with me. The others will stay here to keep the island." The colonel's eye fell on Donal Bean and Alec standing side by side. "Master Bean, carry this news to General Washington at once. It is what you have tarried with me to hear. And you, Alexander, make ready to go with me."

Next Marion called out first one man's name, then another, choosing those who would ride out with him. Oscar, though he was gone at the moment, was to be one of them, according to Marion's orders.

All that Alec could think of was a battle. He heard the man behind him, one who had not been chosen to leave, say, "There will be a battle for certain. I seem to be missing it." He did not sound sorry.

That night, lying on his back, Alec talked long in Gaelic to Donal Bean. He would miss the old man sorely. "Will I see you again, Master Bean?" he asked finally.

"Aye, lad, ye will when the war is ended. I'll come to fetch Jonet away. I meant what I said to her in May."

Alec sighed. How very strange that a man so old as Bean could understand loving someone. In the firefly-lit darkness he told the old Scot of his hopeless affection for Ellen Gilchrist and of her interest in one of Ferguson's redcoat officers. He spoke, too, of his fear that she would think him a coward for leaving Ninety-Six Section and his wounded father.

As he had hoped, Master Bean didn't laugh at him. Alec suspected his grandfather Munn might have, or at least have said something harsh to him. Bean said only, "Until the Gilchrist lass weds this Cornet Ordish, ye have a chance still, Alec *dubh*. Bear that in mind. Lasses change their minds."

"Aye." Alec's one word was bitter. "But what if I am sore wounded in battle in the north?"

"Ach, that is the chance any man who fights must take."

"That could be worse than being killed outright."

Bean's reedy voice was a whisper in the gloom. "Many a brave soldier has said that to himself, my lad."

The next morning the old man and his mules accompanied Colonel Marion, Alec, Oscar, and seventeen other men off the island. Each led his horse over the solid ground that Oscar, going ahead, found for the group. Alec walked beside a skittish Sweet Lass, who snuffled as her hooves sank into the spongy earth. Colonel Marion limped along beside his horse, Ball, just ahead of Alec. By now Alec knew the story of Marion's limping. He'd broken his ankle that winter and been sent out of Charles Towne by the Patriot defenders because he could not walk. He'd taken to the swamps and was the only American commander active in this part of the colony. If Marion had remained in Charles Towne, he would have been imprisoned by the British like the other Patriot officers.

Once they'd passed out of the swamp onto the road, Donal Bean made his farewell to Colonel Marion. Somewhat to Alec's surprise, Marion prayed openly over the old man, then clasped his hand. Bean came last of all to Alec and embraced him. He told him in English, "If ye see Jonet before I do, tell her that I carry the bit of her shawl next to my heart and hope that she sometimes wears the shoe buckles I gave her." Then he was helped by Oscar onto his lead mule. Alec watched him ride off onto a trail that struck out north and east from the road. The last sad look Alec had was not one that reassured him overmuch. The tail of the rear pack mule was switching about wildly as she attempted to drive off ravenous insects. Donal Bean was not escaping the mosquitoes, though he might be escaping battle.

"Mount up," came Marion's words. Alec waited until his colonel started along the trail that led north beside the rushing brown Pee Dee and Oscar swung in behind Marion. When twelve others had fallen in behind Oscar, Alec joined the column of Americans. A sorry, wretched-looking lot they were, more like raiders than soldiers. There was not one complete uniform among them. Most were in muddy rags and pale faced from weeks in the swamp without the sun striking their faces and hands. But all except Alec carried long rifles, and all were well enough mounted. Alec himself sweltered in his buckskin coat, which was rank with grease and stained black at its edges by the acid the cypress trees released into swamp water. His shoes were laughable, warped utterly out of shape by repeated soakings, and his stockings nonexistent. But there was a pair in the sack tied to the saddle that he'd saved to wear for an occasion. Perhaps the occasion would be the battle for possession of Camden Town. Lilias had knit the stockings for him, and like most of her unwilling work they were full of knots. He wondered as he rode, bedeviled on his bare shins and ankles by insects, how she and the others fared? Was Jonet Munn looking into a hearthfire at the moment watching him riding off to war behind the Swamp Fox?

Francis Marion traveled chiefly by night, staying secreted by day in canebrakes or in wooded places alongside the trail that led northwest. He seemed to Alec to have the same instinct to remain hidden by day on firm ground as he'd shown in choosing his lair in the swamp. By now the boy realized that the island he had known was only one of Marion's secret refuges. No man knew the southern and eastern parts of South Carolina so well as he. No matter how closely the British pursued the Swamp Fox, Alec felt certain they would never catch him.

Marion bypassed farms and towns while the rain poured down on the heads of his men and himself. He seemed to like riding in rain that would keep folk to their houses where they could not spy him. Alec hated the rain. July, 1780, was as wet as the spring had been. The streams the Americans forded or swam across were in sullen brown flood. On the third day of march, while they rode by daylight, Alec heard his colonel say to Oscar that they were now almost parallel to Camden Town, passing it on the east. The countryside was becoming hillier, Alec had noted. He took pleasure in this change, though he often cursed the sodden ground beneath Sweet Lass's hooves that made her slip. Even if the journey to Deep River wasn't a pleasant one, he was no longer in the hateful swamp.

Later that same day Marion paused on a hilltop with his soldiers among a grove of trees looking down on the road. They had hastily left it to avoid detection by British troops moving along it. These troops had not marched in silence—much to the contrary. They'd given warning.

Alec was not surprised when Francis Marion summoned him alone to his side to speak with him. Ball and Sweet Lass stood side by side as their riders appraised the redcoats.

The men were not wearing the usual white army knee breeches but short skirts, the kilt of Highland Scots. And they had not been marching to the beat of drum and fife. The skirling of bagpipes was what had first alerted the Americans to the presence of the enemy who walked along the way to Camden Town.

"Who would they be?" Colonel Marion asked Alec, pointing down at them. "I know them to be Scots, but do you know their regiment? Are they Ferguson's men?"

"No, sir. His Americans do not wear the kilt. I've seem them."

The Swamp Fox gave Alec a cool, heavy-lidded glance. "I am of a mind to send you down there, lad. You can speak to them. Ask them where you might find Major Ferguson. Tell them that you want to join his forces."

Alec gaped at his colonel, who went on with a little smile. "No, I do not want you to join Ferguson. I think perhaps you can find out for me where Ferguson might be and perhaps if he also plans to march to Camden Town. Have you the courage for the game? Learn what you can for me of the British troops in Camden."

Alec's knees tightened on Sweet Lass with tension. He stared down at the Scotsmen, who might easily bear the name MacLeod or Munn or Bean. "Yes, Colonel." He tightened his reins, preparing to go down the hill to the Highlanders.

"Not so fast." Marion grabbed at the reins and held them. "Trade horses with Oscar. Do not take the pistol."

Oscar's horse was a large-bodied roan with a hard mouth and swaying gait. Astride the roan, Alec felt rather small. "God bless you and keep you," said Oscar, who had not mounted Sweet Lass.

The boy nodded, took a deep breath, and rode down the

hill as Marion and his soldiers turned about and went further into the trees to hide. A distance from the Scots Alec began to shout, but because of the din of the pipes and the uncertainty of his frightened voice, no one heard him.

He was only several hundred feet from them when one of the Scots spied him and bellowed at the mounted officer who led them. The marchers stopped at a shouted command, and at the same moment the bagpipe droned off to silence.

In that silence, while a fine rain fell, Alec rode forward. "Is this Major Ferguson?" he called out in Gaelic.

The officer cried, "Come forward and identify yourself," in the same tongue.

Alec came at a trot to the man who was as black-browed and black-haired as himself. Under the wary eyes of the officer, piper, and foot soldiers, Alec said, "My name is Alexander MacLeod." He lied, "My home is in the north."

The piper said, "He has the Gaelic." He sounded surprised.

Alec repeated, "Is Major Patrick Ferguson here?"

"He is not," said the officer, whose horse snorted at the approach of Oscar's roan. "Why do ye seek Ferguson?"

"To join his army. I was told Ferguson is a fellow Scot."

"So he is." The officer laughed. "Are ye a king's man, laddie?"

"Aye, my father is. We are Highlanders by descent."

"But Americans, colonials, all the same." The Scottish officer spoke scornfully. He pointed to the west. "Ye'll find braw Ferguson in Ninety-Six Section or west and north of it. He'll have ye, no doubt. He accepts all manner of colonials. My men come from Scotland—each and every one."

"Aye." Alec cast a look over the Scots as if he greatly admired them, and in fact a year ago he would have. He said to the officer, "I rode to the sound of your piping hoping to find Ferguson."

"Na, we go to Camden Town." The officer was touching his blue-shaven chin. "In Camden there are braw soldiers who might take ye as a recruit—though ye be only a colonial. Come with us to Camden and seek out Colonel Tarleton, who enlists men born in the colonies."

Tarleton. The name made Alec want to shiver. "Tarleton? It is not a Scottish name, is it?"

Alec caught a hint of a smile on the officer's face as he shook his head, and he took encouragement from it. How much easier lying was than it used to be. Constant practice had unlimbered his wits and his tongue as well. What of it, too? A ready falsehood was a spy's stock in trade.

"Na, na, sir," Alec told the Scot. "I want to serve under a Scot—not under any Englishman."

He got the effect he desired. He saw how some of the listening Highlanders elbowed one another and heard their flurry of laughter.

Alec added next, "I speak very little English."

The officer chuckled. " 'Tis likely Major Ferguson may have other Gaelic-speaking lads among his Volunteers, so ye'll not lack for company. I could not take ye if I wanted to. But ye can find Ferguson and don a red coat for all that, though I think ye'll miss the battle that's to come soon."

"Battle?" Alec gripped Oscar's roan with his knees, making it move sidewise nearer the officer's horse.

"Aye, near here and soon. The damned rebels are encamped in North Carolina a few days' march away. Take care ye do not fall into their hands." The Scot shrugged. "I much doubt if Major Ferguson will be summoned to Camden Town. There are enough of us there to whip the American scum."

Alec said, "I thank ye and luck to ye."

"Luck to yourself, lad." The officer motioned to his piper, who lifted his mouthpiece to his lips and began a lilting tune Alec knew from his father's playing it. He moved the roan out of the Highlanders' way and stood beside the road as they passed him. The last man, a little fellow with many freckles, gave him a snaggle-toothed grin as he trudged off into the red mire.

Alec took the roan into the trees that were on the other side of the road as if he rode off to Ferguson. He waited until the Scots were out of sight around the shoulder of a low hill. Then, putting his heels to the roan, he hastened over the road and up the hill into the grove that gave shelter to the Swamp Fox and his men.

The camp at Deep River in North Carolina Colony was one of tents set up in a mountain valley. Colonel Marion was given a tent by an American officer. His men had no tents. They made huts out of brush and boughs to cover them from the everlasting rain and infrequent but fiercely hot summer sunshine. At Deep River Francis Marion cooled his heels days on end waiting for General Gates to arrive, and when the general came he sent for Marion or dismissed him as it suited his purpose.

None of Marion's men liked Gates. He sneered openly at Marion and his grimy swamp men. A large, heavy man, Gates wore a fine blue coat and so did his officers, who were ablaze with gold buttons and epaulettes. Everyone in camp knew that the hero of the Battle of Saratoga believed he was a far finer soldier than Francis Marion. Gates had been an officer in the British army before the Revolution began, and his fame after Saratoga, men said, had gone to his head.

Alec preferred Colonel Sumter to Gates, though he saw little of him. In those first few days as he walked around the camp on Deep River Alec took notice of him, though. Sumter was small but appeared to be extremely muscular. The nickname Gamecock fit him. He was as sprightly and jaunty as the fighting bird whose feather he wore in his hat. Alec learned something of the history of the American commander from a youth his age with whom he struck up a friendship the third day he was at Deep River.

The other boy was Joshua Neale, a thin, fair-haired, gray-eyed lad, who'd come to Gates's camp from over the mountains with his father. The Neale farm was located near the Nolichucky River, according to lanky Joshua, when he came over to introduce himself as Alec groomed Sweet Lass.

"What officer do you serve under?" Alec asked.

"No one."

Surprised, Alec paused with the currycomb in his hand. Joshua Neale grinned and went on, "My pa and I come

here to see General Gates and tell him the Indians plague
us where we are. The British are bribing the Indians to
attack our farms on the Nolichucky."

Alec looked at the other boy with new interest. Joshua
was garbed entirely in buckskin and wearing moccasins,
though his hat was a three-cornered one like Alec's own.
He was a mountain man—or would be when he grew a
little older. Alec recalled seeing such men at Master
Deckard's trading post. Here was a chance to talk with one
of them.

"What officer do *you* serve under?" Joshua asked Alec.

"Colonel Marion."

Alec was pleased to see Joshua's eyes fill with admira-
tion, but his words were not so pleasing. "I know who he
is, but if Pa and I planned to stay here with the army, I'd
enlist under Colonel Sumter."

"Would you?" Alec said coldly as he went back to work
on the mare.

"Yes, I would." The mountain boy sat down on a fallen
log. "My pa knew Sumter before we went over the mountains. Sumter is a hell roarer of a man." Joshua shook his
head. "No man rides half so fast or raises gamecocks so
brave as his."

Alec's thoughts went to Jamie Gilchrist. His mouth was
twisted as he asked, "Does Sumter have a cool head?"

"Cool as well water, and he's hard as flint when he sets
himself to it." Then Joshua wanted to know, "Have you
fought? Were you at the taking of Charles Towne?"

"No," Alec spat out the word, wishing Joshua would go
away. He wouldn't tell this boy of Marion's ambushing and

of his own spying. They wouldn't seem glorious deeds to the mountain lad—not like battles.

With a glint in his eyes, Joshua asked, "What have you done? How did you come by such a fine horse? I've seen your Colonel's horse. It's not so good as yours here."

Alec walked around Sweet Lass and spoke from her side as he combed her mane. "I stole her—if that's what you want me to say," he said with great joy. "I stole her from Colonel Tarleton of the king's Green Dragoons."

To Alec's delight, Joshua's mouth fell open in amazement. "How did you do that?"

Alec exaggerated. "How did Alexander MacLeod do such a thing? By trying to kill Tarleton and his men."

The mountain boy snickered. "You did that, and then you stole this horse from Tarleton?"

"So I did." While Alec went on burnishing Sweet Lass to a glistening sleekness, he told the other boy of Jamie's death and of the pokeberries.

Joshua Neale listened round-eyed. "You came over to Colonel Marion after you did that? But you rode out with Loyalists to begin with."

Alec cried, "Would you have stayed with Tarleton after he killed your friend?"

"No, I would not have stayed. I wonder, though, if I would have thought of the pokeberries and stealing the horse." Joshua looked uncertain.

"Let me tell you, Joshua, you don't know what you'll do until the time comes." Alec stopped to consider his words and wipe horsehair from his perspiring face.

He would have lectured Joshua from his experience of

war, but just then a shouted "Josh" made the Neale boy jump to his feet. Alec watched him run to his father. With a wave of the hand Joshua went off with the tall, grim-faced man in the raccoon-skin cap and fringed buckskins. Alec looked after him, smiling. The story of the pokeberries was a new one to the mountain men apparently. Once ashamed of how he'd come by Sweet Lass, Alec was no longer. Donal Bean had convinced him that there were other ways to serve than to shoulder a musket or long rifle and that these other ways could be very important.

Alec rested his arm on the back of the mare, thinking of the battle that was sure to come. Joshua Neale and his father might not take part in it, but he was certain that Colonel Marion would. Marion had promised him a long rifle when that time came.

That same night, as Alec sat by the campfire before he went to bed in the hut he shared with two other swamp men, Oscar came up to him with the command, "Colonel Marion wants you, boy. He's in his tent."

The opening of Marion's tent faced away from Alec's fire, so he had not seen who else had come to it that evening. When he went inside, he found it full of people, and only two of them he knew by name: his colonel and Joshua Neale. Joshua sat on the bare earth at the feet of his father, who had a stool. Francis Marion perched on his camp bed and only nodded when Alec saluted him. Then Alec's eye fell on the short, blue-eyed man with curling brown hair who lounged in the folding chair opposite Marion.

He was Colonel Sumter.

Francis Marion gestured toward the Neale boy. He said

in his musical voice, "It seems you've told your tale of Tarleton well, Alexander. Colonel Sumter has come here to hear it also."

The flush began at Alec's collarbone and rose up over his face. Joshua Neale had told his father, and his father must have told Sumter of today's conversation.

"It was naught at all." Alec was flustered.

"Naught, he says," commented Marion, "but few of the Green Dragoons could take to their horses for three days."

"I have heard that we gained three days' time because the Green Dragoons sampled some bad rum." Sumter's voice was a brisk tenor. He leaned forward, tin cup in hand. Alec heard the sloshing of liquid in it. "It's rum, lad," said the Gamecock. "Your colonel has just given it to me. I trust you have not tampered with it."

"No, sir!" Alec heard his own voice as if from a great distance. He knew as everyone else did that Marion kept a little stoneware bottle of rum under his bed, though he seldom drank himself.

Colonel Marion gave one of his rare soft laughs. "Tell him the story, Alexander."

Alec stood in the center of the tent with everyone watching him, and from there he faltered through the story of Gilchrist's Horse, Jamie's murder, and the plucking of the berries that went into the rum keg.

Sumter began to roar with laughter. "A wit to wonder at, this boy has!"

Alec finished with his escape on Sweet Lass to his home and being given the mare.

Sumter then said, "So ye saved the mare from Tarleton and from Loyalists and fetched her to Colonel Marion.

Why is it that ye went to the Pee Dee River country and did not seek me out? I was nearer to you all the time."

Alec looked at Marion. What could he say?

Marion advised, "Tell him of Major Ferguson and your father."

While Joshua Neale and his father listened and Sumter drank his rum, never taking his eyes from him, Alec told of the attack on his father, of Donal Bean, and his leaving the farm for Marion's camp.

The Gamecock spoke to Marion, not to Alec, at the end of Alec's story. "He has done well, I think." He eyed Alec up and down. "From Ninety-Six Section, eh? Are you a marksman?" he asked Alec.

"Yes, sir, I am."

Sumter told Marion, "I envy you, sir. You've not only got a very fleet horse but a lad with courage and wit." Then he demanded of Alec very suddenly, "Tell me, why didn't you seek to become a courier for me?"

Caught by the repeated question, Alec blurted out, "Because, Colonel Sumter, I'd never heard of you then." Why had the man asked that again? And God above, *what* had he just said?

Red with embarrassment, Alec whirled around and rushed out of the tent, hearing loud laughter behind him. What a rude fool he'd been! And Sumter had praised his cleverness. Alec fled to his hut where he stayed all night, expecting to be summoned by Marion and chastised for his rudeness, but the call never came.

A day later Alec watched the Neales and some other over-the-mountain men riding out of camp. He wondered if they had got what they wanted from General Gates—a solemn promise to come to the Nolichucky River country to fight the Indians. He doubted it. They had sour faces as they left.

That same afternoon Alec watched Colonel Sumter ride away with his forces, many of them with gamecock feathers in their hats.

Yet the Swamp Fox stayed at Deep River.

Francis Marion was still there in August when Gates received excellent news. Sumter was fighting. He had beaten the king's forces at a place called Rocky Mount on the first day of August and driven them out. After General Gates got his large army moving on the march toward South Carolina, another courier came riding from Sumter. He brought the news that the Gamecock had attacked the redcoats at Hanging Rock on the sixth of the month and forced them to withdraw back into Camden with the other British soldiers. There was bad news too, though. Sumter had been wounded in the thigh by a rifle ball.

So apparently the Gamecock would not be present at the battle that was surely brewing and would very soon take place somewhere near Camden Town.

XI

The Couriers

The evening of August 13, as General Gates encamped with the force he referred to as the "Grand Army in South Carolina Colony," Alec's Colonel Marion was summoned once more to the general's tent.

He returned to his own hours later. Alec, who'd lain awake in the dark night, recognized his footsteps as he dragged his injured foot. Alec sat up. At the same moment Oscar, who'd been sleeping near Alec, rose up also.

"Colonel?" Oscar called out softly.

Marion's reply was, "Assemble the men, Oscar. Awaken those that are asleep. I want to speak to them now."

Alec rolled out of his blanket and went with Oscar from soldier to soldier until all who'd come out of the swamp with Marion were gathered together before their commander's tent.

"Ready, Colonel," Alec heard Oscar say from inside, and then the servant came out, followed by Marion.

The Swamp Fox stood with his arms folded. He was scarcely visible in the darkness, but his voice was easily heard though he kept it low. "I have received my orders tonight from General Gates. We are none of us to take part in the battle that he expects to fight soon."

A murmur came from the men, but Oscar hissed, "Silence!"

Marion continued. "General Gates is very sure of victory. His forces outnumber those of the king's army in Camden Town. He knows that when he defeats the army of Lord Cornwallis that the beaten redcoats will try to escape him when he goes on to seize Camden Town."

"They'll run away and come back to fight again for King George," said the man on Alec's left.

"So General Gates believes," said Marion steadily. "He thinks they will try to get away by taking ferries over the rivers. The only way they can cross because of the heavy rains we've had all these last weeks is by boat. And many of them do not have horses—even if they might risk swimming the streams. I am ordered to Williamsburg to take command of the militia there. With you and the Williamsburg militiamen I am to burn every flatboat or ferry we can find on the Santee River so the redcoats cannot escape Gates by crossing it."

One of the swamp men grumbled, "So we will not fire a single ball at the redcoats."

"Not in this battle," Marion answered quietly. "I think that later we shall do more than forage, ambush from the trail, and burn ferryboats."

"When do we go to the Santee?" asked the tall scarecrow of a man, looming up in the dark on Alec's right side.

"At dawn. Good night." And Marion went into his tent. Alec saw his shadow pass in front of his lantern and saw him kneel down in prayer, his hands clasped together. Alec looked away, embarrassed by his unwitting spying on his commander and by his surge of relief at the realization that he wouldn't be fighting in the coming battle.

Alec rode away just after dawn with Colonel Marion and the others while Gates's soldiers, men from Virginia, North Carolina, Delaware, and Maryland, were breakfasting at their campfires. That same morning they would march nearer to Camden Town. Certain of victory to come, they were in high spirits, laughing and jesting. An artilleryman, leaning against the carriage of his cannon, shouted to Marion's group as they rode past him, "Where do you think you're off to so early, swamp boys?" He jerked his thumb toward Camden. "Do you think you will be the first into the town chasing out Tarleton and his greencoats?"

No one answered the artilleryman. Marion led the way out of the camp southward toward Camden for a distance, then turned onto a trail that led toward the Santee and the eastern part of the colony.

They saw no redcoats or any of Tarleton's dragoons that day because, as Marion told his men that night when they camped in a large thicket without any campfires, "The British know that a battle is coming and what direction it will come from." He looked at Alec. "They have their spies as well. I suspect they know we've left the camp. I am sure that many of them have seen us today and ridden with the news to Camden. But twenty men are too few to trouble with—not when battle brews." Marion held up a warning finger. "If General Gates wins his victory, our work on the Santee will assume importance." The colonel muttered at his bone-dry corn bread. "I pray to God that he wins!"

Though they were miles away from Camden, Marion and his swamp men knew when the battle started two days later, at two o'clock in the morning. The far-off booming of cannon came dimly to their ears and made the horses fret and their ears twitch, but Marion did not turn back. He was silent, more silent than usual that day, the sixteenth of August, as he rode for the Santee. The soldiers following him spoke little to one another either. Alec knew their thoughts because they were his own. Who had won the battle? Was it still going on? The thunder of the cannon had ceased, which meant nothing to anyone who could not see the progress of the battle for himself.

When they came some days later into the tiny hamlet of Williamsburg, Marion called Alec to him in the cabin that served as his headquarters. "Ride out tomorrow morning, and learn what you can about the battle," he said. "Then come to me on the Santee with the news. Do not let yourself or the mare be taken. God knows who you might find about in the countryside now that the battle is finished. People will be able to tell you here in Williamsburg where you can find me on the river."

"Yes, sir."

After a night of little rest, thinking about his mission, which might or might not be very dangerous, Alec mounted Sweet Lass in the morning. His pockets stuffed with bread and cheese that Oscar had got for him the night before, he rode back over the trail they'd recently taken. Moving fast, he covered miles before he encountered anyone at all. And this person was a fat man mounted on a large gray horse, with the look of a plowhorse. The man was riding as fast as the gray could manage. Alec halted Sweet Lass in the shelter of fragrant pines and waited with Jamie's pistol in his hand. As he did, he thought how much like a highwayman he must seem. Highwaymen had fine pistols and rode fine swift horses, but they didn't ever wear greasy buckskin, as far as he knew.

The fat man was not a soldier. In spite of his excitement and fright, Alec was smiling. He had yet to gather information by ambushing a man with a pistol. There was a first time for everything. He hoped that this traveler had news of the battle.

As the gray lumbered toward his hiding place, Alec urged Sweet Lass forward into the trail. "Halt or I'll fire," he cried, blocking the trail with the mare's body.

The stranger pulled the gray up only a few feet from Sweet Lass, who twitched but kept her place as Alec cocked the pistol. The rider dropped his reins and raised his hands toward the sky.

"What do you want of me, boy?" he cried out. "I'm a poor man with nothing to steal of any value."

Alec called out to him, "I don't seek your money or your horse. Tell me what you know of the battle near Camden Town."

The fat man's small eyes narrowed. "Who are you? A king's man or a rebel?"

"Who I am is of no matter." Alec found the English

tongue far easier to use by now. "Do you know anything of the battle?"

The stranger bobbed his head. "I do. That is why you find me on this trail away from Camden."

"Are *you* a king's man or a Patriot?" asked Alec. Suddenly he felt a cold chill down the back of his neck. Something was wrong. But what?

"Boy, I am no one's man but my own." Alec saw that the stranger was tilting his left hand toward his hat as if he was waving to it. Alec followed the strange motion with his eyes and noticed the long feather in the hat. It was bronze and black, a gamecock's feather.

Alec said, "I've seen many a feather like yours. At times I think that cock has lost his tail entirely."

The fat man nodded as he stared at Alec's swamp-water-blackened clothing and Sweet Lass. "The cock has lost his tail. My master has plucked the bird clean, and my master has been clean plucked also."

Sumter? Clean plucked? "What is your master's name?" asked Alec.

"Tom, it is. Do you have a master also?"

"I do."

"Where is he now?"

"He is not with me. He sent me to learn what I could of the battle for him."

The fat man swallowed before he spoke, and his words came with effort. "Tell him that the Patriots were beaten very badly by the redcoats, and it is said that General Gates went back into North Carolina."

"*Lost*—to the British?" Alec was astonished.

"More than lost. It was a rout. The redcoats advanced and without firing a rifle, the militia from Virginia and North Carolina turned about and ran away. The men from Delaware and Maryland fired on the redcoats beside their cannon until the king's soldiers killed them with their bayonets and the greencoat cavalry cut them down with sabers."

"The battle was lost!" Alec repeated once more. He shook his head to clear it and force the unwelcome new idea into it. "Did Colonel Sumter come to Camden, too?"

"No. No more than Colonel Marion did. No, poor Tom was not there." Again the hand was waving toward the feather.

Sweat trickled down Alec's sides. The pistol was growing heavier by the moment. He asked harshly, "Where is your master?"

"I do not know." Again the fat stranger swallowed. Alec saw tears on his pockmarked face. "Tom doesn't send me to Williamsburg to seek out his friends. I go there of my own free will, because I don't want to ride to North Carolina." He asked Alec again, "What is your master's name?"

"It is Francis."

"Do you bear a token from him?"

"Yes." Alec reached into his pocket, feeling for the silver button, but did not take it out. "Can you guess what it is?" Alec felt as if he played a ridiculous child's game, but then the pokeberries and the rum had been the same sort of game—and a deadly one.

"A button. There is the number two on it," said the stranger.

"It might be so. Do you know the name of the horse my master rides?"

"He is named Ball. And your master has a servant who is a black man and very large."

Satisfied, Alec wanted to know next, "Where is your master now? The last I heard of him he was at Hanging Rock and was wounded there."

"May I wipe my nose, boy? It runs so."

"Yes, but do not reach for a pistol, I warn you."

The fat man wiped his nose on his coat sleeve, then said, "My master was last seen by anyone at Fishing Creek. I escaped that camp when Tarleton and the Green Dragoons surprised us at midday while we were resting. I saw my master leap up off his camp bed, cut the traces of a wagon horse, and ride off into some trees." Colonel Sumter's man sniffled. "My master wore nothing at all but his linen underdrawers—the day was so hot. I do not know if he even has the blade he used to cut the wagon-horse free. Tarleton may have caught him. I do not know."

"Put your hands down now." Alec reeled mentally under the weight of these two pieces of dreadful news.

The stranger didn't touch the gray's reins yet. "I got away from Fishing Creek. I was a distance from camp in the forest hunting rabbits for supper. I heard the shots and the cries, so I didn't go back but watched from the top of a tree I climbed. I saw it all. Then I stole this horse from a farmer and rode toward Camden hoping to find General Gates there. But on the way I learned that the British had won the battle and Gates had left South Carolina entirely. I knew from hearing my master talking that the Swamp Fox had been sent to the Santee River country. My master said he was to burn boats and ferries." He laughed sourly. "There's no need for that now. No redcoats need to flee from

Camden. The entire up-country is in the hands of the king's armies."

"Yes," said Alec, as he returned the pistol to its holster. He lifted his eyes to the fat man. "My name is Alexander MacLeod, and as you know I serve Colonel Francis Marion. Who are you?"

"My name is Tom, Tom Jessup. I serve Colonel Sumter."

Alec gathered up the mare's reins. "Then come with me back to Williamsburg. You have news to tell Colonel Marion. He won't savor it, but he must hear it."

"What will Marion do?" asked Jessup, sending the gray to trot ahead of Sweet Lass after Alec waved him on.

Alec called up to him, "I don't know, but I suspect he will burn boats until he has some word from another American commander."

Alec and Jessup needed two days to find Francis Marion once they had been to Williamsburg. They came across the Swamp Fox seated on a log on the bank of the Santee, watching Oscar and three others hack a drawn-up dugout canoe apart with axes. Marion got up at Alec's approach with Jessup. He asked, "Who is this, Alexander?"

Jessup spoke for himself. "I come from Colonel Sumter, sir."

"Do you bring news for me? What do you know of the battle near Camden Town?" Marion's question was an eager one.

Alec felt Jessup's eyes on him in dismay. Marion hadn't heard of the defeat. Both Alec and Sumter's man had hoped that the news would outstrip them. One of them now had to inform Marion.

"I want to speak privately with you, Colonel Marion," Jessup told the Swamp Fox. "The boy can hold my horse for me if you give him permission."

"As you wish." Marion's black glance went swiftly from Alec's face to Jessup's. Alec took the gray's reins as Jessup came puffing down off the horse. Alec was delighted that Jessup would have to give the colonel the news, which was only right, come to think on it. Jessup was older. He had been at Fishing Creek, and he had heard at firsthand of the battle result.

Alec stood holding the gray beside the rolling Santee listening to the chopping sounds the axes made but watching his colonel as he listened to Jessup. Francis Marion gave no outward sign of how the news affected him except for keeping his head bowed.

When Sumter's soldier had finished, Marion turned around and beckoned to Alec, who brought Sweet Lass and the gray up to the two men. Francis Marion told him, "It seems I am now the only commander for the Continental Congress in this part of the state, while the British are stronger than ever in Charles Towne and in Camden." He gave Alec a melancholy smile. "We did not think it would come to this, did we?"

"No, sir."

Marion spoke to Jessup. "You are welcome here, if your news is not. Eat and rest. Will you take service under me, or do you want to ride to General Gates?"

"I'll serve you, sir, until Colonel Sumter turns up—if he lives."

Marion eyed the gray, then Sweet Lass. He gazed next at heavy-limbed Jessup, then at Alec. "What direction did

Colonel Sumter seem to take when he rode away from the camp at Fishing Creek?" he asked Jessup.

"Toward North Carolina, sir." He sounded angry.

Francis Marion told Jessup gently, "No, I am not trying to make you say that Colonel Sumter ran away to join Gates like his soldiers who deserted the battle at Camden."

"Thank you, Colonel Marion."

The Swamp Fox warned, "I do not want the news you brought me to get to my men. Not yet. I don't want them to lose heart. Keep your silence. If the men ask what news you fetched, tell them it is secret and comes from General Gates." Marion addressed Alec. "Take Master Jessup to the fire, and let him get some food from Oscar. Then, Alexander, see that you and the mare have some rest. Tomorrow you shall ride out again for me."

"Where do I go this time, sir?"

"To find Colonel Sumter—wherever he may be—or to find out what has happened to him."

Alec's jaw dropped. Sumter could be anywhere in the up-country by now or even over the mountains. He thought of Joshua Neale's father, who had been a friend of the Gamecock.

Marion read Alec's mind. "You found me along the Pee Dee River, lad."

"No, sir, Oscar found me."

Marion told him dryly, "I know Tom Sumter. I do not think the British have him prisoner, and I think wherever he may be he is already gathering men to him to replace those who were killed or wounded or taken captive by Tarleton at Fishing Creek. One of them, I suspect, will find you if you go hunting about the country asking for Sumter."

"Yes, sir." Alec glanced out of the corner of his eye at Jessup, who hadn't waited and who was waddling off with the gray.

The Swamp Fox read the boy's mind once more. "I am sending you because you are light and have this horse and know her well. I require news. I want to know not only where Sumter is but the numbers of his men, and I want to know as swiftly as possible even if you must ride day and night."

"What if I fail to find him, sir?"

"Do not fail. Do not come back until you have the information I need. And do not take any man's word for where he might be. Speak to Sumter himself. Then come find me."

"Yes, sir. Where is Fishing Creek?"

"In the up-country." Marion smiled. "Ask Colonel Sumter's man. He was there."

While Sweet Lass grazed, gaining strength for the journey, Tom Jessup drew a map in the mud of the riverbank for Alec, showing him where Fishing Creek was. He put in other places, too, with the pointed stick. Camden Town and the village of Ninety-Six. Fishing Creek was not so very far from Alec's home.

At daybreak Alec rode away after a blessing from Marion and some last instructions. "Tell no one of your mission. Guard yourself and the mare well, and remember the uses of pokeberries, Alexander."

Traveling as fast he could over sodden trails sticky with mud, Alec passed south of Camden the fourth day after leaving Marion on the Santee. He found the up-country quiet under gray skies, and once he met a boy herding milk cows out of a thicket and asked about the redcoats.

The boy's reply was what Alec had guessed it would be. Many of the king's army had marched out of Camden Town, advancing on Gates in North Carolina, hoping to catch what was left of his Grand Army. Alec presumed that Tarleton had taken his Green Dragoons north with the others. The farm boy knew nothing at all of Patriot commanders. And he was not entirely certain that he was right about the British. He had heard the information from a man who had heard it from another man. Alec knew how reliable such news was, so he became ever watchful for the fearful Colonel Tarleton and his swift cavalry. He was afraid that a tiring Sweet Lass might not be able to outrun the Green Dragoons. If he were caught, Tarleton would remember the mare—if not Alec's face.

Alec kept to trails that were little more than cowpaths—and more than likely unknown to the British—trails that one rider could take and not be spied out. On the fifth day from the Santee, riding more swiftly in familiar country, he rode past the oak where Andrew Munn had been hanged and paused under it for a moment, gazing at the grave beside the trail. Tall grass was growing on it now. Alec shook his head, thinking of how much had taken place since that day only a few months ago. He mumbled the Lord's Prayer once more, then rode on to the Munn cabin. The door hung open and weeds flourished in his grandmother's garden. He didn't wonder that deer had not devoured it. The rank smell of her herbs made Sweet Lass dilate her nostrils and snort.

Jonet Munn was still with the MacLeods, if Major Ferguson hadn't put her into the jail at Ninety-Six because she was a traitor's widow.

Alec passed the Gilchrist farm to the south. He wanted to see his family first for one thing. For another, he was not at all certain what kind of welcome the Gilchrists might give a coward and fugitive to whom they'd presented their hero son's horse and pistol.

The MacLeod hounds greeted Alec with wild yelpings and waving tails as he whistled to them to come to him. Surrounded by the dogs, he rode up to his home, and what he saw made him halt and stand staring. The house was there, but where was the barn? In its place stood nothing but a black rectangle—ashes. To the left of the barn had been a field of wheat when Alec went away to find Marion. The field was there but flattened to the earth, beaten down not by the rain but by something heavy. Only cattle or horses set loose in wheat could do that damage. And no MacLeod would permit animals in a grain field.

Alec rose up in his stirrups and called out in Gaelic, "I be here." His grandmother, not his mother, came out of the house with her shawl up over her head because of the downpour. Stepping through the mud, she walked to Alec and lifted her face up at him, blinking through raindrops. She reached for his hand. "God give ye welcome, Alec *dubh*. I saw that ye were coming here last night. I did not need to hear your dogs to find out. Did ye find the dark water?"

"Aye, Colonel Marion's camp in the swamps. Tell me, how is Father?"

"Little better, I fear. He feeds himself now and puts on

his own breeches when your mother tells him to. He does not speak except to talk of your brother Duncan. He thinks Lilias and I are Duncan."

"And Mother and Lilias?"

"Well enough, and I am well. Ye'll find your mother inside. But your sister's not here." As Alec felt terror rising in him, his grandmother explained not only Lilias's absence but what had happened to the wheat and barn. "The red soldiers burned the barn and drove cattle they'd foraged from the neighbors through the wheat. Lilias lives now in the woods behind the house. She guards what remains of the cattle and the sheep and our horses. She keeps watch there from the top of a tree and blows a horn if she sees redcoats coming. Two blasts if it be them—one if someone we know."

Alec nodded. He had caught the note of a hunting horn as he had ridden up but had not realized it signaled his approach. So Lilias had marked him out, and even so she had not come down to the farm. She had learned caution somewhere. Strange indeed that must seem to her nature! As Alec dismounted, he asked, "Did Ferguson order the barn set fire to?"

"Aye, the red brute himself. I gave him the rough edge of my tongue when he came here ten days ago, and so he punished us. He is my *biast ruadh,* Alec, the man I saw in the flames."

"I knew that from the first, Grandmother. It is a wonder he did not kill ye."

"I will not be shot or hanged," said the old woman with a smile. She added as she took Sweet Lass's reins. "Go see your mother now and then seek Lilias out. I'll talk to ye tonight in the smoke house and ask ye of Donal and the man I sent ye to find."

"I serve that man now, Grandmother."

"I had guessed ye would. And ye have not come here only to see how we fared without ye?"

Alec shook his head. He'd decided that he was going to tell her why he'd come home. After all, she'd sent him to Colonel Marion and she'd known much of Donal Bean's business for General Washington. "I am seeking a man named Thomas Sumter. Do ye know of him?"

"Na, I have not heard his name."

"Have ye been told of Patriot victories at Rocky Mount and Hanging Rock?"

"Na."

"Colonel Sumter won them, as General Gates lost the battle before Camden Town this month. I am hunting for Sumter."

"Then go to see Master Deckard in the village. He knows of ye somewhat. I told him about ye when I bought a long rifle of him secretly and had him bring it here to us in his wagon."

"Aye." Alec smiled at Jonet Munn. His wits did come through her blood. Master Deckard knew many things because many men visited his post. "Is Major Ferguson still at the fort?" he asked her.

"He goes out, and then he comes back again, but the red soldiers he left behind hold the fort." As the mare nuzzled at her shoulder, Jonet Munn said, "Alec *dubh,* there's been news of fighting northwest of here. We had it from the minister of the kirk, who came visiting us last Saturday noon to see your father and pray over him."

Fighting? The Gamecock? The nickname blazed like a torch in Alec's mind. The month had not ended yet, but had Sumter gathered an army already? Possibly. Men might flock to him.

The conversation between Alec and his grandmother broke off all at once as Margaret MacLeod appeared in one of the doorways. "Alec, come inside!" She called out. "Why do ye tarry?"

Old Jonet whispered, "Tell her that ye wandered far and grew homesick—not that ye've been with Francis Marion. It's best she never learn that." As Margaret MacLeod came out bareheaded through the rain, Jonet Munn went on, "Do not spend much time inside with her and your father. Get the mare and yourself out of sight in the woods where Lilias is. Who knows who else might come riding today?"

Margaret MacLeod gazed up at her son after she had flung her arms about him. Her finger traced the dark fuzz on his upper lip. "Ye grow so tall and so braw. But ye be very thin and so very dirty." She caught at his hand. "Come see your father now. Perhaps he'll call ye by name, but if he calls ye Duncan say that ye are Duncan." Pulling him with her, she went on, "And then ye must go to the woods with your sister."

Alec followed along to the door, but as he put his foot on the step he asked, "Mother, how many times has Ferguson come here?"

"Two times, the devil, and one time his young officer came without him. They took almost all of our corn before they burned the barn. They took all of our salt pork."

*   *   *

Ten minutes later Lilias greeted Alec with a frantic hugging on the edge of the woods at the bottom of the hill. She talked to him as they sat together in the shelter the MacLeod women had made out of brush and barrel staves from the Gilchrists. While she talked, Alec heard Sweet Lass grazing outside with the two MacLeod horses and Jonet Munn's old chestnut gelding.

Lilias was wilder than ever and, to his surprise, dressed in an old coat and breeches that once belonged to Duncan. Her feet were bare and her face filthy. Her temper had not changed, though. She spat out her words as she spoke of Ellen. "Sonsy Mistress Ellen came riding here one day with some broth for Father. She asked for ye, and Grandmother Munn told her that ye had gone away rather than serve under Major Ferguson. She gasped and said she was faint. She took the news ill, Alec *dubh*. Where did ye go?"

"To the east of the colony, Lilias." As he had expected, Ellen despised him now.

To his relief, his sister didn't press him with questions about where he had been. She was too full of anger at Ellen. She sniffed and said, as she cracked a hazelnut and offered part of the meat to Alec, "Ellen's fairly besotted on Cornet Ordish. All I can say for him is that he's not so wicked as old Ferguson. Grandmother, too, says that he is not."

Lilias and Jonet Munn seemed to have come to an understanding of sorts at last. Alec asked, "Does Grandmother look into the fire now?"

Lilias shrugged. "She says that we will have a hard winter, but I don't know if that comes from second sight

or from common sense. The redcoats have taken our pigs
and chickens and corn—whatever they could take from
us. I've kept some animals and the horses. God forbid,
we have to eat the horses before the winter's out. Autumn
comes already, Alec *dubh,* and it is not yet September."

He didn't need her words. He'd seen for himself with
his woodsman's and hunter's eye that the summer green
on the trees was turning golden orange. He'd go to the
trader's store and ask old Deckard of Sumter. He'd go
afoot, by night. By her beauty Sweet Lass always attracted
attention wherever he rode her.

But first he would hunt tomorrow for his family. He'd
seen deer as he'd ridden from the east. He'd use the long
rifle Jonet Munn had got from Deckard and kill a deer
for the women to dry as jerky for the coming winter.

The next day Alec hunted. He killed a buck on Gilchrist land and brought meat back in leather bags. Though
once through trees he glimpsed the Gilchrist house, he did
not approach it. While Margaret MacLeod was carrying the
venison off to where it would be cut up and shredded,
Alec spoke softly with his grandmother once more. He'd
told her secretly the evening before of his friendship with
Donal Bean and of his life in the swamp with Marion,
then of Camden Town and Sumter's disappearance.

Today he asked, "Does Deckard know that I serve Colonel Marion? Does he know I am a soldier?"

"Na, but he knows that ye are no more a king's man.
I told him that. Why not tell him that ye wish to find
Colonel Sumter and serve the Patriots under him?"

Aye. That could be the wisest course, indeed.

XII

A Scarlet Coat

That night Alec went to Ninety-Six village. He carefully skirted the fort where the redcoat soldiers held sway and went to the rear door of Master Deckard's store, where candlelight shone from behind a window of oiled cowhide. Master Deckard, a widower, lived alone behind his trading post. He had not gone to bed yet. Candlelight glowed faintly from a second room Alec knew to be the old man's.

Alec rapped softly at the door.

"Who's there?" came the trader's voice.

"MacLeod, Alexander MacLeod."

Alec heard slow footsteps, then the soft words, "If you are the MacLeod boy I knew, you'll remember what color ribbons you got of me last spring."

By now strange and unexpected questions no longer

bothered Alec. "Red silk and rose-colored velvet, Master Deckard."

He heard the bolt drawn back and saw the door opened. Deckard, candle in hand, peered at Alec's face, then opened the door wide enough for the boy to slide through. He grunted once Alec was inside, "So, it is you, Alexander. I do not open my door at night quickly to anyone these days."

Alec thought Deckard looked poorly. He was thinner and the color of his face gone grayish. He asked, "Do you ail, Master Deckard?"

"Not in the body, perhaps in the spirit, as all of us ail these days." Deckard sighed. "It is not easy to maintain a trading post when one is a Patriot and the British hold the village. I am watched. The British would imprison me if there were another trader here, one friendly to their cause. They need me, it seems, and they know that I have friends among the Indians. There is always a soldier in my store during the day." He put the candle down and asked, "What do you want of me, Alexander? Why do you come here tonight?"

Alec shook the rain off his hat without being asked to take it off. "My grandmother said that you have been told that I went over to the Americans?"

"I have been told that. Did you do so because of your father and because of the manner in which young Gilchrist died—or was murdered? I know that sorry tale from Jonet Munn also, though no one else here has heard it as yet. She said Master Gilchrist gave you his son's horse."

Alec opened and closed his mouth. His grandmother

seemed to have said a great deal to the trader when she'd bought the long rifle from him. He wondered if she'd told him the tale of the pokeberries along with the story of Jamie's death. Well, she had smoothed his way somewhat to ask of Sumter. "Yes, sir, I did join the Patriots because of what was done to my father and what Colonel Tarleton did to Jamie—and for more reasons than that. I was at General Gates' camp in North Carolina early this month."

Deckard nodded. His enormous shadow on the white-washed wall nodded also, as he said, "Before the battle at Camden Town?"

So—Deckard knew of the defeat. Alec said, "I was not there. The man I served under was sent away." Sumter, as well as Marion, had left prior to the battle. "I seek him now, sir. I've lost him."

The trader asked quietly, "Who would that be, Alexander?"

"Colonel Sumter, master."

"Where did you lose him?" Clearly Deckard was surprised.

"He was last seen at a place called Fishing Creek. Do you know where he might be now? I thought you might have heard."

"No, Alexander."

"Sumter is reported to be in the up-country, though."

Deckard put his fingers into his beard. "Is he now?"

"Master Deckard, don't you hear travelers talking in your store? Don't the redcoats talk there, too?"

"Not many men talk overmuch these days. Travelers do not take the common roads. It has been a long time since anyone brought furs to me from over the mountains."

The old man nodded again. "Yet I do hear rumors now and then. It is said that there are whole armies of men near to the mountains, Alexander. Perhaps one of them might be your Colonel Sumter's force. I do not know for certain, mind you."

Alec snatched at the words. *Entire armies!* Had Sumter assembled a large force so soon? Or had Deckard been misled? "Where did you hear of armies?" Alec asked.

The old man sat down at his table, staring at the candle flame. "From an Indian, a Cherokee from Georgia. He brought wolf pelts to me the other day—and poor quality they were. He claimed to have seen three armies on this side of the mountains, though what he may have seen was no more than an out-of-doors church meeting. I do not know. I do not speak the Cherokee language as well as I did years ago. Perhaps I didn't understand him."

"Were they king's soldiers? Did they wear red coats?"

"He said that they were not red-jacket men. That I did understand."

Alec sighed. He had learned very little. He told Deckard, "I thank you, sir, and I give you good night." He wondered if the soldiers at Fort Ninety-Six had questioned the wandering Cherokee also. Alec added suddenly, "Grandmother Munn says that Major Ferguson comes and goes at the fort."

"Yes, that red kit fox does. He hunts in the up-country at the moment."

"For Colonel Sumter?"

"For whatever Patriot force he can find. He wants a battle, Alexander. He had no glory at Camden Town, remember. He was not there. Perhaps he knows the whereabouts of the other armies. Major Ferguson does not confide in me. If I speak with any man in his garrison, it is Cornet Ordish."

"He is an American. I've seen him." Alec spoke bitterly.

"All of Ferguson's men are Americans, though some are Gaelic-speaking like yourself." Deckard added dryly, "You are not like them anymore, Alexander. The difference is that you know yourself to be an American."

Thinking of Ellen, Alec asked him, "How do you find this Ordish?"

"Ambitious but not unpleasant." Deckard was smiling. *He knew!* "Gilchrist land is good land. I hear from him that he plans to return here when the war is ended."

Ach, Ellen was surely betrothed to the young Virginian if he planned to return. Aye, old Gilchrist, lacking a son now, would make him his heir.

At the door Alec paused, when Deckard called across the room to him, "Do you still seek to be a trader?"

"Yes, sir."

"Good. I trust you find your Colonel Sumter. If I am still alive when the war is won, come see me. Your English is vastly improved. I can see you've been among Americans."

"I said that I had, Master Deckard."

Alec went out into the night, feeling somewhat annoyed. He had hoped that Deckard could tell him where Sumter was. Instead, if he was to find the American, he would have to ride out and hunt him as Ferguson could be doing. This mission was going to be more difficult than he'd thought, far more so than Colonel Marion had foreseen or he would have sent out more of his men to scout

out Sumter's whereabouts. And to make it even more difficult, there were *three* armies in the north—four including the men serving under Ferguson. Whose men made up the others? Was the Gamecock in the field again? He might not be. He might be dead or he might be secretly held by the British, though Alec doubted that possibility. If they held Sumter a prisoner in Camden Town, they'd spread the news throughout the entire colony to dampen Patriot hopes.

As Alec came around the corner of Deckard's trading post, he noticed that it had begun to rain again. More rain! Never had there been such a wet summer in the history of the colony. His mother had said that very morning that God seemed to be conspiring against the colony to send both ruinous weather and the renewal of the war.

Jamming his hat on his head and pulling it down over his ears, Alec started across the muddy road that lay in front of the trading post. He'd go the long way around and avoid the neighborhood of the fort. In two hours' time, despite the rain, he could be at home, and tomorrow he'd ride out toward the mountains to see what he could learn of Master Deckard's mysterious armies. If he could discover anything that he considered important, even if it did not concern Sumter, he'd go at once to Colonel Marion and try to find him too. Alec let out his breath in exasperation at the life he was leading. It was truly hide-and-seek. He hid from the accursed redcoats, and the Americans hid from him. That armies could appear and disappear might seem strange to anyone who was not familiar with his colony, but not to Alec, who had spent all of his life near dense thickets and heavy woods.

As he stopped in the dark at the edge of the road to re-adjust a shoe that stuck in the mire, he heard a harsh call, "Stop, whoever you be, or I'll fire on you."

A tall dark shape materialized from the side of the village church out from among the gravestones. Alec froze with his foot half out of his shoe. The voice went on, "Who the devil are you?"

"Alexander MacLeod."

"Do you have a permission to be out at night?"

Alec said with a sinking heart, knowing that this person must be a soldier from the fort, "I did not know that I had to have one." Why hadn't Deckard warned him that he had to have a signed paper?

The soldier's next sentence explained Alec's question. "As of nine o'clock tonight no one may go about the village after dark without permission from the fort. It is by Cornet Ordish's orders—and a clever surprise it seems to be. The order will be proclaimed throughout the town in the morning. Fetch the lantern, private."

Alec saw a second and shorter figure come up beside the first. He carried a lantern that showed cracks of yellow light peeping through the heavy metal shutters. The second man pushed a shutter aside and held the lantern to Alec's face.

"Yes, he's the MacLeod whelp. I recall that black hair and that Scots jaw of his from the day we came to his farm with the major. Why is it you never came to join us when the major told you to," he asked Alec. "God be praised, we never drank your father's whiskey, so we didn't find out if it was poisoned or not."

"There was no poison in it," Alec flared at him.

"Perhaps not. But now we have you, don't we, and now you'll join Major Ferguson's Volunteers, won't you?"

"I don't wish to."

The lantern bearer mimicked Alec's words in a falsetto. "I do not wish to. He wants to be a coward and embroider petticoats with the girls or live in the woods as a wild man."

"Come along with us," ordered the first soldier. "We'll take you to the fort, and the officer there will have the say about you. Put on your shoe and fall in ahead of us with your hands on top of your head. Don't try to run off again. Other cowardly lads have been shot dead before they had the honor of putting on the king's red coat."

Red coat! Alec's gorge rose. The idea sickened him as he sloshed along ahead of the two soldiers. All he could think of was the scarlet ribbon he'd bought for Lilias on his father's order and the trickle of blood at the back of MacLeod's head as he lay facedown in the mud. He hated the color red now.

Twenty minutes later the tall heavy gates of Fort Ninety-Six closed behind him and his escort. He remembered the fort. Before the Revolution, while he'd still been a child, he'd walked along the sentryways built into the fifteen-foot-high walls of upright logs. He'd been in and out of the soldiers' barracks and the officers' quarters on that same occasion. The fort had been interesting to him, though not half so interesting as the trading post. His father and Duncan had been with him. Duncan, Alec recalled, had been much taken with the fort and soldiers.

The guardroom, as Alec remembered it, had changed

but little since that day of the MacLeod's visit to it on the invitation of an officer who'd seen service in Scotland and who could speak Gaelic with the MacLeods. There was a picture of King George on one wall and some red coats hanging on pegs on another. There was someone he knew behind a table—a man who seemed as if he were waiting for what the sentries might catch by surprise that night. Ordish, the man Ellen favored over him!

Ordish asked, "Who are you?" His blue eyes were not hostile, only curious, as he waved the two soldiers into the background behind Alec.

Alec took his hands down. "Alexander MacLeod."

Ordish pointed at him. "I know you. You'd be the lad Major Ferguson told to come here and join us after the sergeant was forced to strike your father down. I came after you to your farm and found you gone. What a tongue that grandmother of yours has! She cursed us in Scots. I understood not one word of it, but all the same I knew it for cursing." He laughed.

"My father is witless now." Alec told the Virginian.

"I know that, and I am sorry. That is why I left him at home and didn't bring him to jail here after I found you gone away. Well, you are here now to join as a loyal king's man, are you not?" Ordish took a piece of paper from the top of a stack, wrote on it with a quill, and then redipping the quill into an inkpot, extended the pen to Alec. "Here is your paper of enlistment, MacLeod. Can you write, or do you make an *X?*"

"I can write, but I will not sign your paper."

"So?" Ordish put the quill down on the table. He gave

Alec a somber look and told him, "You are being very foolish. Major Ferguson will be back here soon. I'll leave you for him to deal with. Let me warn you that he will remember, as he remembers everything, that you ran away rather than come here to join us. He does not favor that kind of behavior. Because you are a fellow Scot to him, it could turn out even worse for you." Ordish motioned to the soldiers, who came forward at once.

Alec called out in fury to the Virginian, "What of my father and mother?"

"As long we have you, they will not be harmed—nor your evil-tongued grandmother."

"Will you see that they know where I am? That you have me here at the fort? Will you do that for me?"

"Why should they be informed? Why should I send a message to them?" Ordish was not pleasant now.

"Because they are friends to the Gilchrists. Jamie Gilchrist was my father's good friend. Has no one ever told you that?"

"Yes." Ordish looked at the quill, not at Alec. "I am told that you saved a very fine horse from rebels who killed James Gilchrist."

"Yes, and Master Gilchrist gave the mare to me. I do not have her now." Alec lied desperately, trying to save Sweet Lass and Lilias from any searching party Ordish might send out after the horse. "The mare was stolen from me some days ago. I came here on foot to the village."

The larger of the two soldiers volunteered, " 'Tis true, sir. He was afoot, coming out of old Deckard's living quarters."

"Why were you at the trader's at this hour of the night?" asked Ordish.

Alec lied again. "To fetch him medicines for his rheumatism. My grandmother is a herb wife."

Ordish laughed. "Yes, I have heard that, too. The widow of the rebel Munn, the witch wife, concocts such things. Well, this is of no importance to me. We have you, MacLeod. And we shall hold you fast until Major Ferguson arrives. Take him now." Ordish waved Alec and the two soldiers away.

Alec spent three days in the dim half-underground room that served as the fort's jail. He was alone for two days but on the third a man, a redcoat private, was thrown down the steps to join him. He was a jaunty little man, found guilty of drunkenness on sentry duty. He was talkative, once he had sobered up. As he scratched at a flea bite, he told Alec, "As I see it, you might have some luck, boy. You never joined up so you can't be shot for desertion. But as for me, I know I'm going to get a beating with a whip when Bulldog comes back here. Or I'll be shot. It all depends on Bulldog."

"Bulldog?" Alec's thoughts went to Marion and Sumter —the Swamp Fox and the Gamecock. Ferguson must be Bulldog, though to Alec he was the Red Beast. He wondered if Tarleton had a nickname, too. If not, White Beast would do very well.

While his fellow-prisoner slept, Alec sat in a corner of his prison thinking. By midafternoon he had made a decision. That night he asked the guard who brought him a supper of thin stew to take him to Cornet Ordish or whoever was officer of the guard that evening. He was going to enlist under Ferguson. If he enlisted, he should be allowed to leave the fort. Once out and away from it he'd head for home, get Sweet Lass, and ride off to find Colonel Marion. Or better yet, he'd go to the up-country near the Blue Ridge Mountains hunting Colonel Sumter. This was the only path of escape he could see.

Cornet Ordish was on duty that night. He was fairly cordial to Alec this time, and Alec wondered if he had been talking to the Gilchrists about him. If so Ordish didn't tell him. He gave Alec the quill again, and when Alec had signed his name to the proper paper, he gave him a silver shilling from the metal box of coins kept in a drawer in the table. Alec had accepted the "King's shilling," a token of his enlistment and his loyalty. The coin bore the heavy-jowled face of George III on it. The sight of the king's features made Alec think of his grandfather, and when later in a barracks he donned a scarlet coat at least two sizes too large for him, he cursed the king, Tarleton, Ferguson, Ordish, and everyone else he could think of who served the king. He hoped that his grandmother had cursed Ordish as well. His muttered curses were nothing but wind. Her curse was not a thing he would wish to have.

The thumping of a drum two mornings later informed the garrison that Major Ferguson had returned. The great gates of logs were opened, and Alec, in the hated scarlet coat, stood drawn up in a line to greet his new commander. The Scotsman rode a horse almost as fine as Sweet Lass. Alec wondered if his family knew his whereabouts, inasmuch as old Deckard had not seen him captured and he had not been permitted outside the fort. He knew one thing only—that Lilias would take excellent care of Jamie's mare—and the knowledge gave him comfort.

Patrick Ferguson's stern eyes flicked over his garrison as he rode by, his left arm raised in salute to their formal greeting, the men standing at attention. His right arm was still in the sling of black silk. Alec knew more about Ferguson by now. He was supposedly the best shot in the British army. In a year's time he had learned to shoot and fence with his left hand to compensate for the loss of his right. He had also developed a new type of rifle. Alec had seen one of them but had not handled it, though he had been assured that it was better than any American-made long rifle. There were few of the Ferguson rifles at the fort. The gun was too new and not yet adopted by the king's forces, who clung to the old-style Brown Bess musket.

Alec watched the major dismount close to him and the other newest recruits, who had yet to be issued muskets.

Ferguson, accompanied by two lieutenants and a captain and trailed by Cornet Ordish, came down the line of soldiers while the men who'd marched with him entered the fort. There were wounded among them, limping along, and more wounded in the wagons that came in behind the men. Alec wondered greatly what Patriots the Scottish officer had pitted himself against in the field. Alec stared straight ahead at one particular log in the palisade, praying that Ferguson would not remember him. To his relief, the Scot gave him only a look and went on with his officers. Ordish shot Alec a glance, though, as he passed

by. Alec found him, as Deckard had said, ambitious but
not unpleasant. He was a man who insisted on discipline,
but there seemed little cruelty in him. Alec dismissed
Ordish from his mind, concentrating on Sumter and his
desire to escape Fort Ninety-Six as soon as possible. Things
might change now that Ferguson had returned to take
command.

Alec caught the man's words to his captain as he and
his officers passed behind Alec's line of recruits. "Drill
these men hard to make soldiers of them as quickly as
possible. I'm going to have need of them soon. And see
that only those who joined my forces as willing volunteers
are permitted outside the fort. There are men here who,
I know, did not come to me of their own free wills. I
want no deserters among them. I want every man of them
at my beck and call when I require him!"

Alec's heart stopped beating for a moment. *Caught!* He
was trapped! He had put on King George's red coat for
nothing at all!

Then he heard Ferguson speaking again. "I ride out
again soon to seek rebels near the Blue Ridge Mountains.
When I send for men from here, I want you to march out
with them to join me at once." Turning on his heel, the
Scot walked away, leaving Alec sick at heart. He'd lost
all hope of getting away.

The days that followed were a nightmare to Alec. The
afternoon Ferguson had returned, Alec was forced to
witness the flogging of the man who had been in prison
with him. He was given fifteen lashes, and at the end of
his punishment he collapsed in a heap onto the ground,

his lacerated back streaming blood. Afterward, the intensity of Alec's training doubled. The very sergeant who had clubbed his father taught him how to use a bayonet, once he had demonstrated that he could shoot well enough to please anyone in the fort. The musket he was issued was not half so fine a weapon as the long rifle he had been using for hunting since he was ten years old.

With other recruits, Alec was not allowed out of the fort. He drilled inside its walls, wheeling and turning, constantly shouted at by the sergeant. He was even taught how to fire the fort's cannon and to sponge out the bore afterward to catch any live sparks. While he stood by a cannon one day he watched Ferguson and redcoat soldiers march out once more.

During the whole two weeks of exhausting training Alec learned only one thing about Colonel Sumter, and it lifted his heart. He overheard Ordish and a lieutenant talking once while he was sitting on a bench in a moment of sunshine cleaning his musket. They said that the great sum of twenty guineas had been put on Sumter's head. Anyone who brought Colonel Sumter captive to the British would receive a large reward in gold. Surely the Gamecock was alive—and not only alive, but free, and a thorn in the side of the king's army. Had Sumter been the enemy that Ferguson had fought? If so, Alec never heard the news, and he dared not ask an officer.

A courier came riding to the fort the evening of September 19. Alec watched him ride inside the walls and sprint for the guardroom. Then the sergeant came up behind Alec and ordered him into the barracks, leaving

the boy to wonder all night long about the courier's news.
The next morning Cornet Ordish ordered Alec's group
assembled. As Alec stood in the rain he thought of the time
Colonel Marion had spoken to his men telling them that
they would not be taking part in the Battle of Camden.
Standing in the second rank, feeling miserable, Alec heard
the cornet say, "Tomorrow morning we set out to join
Major Ferguson at Gilbert Town in the north. Fifty men
will march out with three officers. You men will be going."

At last! He was going out of the fort. Once outside, he
might be able to escape. But what if Ferguson planned
to fight a battle? Then, if Alec were unable to escape, he
would have to fire on Patriots. In his heart he made a
vow as he stood in the downpour. He would never do so,
though any one of Ferguson's officers would certainly not
hesitate to shoot him.

That last night another courier came riding to the fort.
Alec's sergeant was asleep. Tiptoeing past him, the boy
went to the door of the barracks and stood unseen in the
blackness. He heard the shrill voice of the boy courier
crying, "I've brought news."

"From Bulldog?" asked the sentry stationed before the
guardroom door.

"No, it comes from the east of the colony."

Colonel Marion? Alec sucked in his breath.

He watched Ordish come out to beckon the dismounting
courier inside, but before the courier entered the guardroom, Alec heard words that thrilled him. "There's been
some sharp fighting, sir, in North Carolina Colony in the
Great White Marsh. It's said to be Marion and his swamp
rats."

Ordish asked eagerly. "Has old Marion been captured then?"

Alec felt his lungs would burst. Then the courier said, "No, he fled back into the swamp. But my message is not about that, sir. It concerns another matter."

At nine o'clock the next morning Cornet Ordish and the other lieutenant led their fifty American Volunteers out of Fort Ninety-Six. They walked behind the officers, who rode at the head of the column. One of the soldiers was a drummer boy who kept up a steady beat for the soldiers to march to. Shouldering his Brown Bess musket, wearing the oversized scarlet coat, Alexander MacLeod came marching among them.

Villagers and some farm folk whom Alec recognized stood on both sides of the line of march. Alec glanced once to the left of him at a housetop. A man dangled from its eaves, his hands tied behind his back. Alec had heard at breakfast that eleven suspected rebels from the Section had been hanged at six o'clock. The courier from the previous night had brought not only news of Marion's exploits at the Great White Marsh but orders from Camden Town. The orders had been to have the rebels confined in the village jail executed. That decision could explain the gathering of people in the village. Some had come to enjoy the spectacle. Others, mourning, had come to take the bodies of the hanged home with them for burial.

Alec marched along in the muddy wagon tracks, his eyes on the thick red-coated back of the man ahead of him until he heard his name being called in Gaelic, and the words, "Look at me, Alec *dubh*."

He looked to his right and saw his mother in the crowd, her shoulders covered with a shawl but her head bare so she could be recognized. She was deadly pale. He hoped she had not witnessed the hangings.

He cried softly to her in Gaelic, "How de ye fare, Mother?"

"Well enough. Where do ye go, Alec?"

Not daring to say Ferguson's name, Alec said over his shoulder as he passed her, "To join the Red Beast, Mother."

The sergeant who had struck Lachlan MacLeod was on Alec's mother now, harrying her, pushing her away while cursing her. "Begone, woman, or you'll suffer for it."

Alec watched her stare past the sergeant at him, then whirl about and run toward the trading post. God be praised neither she nor his grandmother were among the rebels hanged that morning. He'd looked from rooftop to rooftop as he left the village. He'd heard that two women had been hanged along with nine men. So the British did not make war on women!

For three days they were marched hard through a sodden countryside and on the third reached the tiny hamlet of Gilbert Town, a hundred miles from Ninety-Six village. Gilbert Town was a wretched spot with only two cabins, a blacksmith's forge, and one thing else—a very large structure made of green logs. Alec soon learned that it was a pen erected to hold whatever rebel prisoners Ferguson had captured in this northern section of the colony, and he also found out that there were prisoners inside, though he did not enter it.

One of the redcoats who guarded the rebels came to

eat his supper at Alec's campfire that evening. He was a talkative man. "This morning," he told Alec, "Bulldog took one of the prisoners, a backwater man, out of the pen and gave him a horse and sent him back over the mountains with a message to his folk there."

"Backwater men?" Aye, the over-the-mountain men. Alec thought of the Neales, then spat out crumbs of corn bread and asked, trying to keep the eagerness out of his voice, "Is Colonel Sumter supposed to be over the mountains then?"

"Not that I know. Other men, the mountain men. The blacksmith said that they've been coming down out of the hills, giving us a fight, and then running back into the mountains. Bulldog's been trying to catch them, but he hasn't had any luck yet. So now he's warning them to stay home, or he'll take us marching over the mountains himself and burn their farms and hang all of their leaders. I heard what he said to the prisoner that he let go. 'I'll lay waste to you with fire and sword.' "

Alec gnawed thoughtfully at the crust, thinking of the mountaineers he'd seen at Gates's camp, while the guard went on. "The mountain men hate Ferguson because they say the British made allies of the Cherokee Indians and are bribing them to attack the farms over there." The guard gestured toward the north.

Alec wondered if Ferguson had been so very clever in sending a threat to the mountain men. Ferguson was a Scot —not an American frontiersman. He didn't understand such people. The guard droned on. "I heard talk once of those folk from a gunsmith in Philadelphia where I served an apprenticeship before I joined the American Volunteers.

These backwater men are very devils. They will travel two hundred miles by the sun and stars to kill one man they hate. Do you believe it?"

"Aye, it might be true." But then, so would Sumter or Francis Marion.

Ferguson's troops spent another day in rain-soaked tents, but on the morning of the twenty-fifth a courier rode in with news. Soon the camp at Gilbert Town was quickly broken, and the soldiers started back toward Fort Ninety-Six. Ferguson had heard by the courier that Colonel Sumter had appeared at the fort. The Gamecock at Ninety-Six! Alec was thrilled and dismayed at the same time. How could he fire on Sumter's men?

But Ferguson didn't march all the way to the fort. Suddenly he ordered his eleven hundred soldiers to change directions and march east. For three days they broke camp at dawn and marched for short distances, then made camp again.

And in the days that followed not once did they glimpse another force, though rumors were passed up and down the line and around campfires that there were armies about—armies hidden in the woods or just beyond yonder hill. Some men dared to whisper that Bulldog Ferguson was being hunted. But by whom? Still, the frontiersmen among them said they knew by Ferguson's manner.

Alec eyed the major, too, with great interest. Truly Ferguson seemed to be behaving in a strange manner, seldom sleeping, walking about the camp at all hours of the night with his face twitching nervously. He seemed unable to control the spasms in his cheek muscles. One night, in early October, while Alec was watching him, he saw his fellow Scot suddenly swing about and face the north and east. Then he strode off through the long grass with his black officer's cloak billowing out behind him. He had made up his mind to something, Alec sensed.

Ferguson marched his troops out before dawn of the wet morning of October 6, and without food led them at a quick march sixteen long miles toward the blue mountains. Alec had only one quick glimpse of the man as he rode past his group of militiamen, splashing them with mud from his horse's hooves. Ferguson's face was drawn with anxiety as he chewed his lower lip. His gaze was on the mountains —not on his men.

Ferguson called a halt at the bottom of a hill with heavily wooded sides. The hill was a beautiful blaze of gold and red trees set off by the dark green of pines, but the bright autumn beauty meant nothing to Alec, who could only wonder why Ferguson had stopped here.

His stomach was grumbling with hunger when all at once he saw Ferguson, some distance away, rise up in his stirrups and call out words he couldn't hear. But there was no mistaking the man's gesture. The major was pointing to the top of the hill.

Alec's hunger dissolved in panic. A hill. A high place? He asked a grizzled man behind him, who had been a fur trapper throughout North and South Carolina Colonies years earlier, in his youth, "What is this place?"

"They call it King's Mountain, boy."

"What does Major Ferguson plan to do up there?"

"Make a stand atop the hill, I suspect. He can see over the country in any direction from up there." The man snorted. "He means to make the rebels come to him atop King's Mountain!"

Horror rose in Alec's breast. This spot then was surely Jonet Munn's high place.

XIII
At the Top

Alec was angry as he climbed the sixty-foot-high hill. Aye, Major Ferguson was fey, as fey as Jamie. The Scottish officer was envisioning King's Mountain as a fortress he could hold against Colonel Sumter. What he seemed to have forgotten, or perhaps didn't realize, was that the hilltop could also become a death trap for them all if Sumter chose to surround them, starve them into weakness, and then attack them.

In his heart Alec was certain of one thing. This was the high place. And this was where he might die. Whatever happened here, men were surely going to die if Ferguson stayed at the top. And Alec was sure that Bulldog Ferguson would do just that. Ferguson's redcoats would die, but Americans they were in spite of their loyalty to King George, and the Americans who came against them would die. Whoever those Americans might be! Ferguson would not surrender to any army without a battle. He wanted glory. He wanted Americans to come against him.

At his sergeant's commands, Alec cut and piled brush taken from the mountain slope into heaps beside the redcoats who were going to cast musket balls from melted-down lead. He knew there would be no fires to attract attention on the mountaintop after dark. While he watched his sergeant and the others stir the melting lead in an iron pot over their fire, Alec asked himself who would be coming to King's Mountain in search of Ferguson. Colonel Sumter? More than likely it would be Sumter. Or perhaps Colonel Marion? Would they be men Alec knew? Could it be General Gates with the regathered remnants of the army that had fled Camden? Whoever came, one fact remained. The battle to come would be one between colonials —Americans all except for Ferguson himself.

That afternoon, the sixth of October, Patrick Ferguson walked nervously about the camp in the rain. Wrapped in his long cloak, he was a wraith in the mists. Sunk in gloom, Alec watched the man pace the five-hundred-yard length and forty-foot width of the hilltop, hating him. In the twilight Alec went to the northeastern rim beyond Ferguson's tents to see what he could of the countryside below. There was nothing visible but a gray blur under the rain. Earlier he had stood at attention with the other redcoats to hear the major shouting out, "This mountain is safe. From here I defy God almighty and all the rebels out of hell to drive me from it. No army of rebel bandits coming against me can hold together long enough to besiege me. And soon king's soldiers will come to relieve me." He had ended on a wild yelling sentence that made Alec shudder. "I am king of this mountain!"

It had been a frenzied speech, not at all the sort Colonel Marion would have made. Some men had cheered Ferguson. Others had looked from face to face and then stared at their shoes. As for Alec, he had thought throughout of his own colonel, wishing that he could be with Marion attacking Ferguson.

Now, as Alec turned back to the poor shelter of his shared tent, which had been wet for days and stank of mold, he saw the major behind him. He had not known Ferguson was there as he looked out over what he knew from the day's marching was gently rolling countryside.

Ferguson spoke to him very quietly. "You are a Scot, are you not?"

Alec nodded. It was the first time the major had ever addressed him since the terrible day on Alec's own property. He wondered if the man recalled his name, too, and waited to hear it spoken.

All at once Ferguson went into Gaelic. "I am going now to each and every fellow Scot among us," he said, "and asking him the same question before the night is over. Will ye show these colonials how a true Scotsman can stand and fight for King George?" Rain dropped from the front of his three-cornered hat.

Alec stared into his face. No, Ferguson didn't know his name. He doubted if the man remembered smashing his father's whiskey or ordering his sergeant to hit MacLeod with the musket. All Ferguson recalled was that Alec was a Scot, a "fellow Scot." The major's eyes seemed to have sunk back into his head. They were so dilated that they appeared black instead of blue.

Alec, held by their fevered gaze, mumbled, "Aye, sir," in English. He would not speak the Gaelic tongue to this man.

As Ferguson turned away at the call of a lieutenant who stood a distance away in company with Cornet Ordish, Alec sucked in his breath in despair. Fight? Fight hard for this man to bolster up the courage of the other redcoats. God in heaven, no! As Alec gazed at the three officers he thought of his grandparents. He wondered if Jonet Munn had set a curse on the Red Beast as well as on Ordish. He wanted to spin about and run down the mountainside at that moment. If the hilltop had not been bristling with Ferguson's sentries ready to shoot deserters, Alec would surely have rushed down the side of it.

All night it rained, and the next morning the downpour continued until noon. Then the rain stopped, though the skies continued sullen and gray. Around two o'clock a stiff breeze began to blow on the mountaintop. It chilled Alec to the bone and made him long for a fire to warm himself at, but by the major's orders there had been no fires since yesterday, when the musket balls had been molded.

Alec sat miserable next to a soldier near his own age who'd sought him out for company, though Alec was in no mood for talk. The young redcoat, worried as all the others were, rambled on for over an hour about his family. Alec was only half harkening to him, thinking of his family and of Sweet Lass, when suddenly he heard a howling screeching that brought him gasping to his feet.

An Indian war whoop! Alec had never heard the war cry of the Cherokees, but Grandfather Munn had. He had sometimes imitated it for Alec when he was small. Amazed, wondering at the sound of a war whoop at King's Mountain, Alec heard more. They came from many different throats. Had the Cherokees or the Creeks come down from over the mountains or from Georgia Colony against Ferguson? But how could that be? The Indians were supposed to be allies of the British. Did they think the army on the hilltop was American?

Then, intermingled with the war whoops, came the crackling of rifles from below. If these men were Indians, they had firearms.

Alec stood waiting. Redcoat officers began to shout orders to their men. Sword in hand, Cornet Ordish ran past Alec toward Ferguson's tents. The British drums beat a furious alarm. Over the shouting, drumming, and war cries of the attackers rose the high, piercing, ear-wounding note of Ferguson's silver whistle. Alec's companion, his face gone gray, sprinted away to his own unit as Alec's sergeant bellowed at his men. "The rebel devils are below in the trees. Fix your bayonets to your muskets, and follow me." He beckoned to the edge of the mountain nearest him.

Alec fumbled with his blade, fitting it to the musket. Then in a trancelike lumbering run, he joined the men from Ninety-Six in ranks at the southwest end of the mountain-top. Some of them faced west. Alec faced south, his musket ready.

A shouting rose from below. Alec couldn't catch the words, but the language sounded like English. Not Indians! Was it Sumter? Alec's heart blazed with a sudden hope, but then the hope faded. Sumter himself would shoot him down without challenging him because he wore a king's scarlet coat.

So Alec waited among the redcoats, his heart pounding with fright and excitement. He yearned to break free and run down off the hilltop, but his feet refused to obey his wish. He stood in the ranks watching Major Ferguson racing past him on horseback, his sword in his left hand. The Scot yelled as he passed Alec's group of soldiers. "Fire at whatever man you can see below. If they reach the top, attack with your bayonets. Give them King George's steel in their bellies." Ferguson dashed away to cry the same thing to other of his troops.

Alec MacLeod stared at the long, narrow-bladed knife at the end of his musket, then at Ferguson, whose horse was rearing in excitement some fifty yards away. This man was the one he wanted to shoot—not whoever was below. But he didn't lift the musket. He watched Ferguson ride toward the northeast end of the hilltop. Then, at his sergeant's sharp command, Alec looked ahead of him to the southwest edge of King's Mountain. "Run," his brain kept telling him, but still he couldn't move.

The rifle fire crackled from below, and the sound was nearing them minute by minute. Alec guessed what was happening. The attackers, whoever they might be, had come like Indians—approaching in absolute silence and under cover of the morning mists. They were moving from the shelter of one tree to the next, reloading as they came. His red-coated comrades were forced to fire down on moving shadows. The fighting would surely come soon to muskets and bayonets against long rifles in the hands of sharpshooters protected by tree trunks only a few feet away from Ferguson's unsheltered redcoats. They would kill or wound with every shot they fired. Aye, Patrick Ferguson had brought them all to their deaths! The redcoats defending King's Mountain would probably overshoot the attacking Americans. Shooting uphill, the Patriots could scarcely help but make every shot count.

Suddenly Alec saw the Americans scrambling up over his end of the mountain. They came in a swarm, firing as they ran. Alec stayed where he was as the scarlet-coated men who had stood beside him broke ranks and rushed yelling at the attackers with leveled bayonets after they had fired their muskets. In a space of a few seconds Alec was the only one left behind. He was frozen to the spot. The furious shouting of his sergeant didn't reach his ears as he looked at the throngs of struggling men in front of him. No, he could not fire on the attackers!

He turned his head to see what had become of Major Ferguson whose whistle went on shrilling, and at that very moment Alec was struck a sharp blow on his hip. It made him leap into the air, and when he turned his head he saw a snarling Cornet Ordish ready to hit him again with the flat of his sword. The man's face was red with anger, his mouth wide open in a roar, but in the din of shouting, drums, and Indian war whoops, Alec heard not a word Ordish was yelling at him. Alec stared for a split second at the cornet, then threw his musket down. *Now!* He was going to run. Let the Americans fire on him and kill him, but he would neither fire on them nor advance on them with the king's bayonet.

Alec spun on his heel to make for the trees, but as he

did, his corporal, at Ordish's screamed command, shifted his musket and with it struck Alec a hard blow on the left shoulder. Alec was felled in mid-stride. He lurched forward onto his face while redcoats rushed past him, howling defiance. Trying instinctively to save his face from the gravel and sharp rocks of the mountaintop, Alec spread out his arms to break his fall. An instant after he'd gone down, something struck him with great force on his left hand. He glanced at his hand, seeing with horror that the corporal's bayonet was stuck through it and deep into the ground beneath. Then, as he stared at the gravel below it, running scarlet with his own blood, Alec felt a heavy weight come crashing down on top of him. He twisted his neck as far as he could and saw that the corporal was on top of him. The man lay sprawled on Alec's back, his mouth opening and closing like a fish hauled out of a river. He'd been shot the moment after he'd thrust his bayonet through Alec's hand. The corporal's mouth fell open in a last sigh. His eyes glared into Alec's as his bayonet and musket stopped quivering in the center of the boy's hand.

Pinned to the mountaintop by the weight of the musket and the dead corporal, Alec MacLeod witnessed the hourlong battle by lifting his head now and then. He saw Ferguson ride by him twice, rallying his men between fierce assaults of the attackers. Once the major's horse jumped high over Alec and the dead corporal while the boy ground his face into the gravel expecting to be trampled.

And still the attackers came! They fell back into the trees when driven by redcoat bayonets halfway down the hill. They attacked again and again with war whoops and yells.

No one came to Alec to pull out the bayonet. Wounded men were piled up in heaps around Alec as the sharpshooter attackers reached the mountaintop for the third time. Alec heard the cries of Ferguson's wounded, "Quarter, quarter!" Lifting his head again, he thought he could see a white flag through the cloud of gray gunsmoke settling over the ground. The smoke burned his eyes and made him gasp for breath. Through a clear place, as the breeze blew the bitter-smelling grayness away for a moment, Alec saw another man he knew lying dead very near him. He was Cornet Ordish, lying on his side, his sword just out of reach of his hand. There was a small black hole in his brow that a rifle ball had made.

Ordish could not cry for quarter. Nor did Alec MacLeod. He'd already heard the attackers' reply to the words. It was a cry Alec knew all too well from his weeks with the Swamp Fox. It had been "Tarleton's Quarter"—no mercy.

At the end of an hour of attack and withdrawal, the top of the mountain was finally gained in full force by the Americans. Long legs in buckskin trousers ran past Alec toward Ferguson's tents at the northeast end. Alec raised his head to gaze after the running victors. Who were they? Some of them wore cloths tied around their long matted hair. Others had caps of raccoon skin. He recognized them by their great size and their buckskin clothing. There were no blue coats among them. They were not Sumter's men, and not Marion's swamp men. They came to King's Mountain with war whoops and long rifles. Alec knew they must be the over-the-mountain men, the people Ferguson had sent an insulting threat from Gilbert Town. The mountaineers had trailed him as an Indian would an enemy. Aye, Alec told himself. His "fellow Scot" would surely die today. He would never cross the mountains to burn the homes of these fierce fighters and hang their leaders. They had come to the mountain to kill the major.

A sudden crescendo of shouting and rifle fire arose from the opposite end of the hilltop. Over it came Ferguson's wild shrilling as he blew on his whistle. Suddenly the sound ceased, though the crackle of firing went on. So Bulldog Ferguson had been dealt with. No mercy would have been shown to the man. Alec sensed that the major had been killed.

But what of himself? He lay helpless in a red coat and prayed. His grandmother had not told him the dreadful truth to save him grief. He was to be killed here, too—to die with Ferguson.

A long time went by before anyone came to him and lifted the dead corporal off him. The man who did was a brown-bearded mountain man with bloodshot eyes and a gunpowder-blackened face. He stared at Alec's pinioned hand in surprised silence, then kicked Alec to see if he was alive. When Alec groaned, the man took hold of the musket, without saying a word, stepped on Alec's wrist, and in one swift movement pulled the bayonet out. Alec shrieked and fell into the blackness of a faint.

The sound of rifle fire awakened him. Struggling up to consciousness, Alec asked himself if the battle had been renewed? He thought of Tarleton's quarter and drew in his breath in fear. He was alive, but for how long?

Then he heard a hoarse, roaring voice calling out, "Three cheers for Liberty!"

Alec pulled himself to a sitting posture from where he

had been set down against a rock, his left hand throbbing. He looked up to see an enormous man large both in height and girth, standing a little distance away. Coatless in his linen shirt, the man had reddish-yellow hair and carried an unsheathed sword in his hand. He had called for the cheers for Liberty.

As the cheering echoed from every side of him, Alec looked about him. He was at the edge of a huddle of red-coated prisoners seated four deep on the mountaintop. They *had* received quarter. The man next to Alec was sobbing softly, his head in his hands. Armed mountaineers ringed the captured.

The battle of King's Mountain was over and was an American victory. Alec looked back at the man who called for the cheers. He was a complete stranger to him; no one he'd ever seen at Gates's or Marion's camp. He would never forget a man of this size. Alec watched as one of Ferguson's lieutenants came out of a smaller group of prisoners, took off his hat, and gave his sword to the stranger.

Holding two swords, the coatless American spoke again in his hoarse, rough voice. "My name is Campbell, Colonel Campbell. I am elected commander here. You've hunted us and we've hunted you more than once, and then gone home before you could find us again."

Alec snatched at the words. The mysterious armies in the up-country. These were the phantoms, the ghosts Ferguson could not find. Well, they had found him!

Colonel Campbell went on. "We've fought redcoats like you at Cedar Springs, Thicketty Fort, and Musgrove's Mill, and now we've killed your Major Ferguson here at King's Mountain. You are our prisoners. I have been told that

Ferguson had a physician with him in this camp. We brought none with us. When the physician has tended to our wounded, he will see to yours. I warn you, do not try to escape. Our sentries are watching. They will shoot you as we have shot some of you just now for firing on us with concealed weapons. Tomorrow you will go down off this hill with us."

A prisoner seated near Alec hooted, "Before Tarleton gets here with the Green Dragoons?"

The enormous American colonel chuckled. It was an odd sound, one Alec had never thought to hear again. Campbell said, "Do not expect to be rescued. We have had the news. Lord Cornwallis is abed with malaria, and Colonel Tarleton has a fever. They will not be seeking you. And as I have told you, your Major Ferguson is dead. We are going to leave him here on King's Mountain. If you cause us any trouble, we shall also leave you here with him. There's land aplenty for graves. We shall bury our dead up here and yours, also. I have already told my men today, 'For God's sake, quit. It is murder to shoot any more,' but if I am driven to it by your disobedience, I shall permit them to shoot all of you. Be warned."

Even through the great pain in his left hand, Alec was aware of most things around him that evening. Ferguson's physician came to the prisoners at dusk. He bandaged Alec's hand, but first he poured something like liquid fire onto it from out of a brown bottle. By its sharp smell it was turpentine. He said nothing about the wound but went on to the man next to Alec, who had been shot through the calf of his leg. Permitted to lie down and rest by a mountaineer guard, Alec listened to this guard and another talking, as night fell on King's Mountain. Their soft, slow words came to him in spaces between the unheeded pleas and groans of the wounded.

"There was some brave ones among old Ferguson's red-coats," said the first man.

"And there was some cowards, too," muttered the second man. Alec couldn't see his face in the darkness.

He longed to call out to them and tell them that he was not truly one of Ferguson's men—that he had ridden for Francis Marion and been forced into a red coat. But he dared not. He was ringed about by other prisoners. More than one of them would strangle him silently in the night if he told such a story. And what guarantee did he have that the over-the-mountain men would believe anything he said? He had no proof except that some of the surviving militiamen from Ninety-Six Section could identify him by name and would vouch that he was a coward who had been unwilling to serve voluntarily in the king's army and had been forced into it. That would not make the mountain men approve of him and release him. There were others on King's Mountain who had not come willingly to join Ferguson.

The sun came sparkling golden from behind white clouds the next morning as if it approved of the American victory. Still under guard after a painful, restless night, Alec was prodded to his feet from a nightmare in which he was still pinned to the hilltop. He moved away from the rock clumsily with his feet feeling like stumps of wood. It was very cold now on the mountain.

Alec looked about him at the mounds of red-coated dead,

soon to be shoved by Colonel Campbell's mountaineers into the shallow pits being dug. He saw Cornet Ordish's body being dragged by the arms and dumped into one completed pit and then another man thrown in on top of him. As he watched, Alec thought of Jamie's death. It seemed to have taken place far, far back in his childhood—not just four months past.

Major Ferguson's naked corpse lay beside the great pit, face up to the sun, with at least seven rifle balls in him. The Scotsman was going to be left to the turkey buzzards, wild pigs, and the wolves. More than men would be coming to King's Mountain! Alec had heard in the night that the Scot had fallen from his saddle at the first shot he took and had been dragged by one foot in the stirrup. As he had been pulled by his frantic horse along the top of the hill, other mountaineers had fired at him.

Over one hundred fifty of Ferguson's American Volunteers had been killed yesterday but only twenty-eight mountain men. Even fewer mountaineers had been wounded. Colonel Campbell was taking hundreds of redcoat prisoners down off the mountain to God knew where. They were filing off the hilltop now, Alexander MacLeod among them. As Alec passed Ferguson's body he noticed that another, much smaller, pit had been dug for the slain mountaineers. The dead here were laid out in a row and each man covered by a blanket.

Once he'd gone down the mountain trail among trees chipped by musket balls, Alec saw that the mountaineers were burning Ferguson's baggage wagons. The over-the-mountain men had ridden to King's Mountain, then had dismounted and fought afoot. Their horses had been kept by others at the base of the mountain. Some mountaineers were constructing horse litters for their wounded out of blankets and long poles placed on either side of two horses. They were not so considerate of Ferguson's wounded. The mountain men forced the captive redcoats to transport their heavy long rifles for them, first removing the flints so they could not be fired at their owners. In spite of his wounded hand, Alec was given a long rifle to carry. Then at a bellow from Colonel Campbell, the long column of defeated redcoats was started on the march with their watchful buckskin-clad captors riding on each side. Other mountain men had stayed on the hilltop to finish the grisly chore of burying the dead. When Alec left, they had really only started their work with Ferguson's dead.

Wounded redcoats supported each other as best they could that first day of marching away from the mountain. Ahead of Alec two soldiers from New Jersey half carried a man from New York who had had his leg shattered by a rifle ball. Behind him an unwounded soldier, a man of great strength, carried a boy militiaman with a wounded foot. Alec's left hand burned with pain as he walked along. He glanced from time to time at the mountain man riding on his right. He thought he was the same man who had pulled the bayonet from his hand. For the entire sixteen miles of marching that day, this man walked his horse beside Alec, but he never spoke to him, though Alec was aware of his watching him from time to time.

By twos and threes women of the countryside approached to speak with the guards. One, a young girl, asked in Alec's hearing of her brother, who had gone with Ferguson weeks past. The mountaineer riding beside Alec told her sharply,

"Look at the prisoners here as they pass, my girl. If you can't find your brother, go up there and look for him." And he jerked his thumb back over his shoulder at King's Mountain. The girl stepped aside to fasten her eyes on the face of every man who went by her. Alec hoped for a glad cry of recognition from behind him where four hundred other prisoners marched, but he heard none.

No one fed Ferguson's men that day or the next. The only water they had was what they scooped up hastily while they forded streams. In their haste to get away from King's Mountain where an army could come against them as they had come against Ferguson, the mountain men had taken little from the major's supplies. Alec knew the reason. They had believed their commander's tale that Tarleton was ill of a fever as little as Alec had believed it. They were wary of the swift-riding White Beast—though they had killed the red one. They wanted speed. The mountaineers themselves fared ill on the march. They ate only the parched corn they'd brought with them in leather wallets and drank brook water from tin cups.

Because he was very weak from loss of blood, hunger, and marching, Alec was thankful that Campbell forced them to march only two miles the next day. The day afterward the prisoners were turned loose in a sweet-potato patch where they dug food with their bare hands. That afternoon they were allowed to raid a field for the corn in it. This food gave Alec the strength to walk thirty-two miles that day and the next to Gilbert Town, where he had been before.

Here the long rifle Alec had carried was retrieved by its owner. Next he was shut up in the log pen Ferguson had used to confine rebels. Food was brought inside to the prisoners—more uncooked corn on the ear and raw pumpkins.

All of the redcoats were afraid. Alec shared some of their fears that the mountain men might shoot them at any moment of the day or night, but he had another secret terror. He was as much afraid to have Tarleton come riding to the rescue as he feared the backwater men. One of the Green Dragoons, one of Jamie's own troopers, could recognize him and he could be hanged for horse theft. A prisoner had heard from a guard that there would be military trials held for some of the more important of Ferguson's men, those the mountain men suspected of having stirred up the Indians against the mountain settlements in the past. All of Ferguson's officers might be executed. The mountain men wouldn't forgive scalpings of their families and the burnings of their homes. Sick with concern, Alec walked off to a corner of the pen and sat down with his knees drawn up to his chest. He folded his arms and rested his head on them. He might still die—die in this red coat he so hated. Aye, he was ill—and not just from worry and unhappiness.

The diet of raw vegetables had given him a flux of the bowels. His left hand, though its bandage was gray with filth by now, hurt less, though Alec knew that the bayonet had smashed through bones and tendons. He would never again use it with ease. Mercifully he was right-handed, and he didn't think the wound was infected. The wounds many others had taken at King's Mountain were. Each night men died in the pen and were carried out in the morning by the guards. Even those who weren't wounded suffered from griping pains in their bellies and cursed the raw food that was brought to them each day in baskets. Every time he ate raw corn, Alec was reminded of the pokeberries and the rum.

Lord, how small a thing that seemed compared to what had happened atop King's Mountain!

What was going to happen to him now? Would the over-the-mountain men simply walk inside the pen at any moment with their long rifles and shoot every prisoner until all of Ferguson's redcoats were dead? Alec had taken the measure of the mountaineers on the long march with them. He knew their full story by now. They had been infuriated by Major Ferguson's threat that he had dispatched to them with the prisoner from this very pen. They had sent couriers through their mountain settlements, urging a meeting at a special place. Men had come there from many farms and hamlets, and they had decided to come down out of the mountains in a body and attack Bulldog Ferguson before he could march on them. Many had journeyed out of the mountains to smash the king's major, but only 910 men, the best mounted and the finest shots of all, had been chosen by the mountaineers to fight against Ferguson. Now all of these men were very eager to go home, where they were needed for protection against the Indians. Furthermore, Ferguson was dead.

Not regular soldiers, more ruthless than Colonel Marion or Colonel Sumter, they would far rather kill redcoats than wait, feed them, and exchange them for captured Patriot soldiers. Daily they were growing more anxious about their undefended homes. To their way of thinking their work was finished for the moment.

From his now-accustomed sitting place against the logs, Alec looked up on the morning of the fifteenth of October and saw the gates of the pen open. Two mountaineers and a boy entered along with an officer who wore no uniform except for a cockade of fluted white paper in his hat. Alec recognized the very tall man and the boy beside him at once. Joshua Neale and his father! The other mountain man looked at a distance to be the very one who had pulled the bayonet out of Alec's hand. Joshua! Joshua could identify him.

The officer shouted for silence, though not a word had been said since he had entered with the Neales and the other man. Made wary by the officer's appearance, fearing to be shot, the prisoners had fallen silent at once. "I seek a boy named Alexander MacLeod of Ninety-Six Section," the officer called out.

Alec didn't move for several moments. Then with hundreds of men watching him, he got awkwardly to his feet. The officer strode to him through the seated prisoners, followed by the others. He grabbed at Alec's wounded hand, grunted at the sight of the foul bandage, and asked the man beside him, "Walker, is this the lad? Did you take the bayonet out of his hand?"

Alec was looking hopefully at Joshua Neale. Joshua's eyes had roved over Alec's face, but then his gaze had stopped at the sight of the red coat Alec wore. Joshua's father was also staring at him.

While the Neales went on examining Alec, the big man in the fringed and beaded buckskin shirt who had taken the bayonet out of Alec's hand told the officer, "It's the boy. He was the one."

"It is Alexander MacLeod," Joshua told the officer softly. He added, "I guessed it would be Alexander when I heard my father talking about his having black hair and blue eyes." Joshua spat out his next words in fury, "I see that he's a redcoat now. I wouldn't have believed he'd be a redcoat when I saw him at General Gates's camp."

"I'm not. . . ." Alec began.

The officer cut off his words. "Be silent. Let me see your hand."

Using his teeth and good hand, Alec stripped off the bandage that had been put on six days before and held out his hand. He forced himself to look at it. The deep puncture wound was a furious red and ringed about with dried blood, but not infected. The searing turpentine had saved him from that. Alec turned his hand over, showing the corresponding wound on the palm. The sight of it made the American officer grunt and say, "Come with me. Colonel Campbell wants to see you, boy." He motioned to the Neales to follow them.

Alec told Joshua as they went out of the pen, "Joshua, I never saw your father at King's Mountain, and I never saw you there."

"He was there and saw you. You are a traitor. I came here only yesterday." Joshua turned his face away from Alec as they went through the gates.

As Alec followed the men and Joshua through the prisoners, he held his left hand in his right. The unbandaged wound pained him very badly now that the chill air had struck it. He grasped Joshua's words with difficulty. Traitor? They thought he was a traitor. He had never thought that anyone would believe that. Dear God, what would he say now before Colonel Campbell?

Campbell had taken over the same house that Ferguson had used late in September. The officer took Alec by the shoulder and propelled him up some steps into its one room. It was crowded with talking men. Some were standing, their thumbs hooked into their belts within easy reach of Indian-style tomahawks. Others were seated on the floor smoking long clay pipes. The air of the place stank of dirty leather and tobacco.

More enormous than ever in such a cramped space, Colonel Campbell rose up from behind a table. "Bring that boy here to me," he called out.

Alec was pushed by the officer through the crowd to the table before Campbell who had sat down again. Campbell ordered, "Show me your hand, lad." When Alec did, the man nodded and looked to the mountaineer who had pulled out the bayonet. "Is it the boy, Walker?"

"It is, Colonel."

Campbell asked Joshua the same question. Then he said, "Tell me his name."

Joshua said scornfully, "He's Alexander MacLeod." His lip twisted. "It's as Pa and I told you earlier. He was with Colonel Francis Marion when we saw him first time. He says he tried to poison the greencoat Colonel Tarleton with pokeberries in rum."

Campbell let out a snort. "A likely tale, that one! It's the sort of thing a spy might say." The enormous officer went on, "So what do we have here? A lad in a red coat captured at King's Mountain. But not very long ago he was seen at

General Gates's camp by two people whose word I have had good reason to trust for a number of years. They say that at Gates's camp this boy was in the service of the Swamp Fox. Add to this: He was found at King's Mountain with a British bayonet in his hand." Campbell leaned back in his chair. "What's the answer to this riddle, I wonder?"

Alec looked at both the Neales, who were glaring at him with hatred, then at Campbell, whose eyes were cold and questioning. Alec half whispered, "May I tell you, sir?"

At Campbell's mocking nod he said, "I refused to fire on whoever came up there against Ferguson because I am a Patriot, too. I was forced into Ferguson's American Volunteers, but I still serve Colonel Francis Marion. Before God I do, I swear it! I am still his courier, but I was never able to escape from Ferguson. One of his corporals put his bayonet through my hand, so I couldn't escape to you even from the top of the mountain. I knew you might shoot me, but I was still running toward you." Alec stopped. "I hoped," he faltered, "that you'd be Colonel Sumter. He knows me."

Campbell snorted once more. "Do you think that Sumter would accept this story any more than I will—that we are such great fools as that? I think this is what truly took place: You refused to fight at all, and for your cowardice you were bayoneted by one of your own redcoat breed. You are a spy—not a soldier. You spied at Gates's Camp for the British, then came to Ferguson with the news you'd gained there and donned the king's red coat you always wore in your heart." Campbell shook his massive head. "You'll be brought to trial with some of Ferguson's men, and it's my thought that you'll be hanged as a traitor and as a spy. We won't set you free to make your way to Tarleton or Lord Cornwallis and tell them our names and where our homes are. You'll be hanged soon, mind you. We do not make a man wait. It's my plan to leave Gilbert Town as soon as possible."

"Yes, we want to go home now," Joshua Neale tossed at Alec in a fury. Spinning around, Joshua left the house, darting among the mountaineers. After a glance of contempt at Alec, his father went out behind him, shouldering his way through the crowd.

XIV

A Matter of a Feather

Back once more among the prisoners, Alec sat down again and this time turned his face to the wall, not wanting to talk to anyone. Hanging? He had never been able to put the memory of his grandfather's face out of his mind. And now he, too, was to be hanged, but by Patriots. Had Jonet Munn foreseen this very death for him—the same that her husband had suffered? It was a dishonorable death. Alec couldn't even take comfort in cursing King George and dying for his belief as old Munn had done. He suspected he'd be given a trial of sorts by the mountaineers, but judging from Colonel Campbell's manner, it might be no more of a trial than the one Jamie had given his grandfather.

Alec counted deaths in his mind—Duncan, his brother, five years past, Andrew Munn, Jamie, Cornet Ordish,

Major Ferguson, and soon his own—all because the war had come to the colony. Colonel Tarleton lived. Alec was certain that he did. No mere fever would put an end to the White Beast, the man Alec yearned in his heart to get in the sights of a long rifle—or better yet, within range of Jamie's pistol. But now he couldn't find Tarleton. He hoped that someday the Swamp Fox would hear how he had died. Marion would catch the reason for the bayonet through his faithful courier's hand. To him it would signify a brave deed and a death to be mourned.

The trials commenced the next day. Alec saw how prisoners, Ferguson's officers for the most part, were taken out of the pen under guard. Some hours later he and the other men inside heard cheering and shouting at intervals. They knew the noise for what it was. The mountaineers were hanging men they considered more than ordinary redcoat prisoners. Alec could not blame the mountain men, who were avenging tomahawked and scalped children and wives.

But not all of the men taken to trial were hanged. Four returned that afternoon to the palisade. Others clustered about to talk with them, but not Alec, who knew they had been found innocent. Three of them gabbled wildly of their escape, or so he judged from the sight of their mouths spouting words and their gesturing hands. The fourth man knelt praying, murmuring words in some language Alec couldn't identify, though he had gone down onto his knees near him. The fourth man stopped only when the gates were opened and two tall guards carrying long rifles walked in.

One of them bawled out, "Alexander MacLeod of Ninety-Six Section."

Alec got to his feet and, holding his left hand in the

other, came slowly forward through the prisoners. Some eyed him as he passed, but most kept their faces bent on the ground. The praying man called after him in English, "May God help you, boy. I'll pray for you."

His throat a lump of misery, Alec had only time to look behind him and nod to thank the stranger who had escaped the mountaineers' justice.

There were trees around Gilbert Town—many tall and strong enough to bear the weight of a man at a rope's end. Alec expected to be led to one, be lectured by Colonel Campbell, and hanged. He kept his gaze away from the trees as he walked between the guards. By now he had seen enough hanged men to last him a lifetime—and women, too. Aye, Major Ferguson had ordered women hanged at Ninety-Six village, come to think on it.

Alec was taken to the same cabin and pushed inside. It was again packed with lounging mountaineers. He spied out Joshua Neale's father by his extraordinary height as he stood beside Campbell's table. As Alec was propelled there, he thought he scented something other than dirty, sweaty buckskin and tobacco. It was the herb rosemary. Rosemary here? Alec glanced to his left where a long bench had been set up since yesterday.

Five people sat on it now. Joshua Neale at the near end, then the man Walker, who had jerked the bayonet out of his hand. Next there was a fellow with spectacles astride his nose and a three-cornered hat on his head. He was looking intently at his fingernails. Beside him was a slight boy in a coonskin cap, and at the very end a woman wrapped in a long, black mantle. Here? A woman? Colonel Campbell's wife? Or perhaps Joshua's mother come over the mountains too? The perfume of rosemary must come from her clothing. Alec could not see her face because she had the mantle pulled around her head, though he sensed that her eyes were upon him.

Colonel Campbell's voice rose harshly from his great chest as he glared at Alec. "Alexander MacLeod, is it, again?"

Alec felt giddy. His heart was racing and his hand throbbed with pain. He wished he could clutch at the table to support himself, but he feared to. His own voice sounded leagues away as he said, "Yes, sir."

"You are here to be tried for your life, you know."

"I know, sir, but I am not a spy for the king, and I never fired on any one of you on the hilltop. It is because of that that my hand's wounded. I do serve Colonel Marion as his courier." Alec had thought the night before of what he would say if he got the opportunity.

"I can tell you what Colonel Marion looks like, the name of his horse and servant, and what he was doing on the Santee when he sent me off to find Colonel Sumter."

"Any spy who'd been at Gates's camp at Deep River could know those things and any spy could tell me anything at all about Marion's work on the Santee, because I have no idea what that might be. The Neales, father and son, swear to me that they saw you among Colonel Marion's men. They saw you in his tent with Colonel Sumter. How in the devil did you gain their confidence?"

Alec answered, "I served Marion, sir. I rode with messages for him. I was his courier."

"Did you ever meet any of Sumter's men or only Sumter himself?"

Alec thought. Aye, there was one. He hadn't mingled with Sumter's troops at Deep River, but he had met someone else besides the Neales. "Only one man, colonel. He was a courier for Sumter."

Campbell was scowling. "Where did you meet him?"

"On the road to Camden Town after the battle, when Colonel Marion sent me out to get news for him."

"What was this man's name?"

"Jessup, sir. Tom Jessup, he said it was."

"Jessup, Tom Jessup." Campbell's voice rose to a roar. "Is Jessup here?"

"No, but Tom Briggs is!" The man sitting on the bench next to Joshua Neale arose and took off the spectacles he was wearing, putting them into his coat pocket.

Alec gaped. He was Tom Jessup—but greatly changed. He was very much thinner, yet his eyes were the same and so was the line of his mouth. He was not smiling now.

Campbell asked, "Do you say this is Jessup, boy?"

"I think he is, though he did not wear spectacles when I saw him, and he was a fat man then."

Campbell asked the man who had called himself Briggs, "Do you recognize this boy?"

"I do, sir. He is Marion's courier."

The answer made the American colonel grunt. Then he turned his head to look at the bench once more. He called to the thin boy seated beside Briggs. "You, the small lad, get to your feet now."

The boy leaped up. He took off his hat and held it against his chest, then came forward without asking permission, threading his way nimbly among the large-bodied mountaineers. Alec couldn't believe his eyes. First Jessup who was really Briggs and who scarcely seemed the same man at all, and now this boy who was no boy at all. For under the tumble of short dark curls he saw his sister, Lilias.

"*You?*" he managed to whisper, as she flung herself on him and wound her arms about him. Then she flared fiercely at Campbell, "He's my brother, Alec. You'll not hang him. He's no redcoat, and he's no spy for the king."

Campbell ordered sternly, "Have that wild lad removed to the bench and bring the man Briggs here."

As a struggling, biting Lilias was hauled off, Briggs came forward, taking off his hat.

"Briggs, what man do you serve under?" asked Campbell.

"General Sumter, sir."

Briggs smiled at Alec. "I know Alexander MacLeod well enough to recognize him even in a damned red coat, sir. I was in Marion's camp on the Santee River when he ordered MacLeod to ride out and find Colonel Sumter after the defeat at Fishing Creek. I might have been sent in his place, and by rights I should have gone, but this boy had the swifter horse and then I was somewhat heavier, you see. I had a fever for a time and grew thinner after that."

Campbell put in sourly. "It seems MacLeod found Ferguson, not Sumter."

Alec protested. "Sir, Ferguson's men found me!"

"*No,*" Lilias shouted from the bench. "He did not join Ferguson!"

Alec saw the woman seated next to her put her hand on Lilias's knee. At the same time the woman threw back the hood of her mantle. His grandmother! Jonet Munn had come here, too? She put her finger to her lips, asking him for silence. Alec didn't need to be warned to be quiet. He was without speech. He had wondered at the presence of his sister, but his grandmother, too! What were they doing here? How had they come?

Campbell was speaking again. "Briggs, did you ever use the name of Jessup?"

"Yes, sir, I do now and then. All Sumter's couriers have more than one name ready to their lips. I took that name to protect the identity of my family in case the British caught me."

Colonel Campbell nodded, then wanted to know, "Do you know this other boy and the woman?"

Sumter's man nodded in return. "They are from Ninety-Six Section. They are his brother and his grandmother."

In spite of his dangerous situation Alec felt like laughing. Lilias had passed herself off very well as a lad. Doing so would be the sort of thing she would enjoy. She had deceived both Briggs and Campbell.

"So they claim to be," grunted Campbell. "Where did you first meet these two?"

"At General Sumter's camp five days past. They came seeking the general. He sent me off with them when he learned their errand."

Alec couldn't believe his ears. His grandmother and Lilias had found the Gamecock. Where? He shook his head, struck dumb with surprise.

"I thank you, Corporal Briggs. Sit down." Then Campbell called out, after consulting a piece of paper on the table, "Mistress Munn, if you please, come here."

Jonet Munn got up. Erect as a girl, she came to stand next to Alec. She didn't embrace him but only looked very calmly at him out of her strange eyes. Then she fixed those eyes on Campbell.

"Tell me your tale, woman."

Alec shifted his position. In his wildest dreams he had never expected that his sister and grandmother would be present when the mountaineers tried him for treason.

Jonet Munn spoke very softly in English. Alec had never heard her use that language, but she spoke it smoothly. "I shall tell you if you ask me with courtesy, Colonel Campbell."

"Mistress, I do ask you with courtesy." The mountaineer officer was addressing her not in English but Gaelic. Campbell. Of course! The name was as Scottish as MacLeod—or as Ferguson. And the thought had never occurred to Alec.

His grandmother told Colonel Campbell, "I will speak English here, sir, so all may understand me. I believe it will come as a surprise to my grandson that I can speak it with ease. I have always used the Gaelic to my family, because my husband did not like me to speak the tongue of the English."

"Where is your husband, Mistress Munn? It seems odd for a woman your age to be traveling around the countryside without a man."

Jonet Munn smiled. "Dead, hanged by king's troopers earlier this year. Alec saw him hanged. As for having no man, Corporal Briggs guarded us well on our way from General Sumter's camp."

Campbell frowned at both the old woman and at Alec.

Then he asked Jonet Munn, "What brings you to me here?"

"We've come, the three of us, seeking Alexander Mac-Leod, who was forced into Major Ferguson's army." For a moment she stopped, then she went on easily. "First of all, Alec's younger brother here"—she pointed at Lilias—"and I came to King's Mountain following Ferguson's troops. We'd followed Ferguson for days. We climbed to the top while some of your men were still burying the redcoat dead. You had marched away already. We turned over those men who were not yet buried to see their faces. We did not find Alec among them, and no one who was burying the dead soldiers could recall burying a lad such as my grandson. We guessed he had marched off among your prisoners—though by rights he should not be among them at all—so we came down off the mountain."

"But, woman, you didn't follow *us* to see if we held the boy prisoner. You could have done that. Why didn't you?"

"No, Colonel." Jonet Munn shook her head. "I knew that Alec wore a red coat and that you would surely think him to be a true king's soldier. We made our way from King's Mountain to Sumter's camp. I knew that Alec had been sent out weeks past by Colonel Marion to find Sumter."

"How did you find Sumter?" Campbell put one very large hand on the table and leaned back in his chair.

"By means of my wits and by means of this!" She reached into the pocket of the mantle and brought out a green, gold, and black cock's feather. Then she turned to smile at Alec. "Master Deckard, the trader at Ninety-Six village, is a friend of mine and also a strong Patriot. He loaned me his dead wife's warm mantle, and he gave me this feather because he knew its meaning, though I did not." She looked back to Campbell. "Wherever we rode, I showed folk this feather. Surely enough a farmer at last told us where to find Sumter when I waved it under his nose as if it were something that had fallen out of a fine Charles Towne lady's fan." She chuckled. "We'd sought to find a colonel but instead we found a general."

Campbell let out a deep wheezing sigh. He spoke to Joshua Neale's father, who was not quite so grim about the mouth as before. "Tell me the significance of the feather."

"Such a token is often carried by Sumter's people."

Briggs spoke up next. "I can vouch for that if any man can. I carry such a token."

Campbell addressed Jonet Munn once more. "Mistress, did you see General Sumter?"

"Aye, sir."

"What did he say to you?"

Her laughter was a lilting sound in the cabin of rough men, who were hanging onto her every word. "He said to me that he well remembered the clever lad who put pokeberries into the rum Colonel Tarleton and his men drank. He praised our Alec for the deed. He said more than that to me, though."

"What was that, woman?"

Gently Jonet Munn took Alec's wounded hand and held it. "He said that the boy was black-browed, ill-favored, and smelled to high heaven of the swamp, but he said that Colonel Marion found much merit in him." She went on, as Alec's heart swelled, "General Sumter heard that I was seeking Alec, who had been taken away by Ferguson. He knew that Corporal Briggs had met Alec, so he sent Briggs with me. He said that Briggs would be able to pluck Alec out of your lot of prisoners."

Campbell shook his head as he gazed up at Alec. In Gaelic he said, "Aye, the lad is swart and not one bit bonny, but he seems to have wit." Changing to English, he went on to say, "Alexander MacLeod, I believe your tale now of how you came by the bayonet in your hand. You may go with these people who have come looking for you. Where do you propose to go?" His question was for Jonet Munn rather than for Alec.

She said, "Home, once we've put Alec into a better coat and sent him on his way. His breeches are no more white now than the coat I have for him, they are so filthy. No one would know they are the breeches redcoat soldiers wear, and he can take off the gaiters."

"Where will you be going?" Colonel Campbell asked Alec.

"To Colonel Marion, wherever he might be," Alec cried out in joy.

Corporal Briggs put in, "I know where he is—or rather I know where I saw him last. But that was a month past."

Campbell held out his hand to Alec's good one. Alec gave it to him, and Campbell crushed it in his grip. "Tell Colonel Marion what took place atop King's Mountain, boy. Tell him who came there against Ferguson. Tell how we nearly hanged you as a spy. I was set upon doing it."

"I'll tell him, sir."

Jonet Munn added in Gaelic as Campbell released Alec's hand, which now pained him almost as much as the wounded one, "Alec will bear ye no ill will, sir. It is only

right that ye'd consider him a spy and think to hang him."
Campbell replied in the same language, "It's my guess
that ye set a curse on Major Ferguson, did ye not?"

"I had no need to, sir, but I set one on the young officer
who came to us seeking Alec three days after Alec's father
was made witless by Ferguson's orders. What grandmother
wouldn't do such a thing to such a man?"

"Do not curse me, old woman." Campbell's Gaelic words
amused Alec now that he was recovering himself and no
longer terrified of the mountaineers.

Jonet Munn said, "Na, but I should curse ye because ye
did not put a clean cloth on my grandson's hand."

"Such a deed would be coddling prisoners, Mistress
Munn." Campbell's grin had faded. "Why were you following your grandson?"

In Gaelic again Jonet Munn told him, "To help him
escape, Colonel, sir." Campbell gaped and shook his head.
Suddenly she asked him, "Are we free to go now?"

"You are—all of you. Take your horses. You'll find them
where you left them. We are not horse thieves, whatever
else you think of us. I'm told the horse this boy's small
brother rode is a very fine one."

Alec's heart leaped. Sweet Lass? They had brought the
mare with them. He whirled about, making for the open
door. At the threshold, though, he heard Campbell thunder-
ing at him. The words were in English, and they made the
cabin rock with laughter. "They claim you have some wit,
boy, and to poison Tarleton you must have some. But what
of your coat, you young fool? Do you plan to wear that to
seek out Colonel Marion?"

Alec looked in dismay at the scarlet coat. Using his right

hand, he struggled out of it and let it drop to the threshold. Wearing his homespun linen shirt, he ran out of the colonel's headquarters to freedom.

He did not see Joshua Neale slip out behind him and dash behind the cabin.

Jonet Munn, Lilias, and Briggs met him outside as he stood shivering in the wind. Now that he knew he wasn't slated to die today, Alec took note of the weather. The sun shone very brightly, though the October wind was chilling. The four of them waited together until a man and boy came up, leading three horses. One was a clean-limbed black, a horse Alec didn't recognize. He guessed it belonged to Corporal Briggs. Another was the chestnut gelding that the Munns owned. The third was his own beloved Sweet Lass. With a shout of joy Alec ran to her and clasped her about the neck. Affectionately she nuzzled him. As he muttered loving words to her in Gaelic, he became aware that the Neale boy had brought her to him and was holding out her reins to him.

When Alec had taken the reins, Joshua gravely held out his hand. He said very soberly, "If you'd take Colonel Campbell's hand, Alexander, I ask that you take mine. I am glad you weren't hanged."

Alec hesitated, then took Joshua's hand, which was almost as dirty as his.

Joshua jerked his head toward the mountains, blue in the distance. "I live on the Nolichucky River, Alexander. When the war's ended, come visit us." He grinned at Alec. "You'd never believe it by looking at me, but I have a very pretty sister, Alice. She's fair as a lily. I told her once about you and Tarleton and the rum. She thinks you are clever."

Alec smiled at him and said, "I'll come see Alice some-day, but not until the war's ended. There'll be other battles, Joshua. We may have to fight in them, you know."

"I know," said the mountain boy, looking less than happy at the prospect.

Jonet Munn's ringing call in Gaelic reached Alec. "Come away now, Alec *dubh*. I've got bread and meat for ye and a cloth for your hand."

"She's fetched a coat for ye, too, just as she said she would!" shrilled Lilias, "And she's got something more. It belonged to our Jamie."

Jamie's pistol! Jonet Munn had thought of everything!

Alec turned once more to Joshua Neale before he pulled Sweet Lass over to the chestnut. Briggs was already mounted and waiting. Alec spoke to Joshua, "I doubt if you'd believe it, but I have a bonny sister, too!" He jerked his head toward Lilias.

The astonishment on Joshua's face delighted Alec. He guessed why Lilias had cut her hair. To travel more safely around the war-torn up-country with her grand-mother. Someday he might learn whether this idea was his grandmother's or his sister's.

"Her name is Lilias. You must come visiting us."

Alec hauled the mare forward to his family.

Sumter's courier spoke to her as Jonet Munn helped Alec into a snuff-brown coat he'd never seen before and Lilias unbuckled the black gaiters. He suspected Master Deckard had also supplied the coat. Then his grandmother bandaged his hand with an old linen cloth after putting on some sweet-smelling grease from a jar in her cloak pocket. Briggs told him, "Your grandmother here found General Sumter near a place called Cowpens. General Sumter is sending me out again—to seek Colonel Marion wherever he might be. So you can ride with me." He looked hard at Alec. Aye, Briggs could know exactly where Marion was, but he was not about to reveal this secret to Jonet Munn or Lilias.

"First, Alec must eat." Lilias reached into the chestnut's saddlebag and brought out bread and a slab of meat, which she gave to her brother. While he ate, she went around the horse to rummage in the other saddlebag and came back with Jamie's pistol, which she put into Sweet Lass's saddle holster.

After choking down a great chunk of bread, Alec asked her in Gaelic, "Did ye fire it when ye rode Sweet Lass here, Lilias?"

"Na, I had nothing to fire it at." She sounded rather disappointed, he thought. Then she asked him, "What of Ellen's pretty redcoat officer? Is he a prisoner in there, too?" She pointed at the pen.

"Na, he is dead. I saw him buried on King's Mountain before I came down."

"Ochone," came from Jonet Munn. "Alec, ye must ride to visit her when the war is ended. 'Tis said now that the Gilchrists will go to Charles Towne till then. When it is finished, they will come back."

Alec nodded and said to Briggs in English, "Forgive us, that we talk in Gaelic. We are speaking of matters at home."

"Do as you please, MacLeod, but do not take overlong. We have a distance to cover before the sun sets."

As Briggs walked his black horse away, Alec asked swiftly, "How is Father?"

Jonet Munn replied, "Little better—but no worse."

"Grandmother, will ye be safe riding home?"

"Aye, trust to my uncanny eye and two sets of very nimble wits, Alec *dubh*. No man but Master Deckard and no woman but your mother knows that we followed ye and Ferguson."

As he finished the last of the meat, Alec told her, "I've seen the high place and know what ye meant by my left hand. Now tell me true. What lies ahead for me, Grandmother? The Red Beast is dead. The White Beast will not die if only one of the two is to die."

The old woman nodded. "Tarleton will not die but the great honoring he seeks will forever escape from the wicked man. Ye'll see him again. He'll fight against your Colonel Marion as well as against wee, braw General Sumter, Alec, *dubh*. And Tarleton will no more use one of his hands with ease than ye will. Kiss us now, and we'll go home."

Alec kissed them both, then, unthinking, put his hands together to make a stirrup to help his grandmother mount the chestnut. Lilias had already scrambled up. Lacing his fingers together made him cry out in pain as his fingers touched the back of his wounded hand.

At his cry, Joshua Neale ran forward and helped Jonet Munn.

"I thank you, lad," she told him in English. Then she bent from the horse to ask him, "Are there trading posts over the mountains where you live? Would a man who will never follow a plow again find much profit there?"

Joshua took off his hat. "Yes, mistress, there are traders.

We have need of more trading posts—or so my father says."
Alec noted how Joshua peeped shyly at Lilias, who had
caught his eyes on her and had stuck out her tongue at him.

Na, thought Alec, as he mounted Sweet Lass. Lilias
would want the farm they already owned. She was welcome
to it. There wouldn't be any difficulty in informing his
mother that he wanted to be a trader, not a farmer. He
could not do the work of the farm with a maimed hand. If
Joshua wanted to be a farmer, he might someday seek
Lilias out. But given Joshua, the mountaineer, Alec doubted
it. However, Lilias would have no lack of suitors willing to wed her and farm the good land of the MacLeods.
His sister and her husband someday would look after his
father and mother. And, in the meantime, Jonet Munn was
there with them. Alec smiled as his grandmother reined
the chestnut away. He had noticed her shoes as she
mounted. She was wearing Donal Bean's glittering shoe
buckles. He suspected that Donal Bean would pass through
the war unharmed and come riding back in such splendid
finery as he had promised.

He cried out to her, "I thank ye."

Holding tight to Sweet Lass's reins, calming her, Alec
kept his eyes on his grandmother and sister until they'd
gone a distance to the south and west. He sent part of his
heart with them in a silent prayer until Jonet Munn turned
the old horse about so both of them could wave at him.

Taking off his hat, he waved it at them, then turning
Jamie's beautiful mare he trotted through the throng of
mountaineers to where Briggs tarried beyond the prison
palisade.

While he'd waited for Alec, Briggs had put a cock

feather into his hat. Seeing Alec ride toward him, he stood up in his stirrups, yelled, beckoned with his hand toward the south and east, then set spurs to his black.

Alec gave Sweet Lass her head. He knew her mind. She wanted to outstrip the black horse in a race. She sped forward, following the black, racing to wherever Francis Marion might be.

So he, Alexander MacLeod, was taking news of victory to his colonel—welcome news. This time it would not be news at second hand from someone who had not been at any battle at all, such as the news Briggs had brought of Camden.

Colonel Marion should take a very great interest in hearing who had come to King's Mountain. No one could tell that tale to him so well as a man who had been there—a man the Swamp Fox found merit in!

Authors' Notes

HISTORICAL BACKGROUND

The Scots

Each of us has taught American history at one time or another, and each time we have been surprised at the simplistic view of most students regarding the American Revolution. Nine out of ten have thought in very distinct terms such as Patriot and Loyalist, Whig and Tory, Americans and British, redcoats and bluecoats. In fact, the Revolution was a very complex historical event involving people of many, many political persuasions. There were not only colonists of differing faiths but colonists of different backgrounds and traditions. For instance, there were the German settlers in Pennsylvania, the Dutch in New York, the Scots-Irish—men from Ulster—in what is now Tennessee (and was at that time North Carolina) and the Scots Highlanders in both South and North Carolina. Each member of these groups had to come to grips with the issues of the Revolution in the way they affected his group—as well as individually, according to his own ideas and conscience.

In *Who Comes to King's Mountain?* we have chosen to write of the Highland Scots in one particular colony, South Carolina. This is a book we've had in mind for a number of years while we've been writing other novels for young people dealing with the history of England and Scotland. From our previous teaching of United States history we had learned that most of the Highlanders who had emigrated to the Southern colonies chose the side of the British during the Revolutionary War. Knowing something of Scottish historical relationships with England, we wondered greatly at this. Why should the Scots Highlanders, who had so many reasons to hate both the English and the ruling house, support the British? We learned in the course of our research that this same question had also bedeviled other scholars in American history. These scholars were aware of the battles the Scots had fought for centuries against English armies —battles chiefly fought on Scottish soil. From 1603 to 1688 monarchs of Scottish descent had ruled England. In 1688, the last of them, King James II, was driven off his throne by an uprising of the English people. His two daughters ruled after him, one after the other, but he considered them usurpers. In 1714, his younger daughter, Queen Anne, died. The English people offered the crown of England then not to James, but to the German prince who became George I, ancestor of the present royal family of Britain.

Throughout the eighteenth century the descendants of James II claimed the thrones of Scotland and England. Though they lived in exile on the continent, they mustered armies to fight the English. These armies were chiefly composed of Highland Scots, men who gave their loyalty to King James and to his son and grandson.

There was a revolt in Scotland against the English in 1715. It was crushed but later followed by an ineffectual plot in 1719. The Scots suffered for both. In 1745, a third rebellion culminated in a terrible battle, the Battle of Culloden, in which

Bonnie Prince Charlie, the claimant to the throne of George II, led his Highlanders to defeat. The English struck back at the Scots with great savagery. They slaughtered entire families of Highlanders, forbade the Scots to wear the tartans of their clans or the kilt, and transported men (and some women) in chains to the colonies, where they were sold into bondage for seven years as indentured servants. Some Highlanders were, indeed, branded on the face as traitors. These people, like the Andrew and Jonet Munn of our story, would naturally hate the English.

Why then a loyalty to King George III among so many Highland Scots in the American colonies?

For one thing a large number of Highlanders had left Scotland voluntarily for the New World during the 1730's and 1740's because the rocky Highland soil would not support a farmer and his family. These Gaelic-speaking people, though they wore the kilt at times in the New World, had turned their back on their homeland for the most part. Although they often lived in close-knit settlements of their own group, they were not truly involved anymore with Scotland. They liked the good land given them by King George—whether George I, George II, or George III. They supported these kings largely for economic reasons.

We think the reaction of the South Carolina Scots to the Revolution is a facet of American history that will interest young readers, so we have made our Alec MacLeod a colonist of pure Scottish descent. We suspect that there were many young people, like Alec, who were forced to examine their own hearts and choose a side for themselves. The various choices that would have faced them as Highlanders are exemplified by the positions of Alec's father, Jamie Gilchrist, Andrew and Jonet Munn, and Donal Bean.

Perhaps the easiest way to explain the stand taken by Alec's father and Jamie Gilchrist—and granted it is oversimplified—is to say that their adherence to King George III stemmed from the defeats the Scots had suffered in Scotland earlier in the century. The Scots in the Southern colonies of America didn't want to become "four-time losers." Yet, this is exactly what happened to them when the British lost the war. Many of these Scots left the colonies to settle in Canada as exiles at the end of hostilities.

Those who remained, whether they had chosen to fight for the Patriots or for King George III, maintained their Scottishness for many years after the Revolution. Tradition says that the last sermon in Gaelic was delivered to a South Carolina congregation in 1860.

The Irish and Scots are said to be specifically gifted with paranormal talents. Second sight, which would today be called precognition, was accepted as fact among the eighteenth-century Scots and Irish. It was a "gift," bestowed on both women and men, and, though considered uncanny, was accorded respect. Gazing into a fire was one method of divining the future.

South Carolina Colony

Some things we have written about South Carolina in the eighteenth century might raise eyebrows today, but they are attested to in our sources. Readers may feel that it rains a very great deal in this book. Quite true. It did. The spring, summer, and fall of 1780 were unusually rainy, so much so that the British army was often greatly hampered by flooded rivers and muddy roads.

The state was much more heavily wooded in 1780 than it is today. There were many trees and thickets as well as canebrakes standing from twelve to thirty feet high. In 1780, there were a very large number of wild animals in the up-country. A man could live easily as a hunter. At that time there were no large lakes. Although modern South Carolina has several enormous lakes, they are man-made, created during the first half of this century.

Some of the place names we've used might make readers wonder. Charleston was spelled Charles Towne in 1780. Camden was called Camden Town much of the time. Gilbert Town has disappeared completely as a community. Ninety-Six, however, survives, though as a smallish town. Its peculiar name deserves some explanation. It was called Ninety-Six because as a trading spot on the Keowee Trail it was ninety-six miles from an important Indian village farther to the north and west. In the eighteenth century a palisade fort in the shape of a star was erected near the town.

THE PEOPLE WHO APPEAR IN THE BOOK

The British

MAJOR PATRICK FERGUSON was born of an aristocratic Scottish family in 1744 and entered early into a military career. He served in the West Indies for a time and won some renown there as a soldier, but he gained his chief fame as the inventor of a breech-loading rifle in a day when the accepted weapons were muzzle loaded. His rifle was ahead of its time and used only briefly by the king's forces. In 1777, red-haired Ferguson came to America. He was given the post of commander of the American Volunteers, a Loyalist unit, some time later. Wounded in the right arm in the battle of Brandywine, the determined Ferguson learned how to fence and shoot left-handed.

His threat sent to the over-the-mountain men in September, 1780, led to his spectacular death atop King's Mountain. A boy soldier was pinioned through the hand by a bayonet at this battle. After the battle courts-martial were held by Colonel Campbell of some of Ferguson's officers and men who were accused of "crimes of war." Nine were hanged—six of them officers.

We "came" to King's Mountain ourselves. We saw the hilltop and the diorama in the museum and found the entire state park interesting. It is, however, quite difficult to envision the site as a battlefield at all—the park is so peaceful and beautifully maintained. A commemorative marker to Ferguson has been erected there, for he was a distinguished soldier even though he fought on the wrong side so far as we are concerned.

There is one small footnote to Ferguson's career. Some historians refer to him as brevet lieutenant colonel instead of major. At the time of his death he had been officially promoted to the higher rank, but he never received the notification.

COLONEL BANASTRE TARLETON was born in 1754 in Liverpool, England, into a family of well-to-do merchants. He studied at Oxford, then went to London, where he led a wild life of gambling, drinking, and general roistering. In 1775, he purchased a commission in the British army and was ordered to America with other troops. He was at the first, unsuccessful, siege of Charleston. In 1778, he was made a lieutenant colonel and given the command of three troops of Loyalists, the unit that became known as the Green Dragoons because of the color of their coats, and notorious because of their brutal behavior. (Contrary to general opinion, not all of the king's soldiers wore red coats!)

In 1780, Tarleton came again with the British fleet to Charleston. This time he was set ashore outside the city to scour the countryside for horses. He fought in several vital battles in South Carolina, when he was not chasing Francis Marion into swamps or hunting down Colonel Thomas Sumter or looting or burning. Tarleton was at the battle of Moncks Corner, Camden, Fishing Creek, Cowpens, Blackstock, and Guilford Courthouse. Ill with fever during part of the eventful year of 1780, he was not able to ride to Ferguson's relief at King's Mountain. At the battle of Guilford Courthouse in North Carolina, Tarleton's luck ran out. He was shot in the right hand, losing several fingers.

After the war he returned to England. He was never to enjoy great military prominence, the thing he sought. Instead, he became very active in English politics as a member of the House of Commons and as a supporter of the continuance of the slave trade. He was a crony of the wastrel son of King George III. In 1794, Tarleton was appointed to the rank of major-general and sent to Portugal. In 1803, he commanded a military post in Ireland. The year 1812 saw him promoted to the rank of general. Three years later he was created a baronet and in 1820 made a Knight of the Bath. Tarleton, who wed the daughter of a duke, died childless in 1833, honored by the English but almost universally detested in America for his cruelty.

The Americans

BRIGADIER GENERAL FRANCIS MARION was a native of South Carolina. Born in 1732, he went to sea at a tender age but a shipwreck experience with an enraged whale made him give up the sea. In the 1760's he fought Cherokee Indians. In 1770, he was chosen to be Captain of the Second Regiment of South Carolina. He became a strong supporter of the cause of liberty from British rule. After the fall of Charleston in 1780, he took to the swamps he knew so well and from there fought the British. He was not at the battle of Camden, having indeed been ordered by General Gates to burn ferries on the Santee. In September, 1780, he won a victory in the Great White Marsh in North Carolina and at Black Mingo Creek in South Carolina. Later he was chased into a swamp by Tarleton, who had given him his famous nickname, Swamp Fox. In December of that year Marion was made a brigadier general. He fought several battles in 1781. One, the battle of Quinby, was fought in company with Sumter. Later Marion commanded militia at the important battle of Eutaw Springs. In August, he fought his last battle—Fair Lawn. He and his swamp men were considered too bloodthirsty and inelegant to be permitted to take part in the American triumph in recaptured Charleston at the close of the war. Unpaid, unpraised, and as ragged and almost as famished as ever, his South Carolina troops were disbanded and sent home. Then Marion, with Oscar and with his famous horse, Ball, returned to his war-devastated plantation.

Marion served in the legislature of South Carolina for a time. He retained his militia commission, giving it up only the year before his death in 1795.

MAJOR GENERAL THOMAS SUMTER was born in Virginia in 1734. The son of poor parents, Sumter was notorious in his youth for his wild behavior and his devotion to fox hunting, horse racing, gambling, and cockfighting. Yet there was a steadiness in him. He fought in the French and Indian War, then in the Cherokee War. Having learned the Cherokee language, he was sent off with a group of Cherokee to London where he and the Indians were not only the talk of the town but were presented to the king.

Sumter, who suffered from financial problems off and on throughout the 1760's and 1770's, was elected lieutenant colonel of a regiment of riflemen in 1776. He took no great part in the war until 1780, when the British armies reached the South Carolina up-country. He was not at the battle of Camden, though prior to it he had won engagements at Rocky Mount and Hanging Rock. Two days after the defeat at Camden, Colonel Tarleton surprised Sumter in his camp on Fishing Creek, capturing many of his troops and forcing Sumter to leap onto a horse and escape alone.

Sumter gathered more troops in the up-country. In October, he was promoted to the rank of major general. The next month he fought Tarleton at Blackstock. The next year he fought three engagements in February, one in March, another in April, two in May, and two in July.

It is true that he was nicknamed the Gamecock. He was greatly honored in South Carolina after the Revolution. He went not only to the state legislature, but to the United States House of Representatives, and finally to the United States Senate. The longest-lived of all the Patriot generals, he died at the great age of ninety-eight years.

We have had Sumter's couriers carry cock feathers as identification in this novel. This is our own fancy, but it is not outside the realm of possibility at all. Nor is the button of Colonel Marion's that Alec carries as a token of service unlikely, to our way of thinking. Sumter, a flamboyant man, would have chosen something that displayed his nickname, not so the quiet Francis Marion.

COLONEL WILLIAM CAMPBELL, who was of Scots-Irish descent, was born in Virginia in 1745. He was well-educated and, though noted for his violent temper, was elected a captain of militia in Virginia in 1774. He wed the sister of the famous Patriot Patrick Henry. In 1770, Campbell had fought the stirred-up Cherokees; in 1780, he rode with the over-the-mountain men to King's Mountain. He was chosen by vote to be the chief leader of this odd force—though he, himself, was not a mountain man.

After this battle Campbell fought at Guilford Courthouse. Made a brigadier general of militia, he went back to Virginia and served under the renowned Marquis de Lafayette, who favored him. He (Campbell) died of illness in 1781.

(There were other Patriots at King's Mountain who later had very distinguished careers. One was Isaac Shelby, who became first governor of the State of Kentucky. In 1781, he served under Francis Marion. Another was John Sevier who was also with the forces of the Swamp Fox in 1781. Sevier became the first governor of the State of Tennessee.)

BOOKS USED

Source materials for this novel were sometimes very hard to come by. Seemingly California public libraries rarely specialize in South Carolina history, which we know is scarcely to be wondered at. Most of the books we used came through the agencies of university libraries—a goodly number of them through interlibrary loan. We have used the services of Yale University, the University of Illinois, the University of Indiana, the Universities of California at Berkeley, Los Angeles, and Riverside. Some of the books were rare. They had to be read on library premises under the watchful eyes of a librarian. For ordering books for us we specifically thank Ms. Hazel Schupbach, of the University of California, Riverside. We also thank librarian Ms. Zoma Henry, formerly of the Riverside Public Library. We owe our gratitude to Dr. Edwin Gaustad of the University of California, Riverside, history department, for suggesting sources to us. He was most helpful—as was Dr. Patrick Brady of the same department.

We list our sources alphabetically because of their numbers. Most of the books would not interest young readers, and some are, frankly, not very trustworthy. We have two differing versions, for instance, of the color of the uniform Ferguson's American Volunteers actually wore. We have made it red— though one source says green. One book we might suggest to readers for its lively style is *The Story of the Continental Army 1775-1783* by Lynn Montross. (Its former title was *Rag, Tag and Bobtail.*)

We used: *Gamecock, the Life and Campaigns of General Thomas Sumter* and *The Green Dragoon, the Lives of Banastre Tarleton and Mary Robinson* and *Swamp Fox, the Life and Campaigns of General Francis Marion,* all by Robert D. Bass. We also read *The Good Americans* and *The King's Friends,* both by Wallace Brown; *British Military Uniforms* by W. Y. Carman; *History of Edgefield County from the Earliest Settlements to 1897* by John A. Chapman; *The War in the South* by Donald Barr Chidsey; *King's Mountain and Its Heroes* by Lyman Draper; *The Narrative of Colonel David Fanning* by Col. David Fanning; *Colonists from Scotland* by Ian Charles Cargill Graham; and *South Carolina, Annals of Pride and Protest* by William Francis Guess.

Too, we used *The Age of Firearms* by Robert Held; *Colonial Forts of South Carolina* by Larry E. Ivers; *Colonial and Revolutionary History of Upper South Carolina* by Dr. J. B. O. Landrum; *A History of the Upper Country of South Carolina from the Earliest Periods to the Close of the War of Independence* by John L. Logan; *The British Occupation of Charleston* by George Smith McCowen, Jr.; *The History of South Carolina in the Revolution,* 2 vols., by Edward McCrady; *The Story of the Continental Army, 1775-1783* by Lynn Montross; *Weapons of the American Revolution and Accoutrements* by Warren Moore; *The Highland Scots of North Carolina, 1732-1776* by Duane Meyer; *The Irish Brigades in the Service of France* by John Cornelius O'Callaghan; *The American Tory* by William H. Nelson; *The North Carolina Continentals* by Hugh F. Rankin; and *The Old South* by Thomas Jefferson Wertenbaker.

John and Patricia Beatty
August, 1974

Both John and Patricia Beatty were born in Portland, Oregon, and went to Reed College there. After graduation Mrs. Beatty studied at the University of Washington in Seattle, and Dr. Beatty received his M.A. from Stanford University and his Ph.D. from the University of Washington. At the time of his death in 1975, he was a professor at the University of California, his subject being English history of the seventeenth and eighteenth centuries.

The Beattys were married in 1950 and later lived in Wilmington, Delaware, and London, England. Dr. Beatty served in the United States Army in World War II, in the European Theater. He was the holder of the Silver Star and Purple Heart medals and the Combat Infantryman's Badge. Mrs. Beatty has taught high-school English and history and has also held a position as a science and technical librarian. At one time she taught Writing Fiction for Children in the Extension Department of the University of California, Los Angeles. She has had a number of novels published by Morrow about the American West.

At present Patricia Beatty lives in Southern California.